"Did you hate me, Paul?"

Leah gazed directly at Paul as she spoke, her look so open and honest, it was difficult for him to meet her eyes.

"What do you mean?"

"Before," she said, dropping her eyes and gripping her hands tensely in the folds of her napkin. "I must have been a terrible person," she went on in a small tight voice. "I can see by the way the girls look at me. What was I like to you, Paul?"

Paul studied the woman who sat across from him. She had all of Leah's devastating physical beauty and smoldering sex appeal. To his alarm, he found himself battling a sudden desire to lean across the table and kiss her sweetly curving mouth.

Then another image stabbed him—Leah standing in the middle of their bedroom throwing books and makeup bottles at him. He remembered her voice, thick with rage, as she screamed abuse at him.

Would he *ever* know which was the real Leah?

Dear Reader,

Four more fabulous WOMEN WHO DARE are heading your way!

In May, you'll thrill to the time-travel tale Lynn Erickson spins in *Paradox*. When loan executive Emily Jacoby is catapulted back in time during a train wreck, she is thoroughly unnerved by the fate that awaits her. In 1893, Colorado is a harsh and rugged land. Women's rights have yet to be invented, and Will Dutcher, Emily's reluctant host, is making her question her desire to return to her own time.

In June, you'll be reminded that courage can strike at any age. Our heroine in Peg Sutherland's *Late Bloomer* discovers unplumbed depths at the age of forty. After a lifetime of living for others, she realizes that she wants something for herself—college, a career, a *life*. But when a mysterious stranger drifts into town, she discovers to her shock that she also wants *him!*

Sharon Brondos introduces us to spunky Allison Ford in our July WOMEN WHO DARE title, *The Marriage Ticket*. Allison stands up for what she believes in. And she believes in playing fair. Unfortunately, some of her community's leaders don't have the same scruples, and going head-to-head with them lands her in serious trouble.

You'll never forget Leah Temple, the heroine of August's *Another Woman*, by Margot Dalton. This riveting tale of a wife with her husband's murder on her mind will hold you spellbound...and surprised! Don't miss it!

Some of your favorite Superromance authors have also contributed to our spring and summer lineup. Look for books by Pamela Bauer, Debbi Bedford, Dawn Stewardson, Jane Silverwood, Sally Garrett, Bobby Hutchinson and Judith Arnold...to name just a few! Some wonderful Superromance reading awaits you!

Marsha Zinberg
Senior Editor

P.S. Don't forget that you can write to your favorite author

c/o Harlequin Reader Service,
P.O. Box 1297
Buffalo, New York
14240 U.S.A.

ANOTHER WOMAN

Margot Dalton

Harlequin Books

TORONTO • NEW YORK • LONDON
AMSTERDAM • PARIS • SYDNEY • HAMBURG
STOCKHOLM • ATHENS • TOKYO • MILAN
MADRID • WARSAW • BUDAPEST • AUCKLAND

Published August 1993

ISBN 0-373-70558-1

ANOTHER WOMAN

ABOUT THE AUTHOR

Margot Dalton found herself becoming more and more intrigued by *Another Woman* as she wrote the story. "Maybe it's from watching my own children grow up to be interesting, independent adults, or maybe it's just natural for a writer to be fascinated by the complex forces that shape personality," writes Margot.

Margot Dalton has published seven Superromance novels. (*Another Woman* is her eighth.) Her books appear consistently on the Waldenbooks' Romance Bestseller list. As well, this popular author who hails from British Columbia, Canada, has written for Harlequin's Crystal Creek series. Be sure to look for these set-in-Texas stories wherever Harlequin books are sold.

Books by Margot Dalton

HARLEQUIN SUPERROMANCE
508—TUMBLEWEED
511—JUNIPER
533—DANIEL AND THE LION

HARLEQUIN CRYSTAL CREEK
2—COWBOYS AND CABERNET
5—EVEN THE NIGHTS ARE BETTER

Don't miss any of our special offers. Write to us at the following address for information on our newest releases.

Harlequin Reader Service
P.O. Box 1397, Buffalo, NY 14240
Canadian address: P.O. Box 603,
Fort Erie, Ont. L2A 5X3

CHAPTER ONE

SHE WOKE TO A FEELING of warmth, of enclosing softness and safety that was pure happiness. Smiling, eyes closed, she stirred and drifted on the quiet sea of warmth until she realized that there was also a hard knot of pain somewhere—pain that tore and thrust at her.

After that she lay very still, frowning, eyes tightly closed, trying to edge her way around the pain. Slowly she began to understand that the pain was *herself,* was somehow centered in the essence of what she was, while the warmth and softness were something else.

She felt worried then—confused and vaguely frightened. The warmth became heat, shaping itself to her body and pressing against her, pushing her eyelids up, though she was terrified to open them.

But she did, finally, because she had no choice. She lay blinking and staring vacantly, trying to absorb the fact that the warmth was also a light that streamed over her face, so bright that it dazzled and hurt.

The other pain was still there, too, a vast pulsing ache that seemed to encompass everything within her. The softness was something different, something that surrounded her, supple and white and warm.

Gradually her eyes grew more accustomed to the light, and she began to discern shapes and edges, harsh lines, varying shades of gray and pale blue. An object lay beside her, clumsy and inert. She lifted it and held it in front of her eyes, squinting, discovering to her amazement that the thoughts in the painful center of herself could make the object move, make its separate parts fan out and fold back upon themselves.

Hand, she thought, childishly pleased that she could find a word and attach it to the object.

"Hand," she whispered in a husky voice that sounded loud in the bright silence. The pain throbbed and flared briefly. But she barely noticed how much it hurt. She was still entranced at the mysterious connection between the sound, the word and the object in front of her.

"Hand," she murmured again. "Fingers."

She smiled awkwardly, feeling a fresh stab of hurt somewhere as she did so. Carefully she lowered her arm and rolled her head on the softness, trying not to jar the pain and set it off again.

She knew that if she closed her eyes the agony would be lessened, and the harsh light would be replaced by cool, caressing darkness. But she was far too interested in what her eyes were finding, in all the shapes and forms that filled this world she'd awakened to.

Some of the objects had words that went with them, words that she could find readily, like *chair* and *window* and *door.*

Others must have words, too, she thought, but she couldn't track them down, couldn't seem to drag them out of hiding.

She kept trying, knowing somehow that it was very important, that the words were the key to this whole baffling world that she found herself in. But she was so tired, and the pain was getting worse. After a while she gave up and let her eyes drift shut, let the darkness claim her and draw her back into a gently rocking stillness.

When she woke a second time there was something moving in front of her, a large warm object that was like herself but different.

Person, she thought, and then, unexpectedly, *woman.*

"Woman," she murmured aloud, her eyes fixed on the new being that filled most of the space between her and the window.

"Well, well," the other said. "Look who's awake. How you feelin', honey?"

The woman in the bed blinked and stared, trying to concentrate. The person who stood before her was smiling, a big happy smile that showed white teeth against gleaming, dark brown skin. In fact, this person was all white and dark brown, her brown arms and face a stark contrast with the crisp white uniform that covered most of her body.

She looked large and substantial, and full of warmth. The woman in the bed tried to smile back, grateful that she wasn't the only living being in this new world.

"Now, don't you try to smile too big, sweetie," the dark woman said. "You got a real bad cut on that lip, likely gonna hurt some when you smile for the next few days."

She busied herself around the bed, doing mysterious things with glass and metal and paper. "So, how you feelin', Leah?" she said at last, picking up the woman's arm and holding her wrist in a light, expert grasp.

"Lee?" the woman repeated in a halting voice that sounded muffled and indistinct to her own ears.

"Le-ah," the dark woman repeated, pronouncing two firm, separate syllables. "That's your name, right?" she added, consulting a paper clipped to the board that she carried. "Leah Temple. That's your name. Age twenty-seven."

"Leah," the woman repeated. "Name."

She frowned in concentration, studying a small printed square on the ample cliff of bosom that jutted from the other woman's front.

"Doris," she said finally, startled and pleased to find that she could make sense out of the printed symbols. "Name?"

The dark woman smiled down at her. "That's sure my name, honey. Doris Abigail Amelia Walsh. But you can call me Doris."

Leah smiled back again, forgetting the warning about her cut lip and wincing as the pain stabbed her. "Doris," she murmured, loving the name, loving the big dark-skinned woman who looked down at her with such affection.

But the interaction had tired Leah, wearied her beyond bearing. She dreaded the thought of losing Doris, but she couldn't seem to keep herself in the light where the other woman was. She felt her eyelids drop shut again, felt the caressing darkness enclose her, felt herself slide gently down into that other world where there was no light at all, and no pain.

DORIS WALSH, R.N., stood with the morning sunlight streaming across her back, like a golden cloak over her heavy shoulders. She held Leah Temple's slender wrist in her hand, frowning thoughtfully as she studied the woman in the narrow bed.

She was a real beauty, this poor woman, no deny-
ing that. Even better-looking, in Doris's opinion, since
they'd washed off all that garish makeup, cleaned and
trimmed the long, painted nails and cut off most of
that matted bleached hair.

Doris suspected that Leah Temple wasn't going to
be too happy when she regained her senses and realized that her hair had been hacked off. But what
choice did they have? The woman had a bad concussion, possibly even some swelling in the cranial cav-
ity. Tending that long heavy mane of hair just wasn't
practical, even from the standpoint of the pain it
would cause.

Besides, it looked prettier this way, Doris thought,
with all that artificial streaked stuff cut away to show
her natural golden-brown color. The hospital beauti-
cian had given her a casual boyish cut, parted on one
side and combed smoothly across her head, just above
the livid bruise that began at her ear and covered most
of her right temple.

The new haircut accentuated the woman's delicate
bone structure, her finely molded face and the sweet,
pure lines of cheek and chin and brow.

A real beauty, Doris thought, looking at the long,
dense fan of eyelashes against the woman's pale cheek,
remembering those big light brown eyes dappled with
golden highlights.

Gently she lifted the covers back and opened Leah's
hospital gown to examine the sleeping woman's body,
frowning at the bruises on her full, shapely breasts, the
rigid band of tape above her narrow waist that supported her cracked ribs, and her bandaged left arm.
There were other scrapes and bruises on her long, slim

legs and thighs that they hadn't even dressed, just left open to the healing air.

"A real beauty," Doris muttered. "And just such a damned shame." Tenderly she tied the gown, readjusted the blankets and smoothed the sleeping woman's hair across her brow, thinking about their strange little conversation and Leah Temple's puzzlement over her name.

The nurse frowned and turned away, loaded her arms with supplies and moved quietly out into the hallway. She made her way down the wide corridor, her step light and graceful despite her impressive bulk.

Deep in her own thoughts, ignoring the early-morning confusion and tumult of the busy hospital ward, Doris waded through the slanting rectangles of sunlight that flooded the corridor from each open door. At the nursing station she paused, still frowning thoughtfully, and went to the phone to make some calls.

"LEAH? LEAH, can you hear me?"

This time it was a shorter distance up to the light, and not nearly so confusing once she got there. The voice was like a rope that she climbed with painful urgency. At the top she opened her eyes to a scene that was already familiar and objects that had names.

Door, window, hand, face. *Man,* she thought, studying the face. Not Doris.

Leah felt a stab of disappointment, a childlike longing for Doris with her dark smiling face and gentle hands. She tensed herself against the pain and waited, studying this new face.

The man was as pale as Doris had been dark. Even the stuff on his head was white, what little of it there was, and his eyes were no color at all, just flashes of light from squares of glass that fronted them.

Leah stared, wondering in horror if some people had light instead of eyes. She was relieved when he shifted in his chair and the light subsided, revealing circles of piercing gray behind the glass.

"Leah, do you know my name?"

Leah frowned, recalling the only names she knew. "Doris?" she ventured timidly. "Leah?"

The man studied her face, leaning forward intently. "Dr. Holcross, Leah. I'm Dr. Holcross, but you've always called me Ken."

"Ken," she repeated, wincing at the unexpected sharpness of the name. It drove like a little pointed spike right into the center of her head where the pain was the worst.

The doctor continued to gaze at her, his gray eyes full of interest.

"Hurts," she told him, lifting her right arm toward her head, then letting her hand fall limply back onto the bed.

"Does it? Where do you hurt the most, Leah?"

She frowned, anxious to give the correct answer but bewildered by the complexity of the man's question.

Leah wasn't at all sure what comprised her own body, though she was beginning to understand how a body looked on other people, like Ken and Doris. She remembered her earlier suspicion that all the parts that were painful formed her body, and whatever was warm and soft was something else. ·

"Everywhere," she said finally, hoping this was the correct answer. "Hurts everywhere."

Dr. Holcross nodded thoughtfully, then leaned forward again and took a narrow silver cylinder from his pocket. Leah was fascinated to discover that the cylinder trapped a ray of light and the doctor could control it, turning the brightness on and off at will.

"Light," she said, smiling up at him.

"Yes," he agreed, giving her a surprised glance, then shining the light into her right eye. "Look straight ahead, Leah, just past my ear. Good. Now the other one..."

He paused, settled back and put the light in his pocket while Leah watched him in silence.

"Leah," he said, "how much do you remember of what happened yesterday?"

She frowned again, struggling with the concepts of "yesterday" and "remember." She had a vague idea what the doctor meant, but there was nothing inside her head she could give him, except...

"Woke up," she said at last. "Saw Doris."

Ken Holcross tapped his blunt fingers against the arm of his chair. "All right," he said. "I guess you have no memory of the... accident. Probably just as well," he added with a sudden grim edge to his voice. "But what about before, Leah?"

"Before?"

"Last week. A month ago. Do you remember last month when you came to see me, Leah? Do you remember what we talked about at your last visit?"

Leah stared at his pale face, completely unable to grasp what he was saying. "Last visit?" she echoed blankly.

The doctor gazed at her in silence. "Leah," he said at last, trying another tactic, "did you know that they've cut your hair? I don't believe I've ever seen you with short hair."

She returned his gaze, struggling to isolate the word. *Hair,* she thought, looking at the fluff of white on the doctor's head, then lifting her hand in the direction of her own, touching it experimentally with her fingers.

"Hair?" she asked.

"Yes, Leah," he said, watching her with that same intent look. "They've cut your beautiful long hair almost as short as a boy's. What do you think of that?"

Leah gazed at him, wondering what to say. Doris had hair that looked much the same as hers felt. And the doctor had almost no hair at all. Leah couldn't imagine hair that was long.

She frowned suddenly, wondering what color her own hair was. Black, like the shining, clipped mop of curls that Doris sported? Or white, like Ken's?

She wanted to ask, but she couldn't find the words to form the question. Besides, the doctor was still gazing at her, examining her face with that strange, thoughtful expression. He leaned toward her, taking his flashlight from its nest of white again. "Leah," he said softly, "I want you to look at the light, okay? Watch the light, and don't take your eyes off it. Keep watching the light, Leah. See how slowly it's moving? Watch it moving slowly, slowly in front of your eyes...."

Soon his face was gone, along with the little silver light and the larger light behind him, and she was hurtling down head over heels, sinking and falling and tumbling once again into the warm, sweet darkness.

NEXT TIME SHE WOKE Leah felt rested and peaceful, soothed by the softness beyond the window. The warm light lay in soft pools on the floor and gleamed in a friendly way against the chrome bars at the side of the bed.

Leah smiled, then frowned, remembering the man called Ken, his tiny silver light and disturbing questions. She wondered what they meant, all those questions.

Was there another world besides this one, a world that Leah knew nothing about? How many people lived in all these different worlds and what were they like? Were there other kinds of people than Ken and Doris?

Had Leah herself once occupied some other world, and then somehow gotten lost in this one? Suddenly Leah felt a chill of fear, a sense of displacement and isolation that clouded her mind and took away all the gentle warmth of the day. She trembled in the grip of rising panic, struggling to contain her fear, to prepare herself for whatever came next.

While she lay with her eyes closed, holding the edge of the blanket tight in her fingers, she heard the door open and peeped up fearfully.

The person who came into her room was somebody altogether new, not Doris and not Ken. Leah forgot her panic and blinked in astonishment, marveling at how many different kinds of people there seemed to be.

Leah understood that this one was like herself and Doris, also female, but small, with long golden hair and light blue eyes. She wore a gown the same pale blue as the walls, and carried a tray covered with shining metal domes.

Leah gazed at the woman, then at the tray, and became aware of a great aching discomfort within her, something that wasn't exactly painful but still over-whelming in its urgency.

"Are you hungry, Leah?" the golden-haired woman asked with a smile.

"Hungry," Leah repeated. "Yes," she said, realizing that this was the truth, that the woman had identified her problem.

"Good, because there's a nice meal for you here. Do you like tuna casserole?"

Leah frowned, searching for an answer. "I don't know," she said.

"Well, I know what people think about hospital food, but this is pretty good, actually. I often order it myself, down in the cafeteria. Now, let's see. Would you like milk in your tea?"

"I don't know," Leah said again, feeling another little surge of panic. So many questions, and she never had answers. These people must be so disappointed in her.

The golden-haired woman glanced at her nervously, then looked over her shoulder, her face clearing in relief when she saw Doris come bustling into the room.

Leah, too, almost laughed aloud with delight when she saw the familiar dark face and warm, beaming smile of the white-clad nurse.

"Doris," she said. "I'm hungry!"

"Of course you are, sweetie." Doris grasped Leah's hand and smiled down at her. "Amy, you go on and have your own lunch, okay?" she added. "I'll look after Mrs. Temple."

The smaller woman nodded gratefully and hurried out of the room, leaving the nurse to lift the domes and set the utensils out in front of Leah.

"First, let's crank this bed up a little higher, all right? Hold on, Leah, you're going for a ride," Doris said, doing something mysterious at the foot of the bed that brought Leah slowly and magically to a sitting position.

The room dissolved in broken circles of color and Doris turned into a warm brown-and-white blur.

"Dizzy? Just sit still a minute with your eyes closed and it'll pass. You really need some food in your stomach, girl. Now, look here."

Leah obeyed, discovering to her astonishment that Doris was indeed right. The spell of vertigo had already passed and the room seemed clear and bright, its contents even more interesting from this new angle.

She stared curiously at the big woman, wondering how Doris knew all about what was inside Leah's head, while Leah had no similar knowledge about Doris. She wanted to ask, but again it was too difficult to frame the question.

Instead she concentrated on the small metal object that Doris was holding in front of her eyes with a questioning glance.

Leah struggled through a whole list of words, rummaging amongst them like somebody trying to find the right object in a drawer.

"Fork," she said finally, and felt a glow of happiness when Doris smiled her approval.

"Good girl. This one?"

"Spoon. Knife," Leah added before Doris could pick up the last one.

"Smarty. Now, are you right-handed, Leah?"

Leah stared, her confidence ebbing.

"Never mind. You have to be right-handed for a while, anyhow, since you can't use that left arm with

such a big bandage on it, can you? Now, do you remember how to hold a fork, honey?''

Leah frowned, taking the fork from Doris and
palming it awkwardly, looking at the other woman
with a helpless expression.

"Sorry," she whispered. "I'm so sorry...."

"Don't be silly," Doris said briskly. "Like this,
see?" She positioned the fork in the younger woman's slender hand and closed her fingers over it.
"Good. Now, this one supports it, and these two hold
and guide it. You understand, Leah?"

Leah nodded, struggling to hold the fork as Doris
demonstrated, plunging it experimentally through the
air a couple of times.

"What a smart girl," Doris observed with warm
admiration, making Leah feel absurdly happy again.
"Now, try this. It's tuna casserole."

"I know."

"You do?" Doris gave her a quick, alert glance.
"How'd you know that, Leah?"

"Amy told me."

"Oh." Doris was silent as she watched Leah struggle awkwardly to load some casserole onto her fork.
"Leah, what's tuna?" she asked casually.

Leah pondered, still struggling with the tricky business of getting the food balanced on her fork. "Water?" she ventured at last. "Something to do with
water?"

"Close enough. Careful, now, hotshot...good!"

Doris beamed as her charge landed the fork directly in her mouth, then watched while Leah chewed
and swallowed.

"I like tuna casserole," Leah announced finally, with the air of someone making an important discovery.

"Good. That's something else we know, isn't it? Let's see if you like turnips."

"Which are turnips?"

"This little pile here. What color is it, Leah?"

"Orange," Leah said promptly, having already learned that colors were among the easiest words to find. More confident now, she stabbed the fork into the mushy pile of orange, guided some to her mouth and spat it promptly back onto the plate.

"Oof," she said apologetically as Doris chuckled and wiped her mouth with a napkin. "Awful. Just awful."

"And *now* we know that you don't like turnips," Doris said cheerfully. "But we don't spit them out, sweetie," she added gently. "If we happen to eat something we don't like, we just swallow it and have a real quick drink of water, and make sure we don't eat any more of it. Okay?"

"I know," Leah said, feeling a hot, miserable flood of shame. "It's not right to spit food out. I know."

Doris looked at the flushed, unhappy face of the beautiful woman in front of her. "You know that, do you, honey? You even feel embarrassed, don't you? Now, isn't that interesting," the nurse murmured, mostly to herself. "Isn't that interesting, that you'd still know enough to be embarrassed."

But Leah was fully absorbed by now in the struggle to load more tuna casserole onto her fork. She felt ravenous all at once, hollow and aching with hunger, and the smell of the toasty, oozing mass on her plate was so delightful that it gave her a sensation close to pain.

While Doris watched, helping occasionally and offering advice, Leah ate her meal, devouring everything but the turnips. She delighted in the surprising tang of tomato, enjoyed the crisp texture of her toast, decided solemnly that she preferred coffee to tea, and giggled like a child when she encountered the dish of gelatin dessert. "It *wiggles*," she said, giving Doris a look of awed delight. "Look, Doris! See how it wiggles? And it's red. And it tastes so *good*," she added, swallowing a mouthful and closing her eyes in bliss.

Doris watched in silence. Leah was surprised to see the big woman swipe a hand across her eyes.

"Doris?" she asked in alarm, forgetting the wonder of her dessert for a moment.

"Oh, don't mind me, sweetie. I just keep thinking about all the things you've still got to discover. I hope your life doesn't hold any worse surprises than turnips, that's all."

Leah gazed up at her, eating the delicious, chilly confection in thoughtful silence.

"Don't mind me," Doris repeated. "You just keep enjoying your dessert, Leah. That stuff comes in all colors, you know," she added cheerfully. "Green and yellow and orange, even stripes...everything you could think of."

Leah gazed at the nurse, wide-eyed with amazement. "Really?" she breathed. "Do they all taste just as good as this?"

"Every one of 'em. Now, let's get you into the bathroom, honey. You need to get all cleaned up and ready, because you know what I heard? I heard that your husband's coming by to see you in a little while.

You want to be all clean and pretty for your husband, right, Leah?''

Leah nodded automatically, stunned by this piece of information. She continued to puzzle over it while Doris helped her from the bed, put a strong arm around her and supported her into the bathroom. In this new position, away from the warm softness of the bed, Leah was able to form a better conception of her own body. She discovered that she'd been right in her earlier appraisal. Every part of her throbbed with some kind of pain, from the floor all the way up to the top where her head was.

''Hurts,'' Leah told Doris after they finished their tasks in the bathroom. She gritted her teeth and tried to smile. ''Hurts everywhere, Doris.''

''You bet it does. And lying in that bed won't help, either, just makes you stiffen up. When your husband comes by, you should get him to take you for a nice walk down to the lounge or something.''

''Husband,'' Leah repeated, feeling a little chill of fear.

Doris walked her back into the room, lifted her effortlessly and tucked her into the freshly made bed. Leah nestled with a sigh into the familiar welcoming softness, letting her pain-racked body sink slowly back into comfort.

''Do you remember your husband at all, Leah?'' Doris asked, bending forward and smoothing Leah's hair with her hand.

''Husband,'' Léah echoed, searching though the piles and masses of words that littered her brain. She shook her head in confusion. There was a general idea of what a husband was, but it didn't seem to apply to anything that Leah could identify.

"His name is Paul," Doris said. "Paul Temple. He dropped by the nursing station this morning but you were sleeping, so he said he'd come back later. The little nursing aides were all aflutter, believe me."

"Why?" Leah asked.

"Because, honey, your Paul is just about the most gorgeous hunk of man any of us has ever seen, that's why."

Leah stared at her friend. She had a fair idea what gorgeous meant, but no concept of what caused a man to be described that way.

"Is Ken?" she asked finally.

"Ken who? What are you saying, Leah?"

"The doctor. The one with the light. Is he gorgeous?"

"Dr. Holcross?" Doris laughed, a booming cascade of mirth that sounded warm and rich, the way the tuna casserole tasted. "No," she said finally, wiping her eyes. "No, sweetie, Dr. Holcross is a real nice man, but he's not exactly what you'd call gorgeous."

Somebody called from the hallway and Doris straightened reluctantly, still chuckling. "Gotta go. I'll see you in a little while, Leah. You can go back to sleep if you like."

Leah shook her head, wincing at the sudden stab of pain. She had a panicky feeling that it was wrong, somehow, to spend so much time in the comfortable, oblivious darkness. Out in the other world, this one that was full of light, there was so much to learn and she couldn't learn it all unless she stayed awake and concentrated.

Doris nodded, apparently reading her thoughts again. She drew a small stack of colored paper from somewhere beside the bed.

"Here're some magazines," she said. "We know you can read, because you read my name tag this morning, didn't you?" Leah took the papers and held them, watching while Doris hurried from the room, her big heavy form brisk with purpose.

Then she leafed though the magazines, gazing at them in bemused silence.

Doris was right, as usual. Leah could read, could make sense of the printed words and sometimes find images in her mind that matched them. But they seemed so bizarre, like random scraps of dreams, so strange and difficult to understand that her eyes swam with confusion and her head began to ache horribly.

After a while she dropped the magazines onto the blanket and gave herself up to exhaustion, letting the warm darkness reach up and draw her back into merciful oblivion.

WHEN SHE WOKE, somebody was once again standing between her and the window, just as Doris had been when Leah first saw her.

Leah blinked and gazed, trying to separate light from darkness, to form a clear picture of the man who stood beside her. As her eyes adjusted, details began to register and she realized that this new person was completely unlike any she'd ever seen before.

He wore a brown leather jacket and blue jeans, not a hospital uniform. He was tall, far taller than Ken or Doris, and so broad-shouldered that his body seemed to fill the whole window. But he wasn't fat and comfortably soft like Doris. In fact, parts of him looked slim and lean, hard as bone, while other parts were wide and muscular.

His face was hard, too, with clean planes that glowed in the waning light. His hair was a smooth cap of pure gold, lying thick and shining across his finely shaped head and against his neck.

But unlike the golden-haired woman who'd brought the food, he didn't have blue eyes. This man's eyes, set beneath dark, soft lashes, were a color that Leah couldn't name, a strange mixture of blue and brown, of sparkling gold and green, eyes so beautiful that they took her breath away.

Leah gazed up at him, shaken by the tide of feeling that surged though her. This was something new, this feeling, similar to what she felt for Doris but far more intense.

Still, it was strangely different, too. Whenever she saw Doris, Leah felt a flood of warmth and a pleasant sense of happiness and safety. This big man in the leather jacket made her feel hot and tingly, breathless and excited and full of vague hungers and yearnings that she couldn't identify.

She trembled under the covers, searching for words that she could say to him, wondering how to ask who he was and why he was standing by her bed. But at that moment he realized that she was awake and he leaned over to examine her, so near that Leah could see the texture of his tanned skin, the gleam of golden stubble on his hard jaw and the way his shining hair fell softly across his forehead. He looked down at her intently and she shuddered, gazing back at him in confusion, wondering what kind of nightmare she was caught up in.

The man's beautiful jewel-colored eyes were cold and bitter, his sculpted face taut with hatred.

CHAPTER TWO

"Was she raped, Ken?"

Dr. Kenneth Holcross lifted his head and stared at the tall, golden-haired man across the desk. He hesitated, wondering how any man could ask that particular question in such a cold and unemotional fashion.

Especially when it was *his own wife* he was talking about...

But when the doctor looked into Paul Temple's eyes, he realized that the man wasn't calm at all, was in fact fighting to keep his emotions under rigid control.

"Why do you ask, Paul?" Ken Holcross said quietly. "What makes you suspect she might have been raped?"

The younger man shrugged and leaned back in his chair, gripping the wooden arms so hard that his knuckles were white against his tanned skin.

"The police told me she was found in an alley at one o'clock in the morning, badly beaten and unconscious. Considering the area of the city she was in, and the fact that her rings were still on her fingers and nothing had been stolen from her handbag, it's reasonable to assume that it was a sexual attack, isn't it?"

Ken Holcross was silent, twisting his pen in his hands and looking thoughtfully at the bitter, handsome face of the other man.

"Especially the way she was dressed," Paul Temple went on in a lower tone, speaking reluctantly, as if the words were being dragged from him.

"How was she dressed, Paul?"

"The same as always, only worse," Paul said harshly. "Come on, Ken, you know how she dresses! When this happened she was wearing a red leather miniskirt, a black see-through blouse with no bra, high-heeled sandals and seamed nylon stockings."

The doctor nodded, his face carefully noncommittal. "So?" he asked.

"So," Paul Temple said angrily, "if she chooses to hang out after midnight in an area of town like that, dressed like a tramp, what does she expect?"

"Paul," the other man said gently, "that's unworthy of you. You're a smarter man than that, and much more compassionate. I can't believe that you think a woman who dresses provocatively deserves to be raped."

The younger man shook his head wearily. "I'm not debating over what Leah deserves, Ken. Not to say that it isn't an interesting question," he added with another bitter twist of his mouth. "I'm just asking you if the medical examination shows that she was raped."

"No," Dr. Holcross said. "We think the police must have interrupted the assault before her attackers finished with her. She was lucky to get away with nothing more than a severe beating."

"Lucky," Paul echoed tonelessly.

"Probably. Her injuries are quite extensive, but mostly superficial. She has some deep internal bruising and quite a few shallow wounds on her legs and torso. Her left radius is cracked...that's the outer bone in the forearm?"

He raised a questioning eyebrow. Paul nodded, watching the doctor's face intently. "The arm will have to be supported for a couple of weeks. Apart from that, and taping the ribs, there's not a lot we can do for her."

Paul gazed at the elderly psychologist, his face taut with anger.

"What about this phony new act of hers?" he burst out finally.

"What act, Paul?" the doctor said gently.

The young man shifted restlessly in his chair, his big body tense with emotion. "Come *on*, Ken," he said in low, furious tones. "I stopped in to see her yesterday and she pretended she didn't even know who I was. She talked like a complete idiot."

"She's not a complete idiot, Paul. I can assure you of that."

"Oh, God, I know *that*," Paul said grimly. "Hell, Ken, you think I don't know how smart she is? The woman's like a goddamn snake. She's so cunning and devious, she truly thinks she can get away with anything. But this . . . this is too much!"

"You think she's faking the amnesia?"

"That's what you call it? Amnesia? I call it a scam, Ken. If what you say is true, and she wasn't the victim of a sexual assault, then I think this is just another typical Leah-type effort to protect her position."

The doctor gazed mildly at Paul. "Right now, Leah Temple doesn't look like a woman who's done a particularly outstanding job of protecting her position, does she?"

"Maybe she does," Paul said stubbornly. "Ken, I doubt that she's told you this, but I'm ready to throw her out. In fact, I had divorce papers served on her last

week, and she has less than three more days to respond to them. Don't you think this is just a handy
little device to sidestep that particular problem?''

Ken Holcross gazed at the angry young man in silence for a moment. ''Let me get this straight, Paul.
Are you suggesting that she hired someone to beat her
up? She paid someone to break her bones and disfig-
ure her body, just to postpone a divorce hearing?''

Paul shrugged, his face still drawn in cold, bitter
lines. ''It sounds plausible to me, knowing Leah.
Maybe she told them to rough her up a bit, and things
got out of hand. The kind of people she hangs around
with, things are always getting out of hand.''

''But what would be her motive?''

''Dammit, Ken, isn't it obvious? She knows she's
got just a few more days and then I'll be tossing her
out on the street. That's the last thing she wants. Not
because she cares a damn about me,'' Paul Temple
added with a mirthless smile. ''Just because she
doesn't want to be stuck out there in the cold world
without all that lovely money.''

''But wouldn't Leah do pretty well in a divorce settlement?''

''My lawyers say she won't. Most of it's family
money, Ken. I had it before I married her, so she isn't
entitled to any of it. And in the five years we've been
married, the business hasn't earned a tremendous
profit, you know. What there was, she's spent twice
over. She'll be lucky to get away with pocket money
for a year or two, especially considering the way she's
behaved.''

Ken Holcross nodded reluctantly. ''Leah has done
some very foolish things.''

"Foolish!" the other man echoed. "My God, Ken..."

After a moment's silence Dr. Holcross looked up, his pale gray eyes meeting the other man's brilliant hazel glance. "So what do you think, Paul? You think she seized this opportunity to fake an amnesiac attack so you'd be prevented from going ahead with a divorce action right now?"

"That's what I think. Come on, Ken, look at her record. This is just like that phony suicide attempt and all the other crap we've been through over the years. Leah's the most manipulative woman you'll ever meet. Nothing is beyond her. And this," Paul concluded, "is just her latest ploy."

"I don't agree," Dr. Holcross said finally. "I think it's genuine."

Paul stared at him, aghast. "You're kidding."

The doctor shook his head. "I'm afraid not, Paul. I'm used to Leah, you know. I've been dealing with her on a regular basis for quite a long time. I'm familiar with how she reacts, particularly under hypnosis."

"You've put her under? Since this accident, I mean?"

Dr. Holcross nodded. "Twice. And I've also given her an extensive examination and called in another consultant. Paul, her most basic personal memories are fragmented and disordered, even under hypnosis, which is consistent with psychogenic amnesia. In fact, some of her particularly traumatic childhood events, ones that we've recovered only recently, now seem to have vanished altogether. It's an astonishing degree of amnesia. Virtually total.

Paul shook his head. "That's crap, Ken. Look, she's heard tapes of herself under hypnosis, and she's smart enough to study up on the symptoms of amnesia. Couldn't she fake the hypnotic state, too, and then while she's pretending to be under, deliberately feed you what she wants you to hear?"

"I don't believe that she—"

"I'm not asking what you believe, Ken. I'm asking you what's possible."

"Yes," the doctor said quietly. "Yes, Paul, it's possible that she could be faking. But I don't happen to believe she is. And that's how it's going to go into the psychological evaluation."

"Don't tell me you're reporting this as a genuine case of amnesia?"

"Yes, I am."

"Oh, *hell!*" Paul Temple flung himself out of the chair and began to pace the doctor's office, his big body as lithe and powerful as a caged tiger's.

Ken Holcross sat behind his broad, littered desk and watched the angry young man. His bland face was unrevealing, his gray eyes pale and still behind the thick glasses.

"Where does this leave me, Ken?" Paul Temple asked, turning to look at the doctor, his features twisted with anguish. "If you report her case as genuine, then I'll have to take her home and look after her, won't I? How can I just...dump her somewhere? Ken, I know it sounds brutal considering the shape she's in, but you just don't know how much I despise that woman."

"There's no need for her to remain in hospital," the doctor said gently. "And I think it *would* speed the recovery of her memory if she could be in familiar surroundings, Paul. Most amnesiacs begin to recover their identity almost immediately, although Leah's memory loss is unusually profound just now. I think the most compassionate course of action would be to take her home for a few weeks, let her regain her strength and then make a decision after that."

"A few weeks," Paul Temple repeated, his face bleak.

"It won't be so bad, Paul. You can stand having her around for a month, and by that time she'll be better equipped to manage on her own. Right now, she's got such a lot to learn."

"Does she need some kind of full-time nurse? Should I hire somebody for the time she'll be there?"

The doctor considered that. "I don't think so," he said finally. "You still have that couple living there, don't you?"

"Bob and Anna. They have a house of their own on my property, and Anna looks after most of the housekeeping for both places. Leah's never been much of a homemaker," Paul added with a mirthless smile.

"Well, that should be enough, as long as there's someone around. Mostly she just needs someone to talk with, to tell her things. As a matter of fact...Bob and Anna have a couple of children, don't they?"

"Two little girls. Not so little, actually. Allie's about ten, and Bonnie's a couple of years older. Just about a teenager now, I suppose."

"Well, that would be ideal. Two girls that age, if they have the patience to spend some time talking with Leah, that's the best therapy we could hope for."

Paul shook his head. "Ken, those kids aren't exactly crazy about Leah. She's not a motherly type, you know. She's been pretty damned harsh with them over the years, and they don't like her one bit."

"Kids are quick to forgive. They usually have a lot more compassion than we give them credit for. They'll soon realize that Leah is sick, and that she needs help."

Paul Temple gazed in disbelief at the psychologist. "God, you've really bought this whole thing, haven't you? She's got you, Ken. Hook, line and sinker."

"I believe she has genuine massive amnesia, Paul. And I have a considerable weight of professional training and experience on which to base that diagnosis."

The younger man sank restlessly back into his chair and then leaned forward, his hands tensed. "Okay," he said. "Just for the sake of argument, let's say it's true. Let's say she's really lost her memory. What does that mean, Ken? What happens next? Does it all come back in a blinding flash one morning, or what?"

"That's the typical scenario in movies and books, but it doesn't happen like that very often, I'm afraid. Usually the return of memory is ragged and sporadic. Sometimes, though very rarely, the memory loss is irreversible. And in a case like Leah's it's especially difficult to form a realistic diagnosis."

"Why?"

"Because we're still not sure about causation. She has a concussion, Paul, which has caused some slight inter-cranial swelling. We've been monitoring that very closely. But she's also been under a lot of emotional pressure for a long time, and now you tell me that's been compounded by the stress of an impending divorce. So there could be multiple causes for this amnesia, both physiological and emotional. In cases like that, the picture becomes much more complex. In fact, there are so many anomalies that it's hard to draw any kind of clinical profile.''

"So anything could happen?"

"Anything."

Paul was silent a moment, thinking. "I just can't bring myself to believe it," he said finally. "Doesn't it strike you as odd that she claims to have completely lost her memory, but she still knows how to talk and feed herself and everything? The nurse says she can even *read,* for God's sake. Isn't that just a little suspicious to you?"

"Not at all." Dr. Holcross hesitated, frowning thoughtfully. "Let me put it to you this way," he said at last. "The mental state of a true amnesiac is rather like this, Paul. It's similar to the condition of somebody who's lived for years on another planet and spent all his time learning about us here on Earth. He's stored all kinds of facts about the language, the habits and customs, even the history and geography, but he's never experienced any of it in a personal sense. If you asked an amnesiac what snow was, he'd probably be able to search his mental stores and tell you that it's frozen precipitation, it's white and it comes in the winter. But he wouldn't have the slightest recollection of how it feels to walk on crunchy new snow or to have snowflakes falling on his face."

Paul stared at the elderly doctor. "That's so hard to grasp, Ken. How could they remember one but not the other?"

"Because what they've lost, usually, is personal memory, not general memory. We still don't really know all that much about the working of the brain, but there seem to be different storage and retrieval mechanisms for different types of memory. On the basis of the examination I've done so far, I'd say that Leah is a classic example of selective amnesia.''

"Oh, I agree with that. She always has been,'' Paul said grimly. "Just try to get the truth out of her some time, and see how conveniently she forgets all the parts she wants to avoid.''

"Paul,'' the doctor said gently, "you know that's not what I'm talking about.''

"Sure, I know. I just can't believe any of this, Ken. I still think the whole thing is another of her little scams, and I resent like hell the fact that she's getting away with it so successfully. I just hate the idea that she's probably laughing at all of us behind those wide, innocent eyes.''

The doctor picked his pen up again and eyed it thoughtfully. "Speaking of innocence, Paul, that was something else I wanted to warn you about.''

"What do you mean?''

"It's my belief that Leah has no personal memory of any kind. She's much like a little child, in that everything that happens to her is happening for the first time. It's important for those around her to bear that in mind so she's not traumatized by the things she experiences.''

Paul stared intently at the other man, clearly caught by something in his tone. "What are you saying, Ken? What exactly are you trying to tell me?''

"I'm just warning you,'' Dr. Holcross repeated carefully. "I know you don't believe what I've told you about Leah's condition, and I can certainly understand your anger and bitterness. But if my diagnosis is correct, and I believe that it is, then it's something you really have to bear in mind in your... your dealings with her," the doctor concluded, looking a little awkward for the first time in the interview.

Paul leaned back, his brilliant hazel eyes still fixed on the other's face. "I get it," he said slowly. "I understand, Ken. You're telling me...my God!" he said with a brief, harsh laugh. "You're telling me that she's a virgin. Isn't that right?"

"By most standards, yes," the doctor said firmly. "Not physically, of course, but mentally and emotionally. I believe she won't have the slightest recollection of sexual experience. It could be very traumatic if she were approached in...in a careless manner," the doctor concluded after another uncomfortable pause.

"Ken, she's covered with bandages. I'm not a complete monster, you know."

"Her injuries are going to heal rapidly," the doctor said. "But her memory will recover more slowly, if at all. And in an emotional sense, she's going to be absolutely vulnerable."

"Oh, hell," Paul muttered. "This is all just so bizarre, you know? Leah Temple, a *virgin*. My God." He fell silent, his handsome face twisted once more into hard lines of bitterness and pain.

"I'm not just speaking about sexual matters, Paul," the doctor ventured after another brief silence. "I'm warning you about traumas of any kind. She really needs to be protected just now."

"Not from me, Ken," the younger man said, rising abruptly and giving the doctor a curt nod. "She's absolutely safe with me. I haven't touched the woman for over a year, and I can assure you that I don't intend to start now. In fact, nothing could induce me to touch her. You don't need to have any worries on that score, believe me.''

With another brief nod he turned and was gone, his broad shoulders disappearing through the door, his footsteps echoing faintly in the tiled corridor.

Ken Holcross sat at his desk in silence, staring at the chair the tall young man had recently occupied, his bland, pleasant face creased with concern.

PAUL TEMPLE PARKED his low-slung sports car at the edge of the road and got out slowly, turning up the collar of his jacket against the biting April wind and plunging his hands deep into his pockets.

He walked down the grassy embankment and stood by the edge of the prairie river, gazing at the lacy swirls of thinning ice that clung like fragile lace to the rocks along the shore.

Clouds massed overhead, pearl-laden galleons drifting smoothly in a dazzling sapphire sea. A breeze blew off the water, fresh and tangy with the scents of damp earth and new grass and flowers waiting to be born. Everything about the April morning carried sweetness and promise, a joyous sense of hope and renewal.

But the beauty of the day was lost on Paul. His face was restless and miserable, his big body slumped with despair. He kicked idly at the pebbles on the damp gravel beach, thinking about his interview with Ken Holcross.

Paul wasn't at all proud of the way he'd conducted himself, the things he'd said or the emotions he'd revealed. He hunched his shoulders and lifted his eyes briefly to watch a hawk soaring overhead, then gazed moodily at the water again.

That was the worst thing about his marriage to Leah, he thought, remembering the conversation with a brief shudder of distaste. Life with that woman had turned him into a different man, one that he often despised. He hadn't always been like this, so coldly unforgiving.

But, he told himself in despair, a man could only take so much. How many times could he endure humiliation and anguish without turning brutally cold?

He thought of the doctor's diagnosis, and of Leah looking so pale and fragile in the hospital bed, with her strange boyish haircut and those beautiful, piteous eyes that concealed the soul of a monster.

It had been her eyes that had drawn him first, years ago when he'd gone to a lounge one night with a couple of business associates and she'd served them their drinks. Paul Temple had gazed up at her, spellbound by her beauty. He'd never seen eyes like that, huge brown eyes with sparkling golden highlights, set beneath a dense fringe of dark lashes. He'd been so young then, just twenty-five, and it hadn't taken him long to notice that she had a face and body to match those lovely eyes. In fact, there was something about her physical person that drew him with an irresistible force. She had a smoldering sexual appeal; her body seemed to whisper a breathtaking, secret promise every time she moved.

By the time he'd been back to the lounge a few more times, he was obsessed by her. She filled his dreams and his waking thoughts to the exclusion of everything else, and all he wanted was to possess her. He had no parents or family to warn him about the liaison, although some of his friends certainly tried.

"Paul, what the hell do you know about her, really? You're planning to marry this woman, make her heir to a fortune like yours, and you don't even know who she is? You're crazy, man."

It was true that he knew very little about Leah when he married her. Oddly enough, after five years of marriage he still knew very little. He certainly didn't know as much about her as Ken Holcross did. The doctor occasionally hinted at childhood trauma, terrible experiences that Leah tried to repress, but she never talked to Paul about her family or her past.

"I have no family, just like you," she told him cheerfully. "If you can't accept that, too bad. What you see is what you get."

He'd loved her then, loved her gallantry and her jaunty bravado about her own life. Paul Temple had led a wealthy, privileged existence, an only son born late in the life of doting parents. He'd never known a moment's need in all his life, and very little sorrow until his early twenties when his parents died of cancer within six months of each other, leaving him enormously wealthy and very much alone.

He couldn't imagine what Leah's life must have been like before she met him. He was awed by the degree of courage it must have taken for a young woman to look after herself all alone in the city, slinging drinks and pocketing her tips, keeping herself cheerful and attractive all the time, getting back and forth to her college classes in the daytime and going to work at night.

Later, of course, he learned that she'd lied about the college courses. She'd never been to college at all, except to take a night course in bartending. She'd invented the college-student persona just to impress him, lied about that as easily as she did about everything else.

Leah Temple was a pathological liar, a woman who manufactured elaborate webs of deceit just for the fun of it. She craved danger, intrigue and the sensation of living her life on the brink of destruction. Leah's idea of excitement was to walk a razor's edge just above a dark abyss filled with monsters.

Life with Paul Temple soon bored her. The money was a novelty for a while, but not enough to soothe her restless, questing spirit. And despite his wealth, Paul was a home-loving man who craved closeness and warmth in his marriage, who loved the simple pleasures of nature and conversation and the gentle passage of the seasons. He'd married with a kind of innocent confidence that his wife would share these dreams, and that together they'd build a warm, secure, loving home, a place for children to grow up in happiness.

But there never were any children, and his marriage to Leah had rapidly become a grim nightmare of trauma and turmoil, of dramatic near-disasters and embarrassing brushes with the law, of shoddy deceptions and fits of rage and bitter screaming arguments that left Paul shaken and ashamed.

He would have divorced her years earlier except for those strange enchanting periods when a different Leah sometimes appeared, a sweet, playful, irresistible gamine who was able to entrance him all over again. Paul never knew when these brief episodes would happen and they always took him by surprise, making him twice as miserable when she reverted to the cold, manipulative woman that he hated.

But most painful of all was the fact that, despite the squalid horror of his marriage, he still craved her physically. Even though their sexual relationship had long since deteriorated into bitter emptiness, he couldn't quite get over the helpless yearning for the only body that had ever satisfied him so deeply.

Paul hated himself for this weakness and kept himself sternly removed from his wife's physical presence. It was no exaggeration when he told the doctor that he hadn't touched Leah in more than a year. But nobody would ever know what it had cost him, how fiercely he sometimes longed to push his way into her room and take her by force.

Of course, there wouldn't have to be any force. She'd probably resist a little at first, just to get him excited, then give in and savage him in return, laughing with cruel pleasure at his brutality, the moonlight shining on her slim white throat, those golden-brown eyes glistening in the darkness. . . .

Paul swallowed hard and shook himself to dislodge the image, feeling unclean and miserable. He thought about Dr. Holcross's gentle warning that Leah was now an emotional virgin.

"A *virgin*," he muttered aloud, and heard her mocking laughter in the gentle springtime breeze.

Paul shuddered and gazed blindly out across the water. He had a sudden powerful urge to get into his car and drive back to tell Dr. Holcross that he couldn't possibly take that woman into his house again.

He'd felt so good this past month, after finally making the firm decision to divorce her. For the first time in years he'd felt clean and free, hopeful that his nightmare would end and he'd have a decent life again. The thought of wading back into all that misery was almost more than he could bear.

Wearily he recalled the conversation and Ken's insistence that Leah's condition was genuine.

What if it was? What if she was truly amnesiac, without the most basic knowledge of herself and her place in the world, as helpless and vulnerable as the doctor claimed? What kind of monster would a husband have to be, to turn a woman out under such conditions?

As much of a monster as she is, Paul thought bitterly. *She'd do the same thing to me in a minute if it suited her purposes.*

But he knew he couldn't be so merciless. If he began fitting his actions to hers, then she would have succeeded in making him utterly corrupt and his life would be worthless.

Paul's face hardened.

Let her come home, he decided. Let her come home for a month and be forced to maintain this whole charade. The minute she let her guard down, he'd catch her at it and throw her out. In the meantime, he could probably even enjoy watching her struggle to keep up an appearance of innocence and confusion.

Paul's mouth twisted in a humorless smile and his jaw tightened. He turned and climbed the grassy embankment, heading back to his little car, still heedless of the mellow beauty of the rich sleeping prairie.

"THIS CITY we're living in is called Calgary," Doris said in a casual, informative voice. "What province is it in, Leah?"

"Alberta," Leah said obediently. "Canada?" she added, sitting cross-legged on the bed and watching

Doris pack toiletries into a small tan leather bag fitted with compartments.

"That's right. You know, this is such beautiful luggage," Doris commented. "It must've cost thousands of dollars if you've got a whole matched set. Do you?" she asked, glancing up.

"I don't know," Leah said, leaning forward and looking curiously at the leather bag. "Where did it come from?"

"Your husband brought it, along with some personal things and some clothes for you to wear when you go home. It has your initials on it. See, LJT in gold right there by the handle."

"Oh," Leah said, settling back onto the bed again with a troubled expression.

"Don't you remember, Leah?" Doris looked with concern at her patient. "He came yesterday when you were asleep and brought that jumpsuit you're wearing, and some shoes, and your makeup kit and hairbrushes...."

But Leah wasn't listening. She sat tensely in the middle of the bed, watching Doris's brown hands as the nurse packed things into the leather bag.

"I don't want to go, Doris," she said abruptly.

"Where?"

"Wherever he lives. I don't want to go there. I want to stay at the hospital."

"Honey, that's your home," Doris said gently. "It's not just where he lives, it's where you live, too. And they tell me it's a really beautiful place."

"What's it like?"

"Well, let me see. It's a big house out in the country, about fifteen miles from the city limits."

Leah frowned. "Is he a farmer?"

"Your husband?" Doris chuckled. "Not really, Leah. More like a hobby farmer, I guess you'd call him. He just keeps that little property out there for the fun of it. He's the owner and managing director of a company that manufactures special equipment for oil fields all over the world. He's just about one of the richest men around, so I hear."

Leah pondered the meaning of "rich" for a few moments, then abandoned the effort. "I wish you could come," she said shyly to Doris. "I'd feel so much better if you'd be there."

Doris laughed and reached over to pat Leah's pale cheek. "Honey, I'm sure gonna miss you, too, but you'll be fine at home. There's a woman who lives out there full time, and a couple of kids, too, so I hear. About the age of my kids, they are."

Leah brightened, looking with interest at the big woman. "Do you have children, Doris?"

"I sure do. A boy and a girl, just getting to the awful age."

"That must be so nice, having children," Leah said. She paused shyly. "I don't suppose...Doris, have I ever had children?"

Doris hesitated, looking with gentle compassion into the woman's beautiful, pleading eyes, wondering what to say.

Leah Temple's medical records indicated that she had never borne a child. Dr. Holcross said she'd been taking birth control pills throughout her marriage, a fact that she had concealed from her husband. Apparently Paul Temple wanted children and his wife didn't.

That was something else to discuss with the doctor, Doris thought, making a quick mental note. Somebody certainly needed to explain to Leah Temple what her various medications were for.

"No, honey," the nurse said aloud, her broad face impassive. "No, you've never had children."

"I wonder why I didn't. I think that would just be so nice, having a little baby to hold," Leah said in that same wistful tone. "Is it really a wonderful feeling, Doris?"

"Yes," Doris said, pausing with a scrap of lacy underwear in her hands, smiling into the distance. "Yes, it's really a wonderful feeling. Now," she added briskly, changing the subject, "let's go over all this one more time, Leah. You've read this list I made up for you?"

Leah nodded.

"Good. And you know all the things I told you about looking after yourself, and what to expect from your body?"

Again the woman nodded obediently.

"Okay," Doris said. "You're a real smart girl, Leah, and you learn so fast that I'm not all that worried about you. But I wrote down my number here at the hospital if you need anything, and the shifts I'll be working so you can get in touch with me. And if there's anything you're not sure about, and you can't get hold of me, you can always ask the woman who lives there at your place. She'll be glad to help you, I'm sure."

"Anna," Leah murmured tonelessly. "Her name is Anna McBride."

"That's right. And her husband?"

"Bob."

"And the girls?"

"Let me see. Bonnie, that's the older one. And...and Allie?"

"Right. That's what Dr. Holcross says here on the list. And your husband?"

"Paul Temple."

"And why the long face?" Doris asked, looking keenly at Leah's lovely oval face with its fading stain of bruises.

"Oh, Doris..." Leah choked and turned away, gazing blindly out the window, her golden-brown eyes sparkling with sudden tears.

Doris sat on the bed and cuddled the slender woman like a child, drawing her into an ample bosom and patting her trembling back. "Now, what's all this?" she murmured. "What's the matter, honey?"

Leah sobbed briefly against the comfortable bulk of the big nurse, then drew away and bit her lip, struggling to regain her composure. "It's him," she whispered at last. "Paul. My...my husband."

"What about him?" Doris asked briskly.

"He hates me, Doris!" Leah said, gazing up at the other woman, her eyes dark with misery. "He just hates me."

"Of course he doesn't hate you. Whatever gave you such a silly idea?"

"I can tell," Leah said. "He can't stand me. He thinks I'm an awful person."

"Now, that's just silly," Doris said comfortably. "I understand the two of you have been going through some problems in your marriage, but that doesn't mean he hates you, Leah. Lots of times married people have fights and squabbles, and then they make up and it's just like before. Why, it happens with my husband and me all the time."

"But you should see the way he looks at me," Leah whispered, gazing at Doris with a helpless, pleading expression, her eyes full of childlike pain. "He's been here twice, and both times I just wanted him to go away because it's so obvious that he . . . he . . ."

"Now, just forget all this," Doris said sternly. "You just put all this right out of your mind and concentrate on getting better, and don't worry about such nonsense. He doesn't hate you, Leah. He just doesn't understand everything about your condition, so it's probably a little upsetting to him. Now, you're going to go home, and you're going to stop fretting and start getting your memory back, and things are going to be just fine. Do you hear me?"

"Yes," Leah said. "But what if he—"

"No 'buts.' You just do what I say, and don't let me hear any more about people hating each other. Come on now, it's naptime."

Doris moved briskly around the small private room, drawing the drapes, plumping pillows and tucking Leah under a soft mound of blankets.

She gathered her charts and headed for the door, pausing to smile at the slender form lying quietly beneath the blankets.

Then she went out into the hallway and headed for the nursing station, her broad face troubled and thoughtful, resolving to have another little talk with the doctor about Leah Temple and her husband before the poor woman went home with him tomorrow.

CHAPTER THREE

"He's bringing her home today. This afternoon, right after lunch."

Bonnie McBride nodded and munched on part of a chocolate doughnut, then stuffed the remainder greedily into her mouth and reached for another, anxious to eat as many as she could before her mother came back and caught her.

"I *know* that, stupid," she said to her younger sister, talking with her mouth full. "Mom told us yesterday."

"Oh, yeah? Well, I bet you don't know *this*, smarty." Allie McBride, aged ten, lowered her screwdriver to the table and leaned on her elbows, gazing across at her sister.

"What?" Bonnie asked cautiously.

"She's crazy," Allie said with a smug expression. "Nuts. Wacko."

"Mrs. *Temple?*" Bonnie said, staring in disbelief.

"Yeah." Allie picked up her screwdriver and frowned at the front-wheel assembly of her skateboard. "I think it's one of these bearings," she said thoughtfully. "I better get Dad to look at it."

Bonnie sat with a doughnut forgotten in her plump hand, still gazing in astonishment at her younger sister.

Allie McBride was thin, freckled and boyish, with pale red hair and dark green eyes. She would no doubt be beautiful someday, but right now, dressed in a ragged black T-shirt, faded patched jeans and scuffed high-top sneakers, and sporting a smear of grease across her snub nose, Allie didn't look all that great.

Especially with such a smug expression on her face, Bonnie thought with distaste.

"I don't believe you," she said calmly, reaching for another doughnut. "You're just making it up. You lie all the time, Allie."

"Yeah?" Allie said with some belligerence. "That's what *you* think. If you don't stop gobbling those doughnuts, Mom's gonna kill you," she added in a careless, detached manner, squinting down at the faulty metal bearings.

"Shut up," Bonnie said automatically. "Who told you?" she asked after pausing to chew and swallow, then looking closely at the remaining doughnuts in the package.

"That she's nuts? I heard Mom talking to the hospital on the phone. They were telling her how she needs to be looked after and stuff. I guess she got knocked real hard on the head and it made her crazy. Right out of her gourd."

"I don't believe it," Bonnie repeated.

Her face and voice were calm, but her mind reeled with shock. She thought of Leah Temple, so slim and glamorous with her beautiful eyes and hair and stylish, scented clothes, her mocking smile and cold silvery laughter.

"Hey, where'd you get all that makeup?" Allie asked suddenly, looking closely at her sister. "Jeez, look at you, Bonnie! You got on eye shadow and mascara and everything."

Bonnie's plump face flushed with annoyance. "Shut up!" she hissed, glancing nervously over her shoulder into the other room where a vacuum cleaner whirred.

"You went in her room while she was gone, didn't you?" Allie said, unimpressed by her sister's fierce glare. "You stole all that stuff from Mrs. Temple's room, right? Wait'll Mom finds out, Bonnie. You're dead meat. You're toast."

"I didn't steal it!" Bonnie whispered furiously, her round, dimpled face twisting with the force of her emotion. "It was in her *garbage!* She always throws away stuff she hasn't hardly used, and I just took some of it from the wastebasket in her room before Mom cleaned in there."

"It's a good thing she's crazy," Allie said calmly, "or she'd know right away that you were messing with her stuff while she was gone, and would you ever be sorry."

"Who's crazy?" Anna McBride asked, moving briskly through the room with a cloth and a jar of furniture polish.

The girls exchanged an awkward glance. A look of unpleasant triumph dawned in Bonnie's eyes. "Mrs. Temple," she told her mother with an air of innocence. "Allie heard you talking to somebody on the phone. She says they were telling you that Mrs. Temple's crazy."

Bonnie exchanged another brief glance with her sister, who glared horribly and twisted uneasily in her chair. Bonnie, meanwhile, lowered her eyes in demure silence and waited for the storm to break.

Anna McBride's pleasant freckled face turned pink with annoyance. She stood with her hands on her hips and glared at her younger daughter, who had inherited Anna's own wiry frame and distinctive coloring.

"Alicia McBride! Have you been listening on the other phone again? Answer me!"

"I wasn't listening," Allie said sullenly. "I just picked it up to call Robbie, and you were talking and I sort of overheard. I heard that nurse telling you how Mrs. Temple was crazy."

"She didn't say that at all," Anna said firmly. "Mrs. Temple is suffering from memory loss, that's all. We're all going to have to be very nice to her for a while, and help her get better."

"Memory loss?" Allie asked, twisting in her chair and gazing up at her mother, the screwdriver dangling from one dirty hand. "What's that?"

"Just what I said. Apparently she can't remember much of anything just now, but they're sure that things will come back to her soon."

"Not even her own *name?*" Allie asked. "Did she forget stuff like her own name, and all that, Mom? Does she remember us?"

"I don't know," Anna said briskly. "We'll just have to wait until Paul brings her home and see what she's like."

"She's a creep," Allie said calmly. "I hate her. Paul's nice, but not her. I hate her guts."

"Allie!" her mother protested, but her glance was already straying back into the living room where the vacuum cleaner waited.

Bonnie peeped up at her mother's face, disappointed that Allie was apparently getting off so easily. "Don't you hate it when Allie listens on the phone,

Mom?'' she ventured, ignoring another fearful glare from her sister. "I wish she'd stop doing it."

Anna looked down at her elder daughter in a harried, distracted manner, then bent to peer more closely. "Bonita!" she said. "What is all that awful stuff on your face? Go right this instant and wash it off. And did you eat all those doughnuts? Oh, *Bonnie,*" Anna said, her anger fading abruptly into sadness.

Bonnie stared coldly at Allie, who was grinning back at her sister with a secret look of gloating triumph.

"Go wash your face, Bonnie," Anna repeated wearily. "And then walk down for the mail. You could use the exercise, after all those calories."

Slowly, drowning in shame and misery, Bonnie went into the hall bathroom and scrubbed the makeup from her face. Then she trudged out through the back door and down the lane toward the mailbox.

Bonnie McBride was two months from her thirteenth birthday. She had her father's small sturdy form, his fair hair and blue eyes, and a face so pretty that it was almost angelic. But her good looks were lost in the mounds of pudgy flesh that plumped her cheeks, sagged around her middle and made her legs rub together when she walked.

She moved reluctantly away from the house, her beautiful long hair glinting in the sunlight, her fat body swaying awkwardly. As she walked, Bonnie thought about the astonishing news that Leah Temple had something wrong with her head.

Amnesia, Bonnie thought. That was what they called it when you couldn't remember things about yourself. She knew about the medical condition, but she couldn't imagine it, somehow, in connection with the woman who was mistress of this estate they lived on.

Leah Temple had always loomed large in Bonnie's eyes—a mythic figure like one of the cruel goddesses of ancient times. Everything Leah did wàs beautiful and enticing and bad. Yes, Bonnie knew that the woman was bad, but her evil was awe-inspiring, somehow—almost overwhelming in its beauty and audacity.

Bonnie just couldn't imagine Leah Temple being hurt or helpless, needing assistance from anybody.

She rubbed at her eyes, where some of the mascara still burned and stung after her hasty washing.

Anger at her sister flared briefly, then subsided into relief when she thought about Allie's news. Bonnie had in fact been feeling some urgent concern about the prospect of Mrs. Temple coming home and discovering that Bonnie had been in her room.

Because not *everything* Bonnie had taken had been in the wastebasket. Most of it, yes, but Bonnie had also helped herself to a few of the things that crowded a gold-and-crystal tray on the vast dresser. She'd even rummaged breathlessly in a couple of the bureau drawers, gazing with a kind of helpless anguish at the tiny lacy wisps of bras and panties.

Allie was right, Bonnie thought miserably. If Mrs. Temple ever knew that Bonnie had been in her things, she'd be furious. Not that she needed the things herself. Leah Temple was careless and wasteful, often throwing things out simply because she was tired of them, or giving away the most expensive items apparently on a whim.

When she was younger Bonnie used to hang around the big house while her mother cleaned, hoping that Leah would choose to part with a crystal necklace, a pretty silk scarf or an unused bottle of perfume.

But lately, just before the accident that landed her in the hospital, Leah hadn't been in the mood to give away much of anything. In fact, for months now she'd been deliberately mean to Bonnie whenever she saw the girl, asking her when she was going to grow tall enough for her weight, or how long she planned to carry around all that baby fat.

"Fat's okay for babies," Leah had said once to Bonnie, with a cruel twist of that beautiful mouth. "But it's sure ugly on girls and women. You really should do something about that, kid. You're getting to be a real little tubbo."

Bonnie caught her breath, remembering. She was still shattered by the viciousness of that remark, still chilled with agony whenever she thought of it.

The funny thing was, she hadn't even been all that fat when Leah Temple had said what she did. That had been a few months ago, when Bonnie was just five or ten pounds overweight.

Every time she remembered Leah's careless words, Bonnie hurt so much she couldn't bear the pain, and the really strange part was that the only way to console herself seemed to be with food. She felt better when she was chewing and swallowing, found comfort in the food, comfort that kept Leah's mocking laughter and cruel golden-brown eyes far away from her. And now, Bonnie thought miserably, remembering the pile of doughnuts she'd just eaten, she was more than thirty pounds overweight, and gaining all the time, and there didn't seem to be a single thing she could do about it.

Hot tears blinded her eyes. She pounded at her sides with her fists, hating herself, hating the ugly walls of flesh that imprisoned her, hating her sister and Leah Temple and everybody else who said cruel, hurtful things.

She took the mail from the box, flipping through it listlessly to see if there was anything for her, even though she seldom got any mail.

Allie got mail all the time, because she sent away for everything from free brochures on the environment to magic pens that could work underwater.

"Dear Sirs," Allie would write in a laborious hand, sitting at the kitchen table with a pencil clutched in her grubby fist. "I would appreciate it very much if you would send me..."

"Stupid kid," Bonnie muttered aloud, still burning with shame over the business of the makeup and her mother's comments about the doughnuts she'd eaten.

She quickened her steps, remembering a big chocolate bar she'd hidden in her bedside table just the day before, yearning with sudden passion for the dark richness of the chocolate, the comforting taste and texture of it.

Bonnie was so absorbed in the thought of the chocolate, and how to get it out of the house without being caught, that she didn't hear the truck pull up behind her.

"Well, hi there," a familiar voice said.

Bonnie's heart leaped and then began to hammer painfully in her chest. She flushed and turned around, struggling for an air of nonchalance.

"Hi, Jody," she said, hoping her voice sounded cool and lofty like the ladies on television.

Jody Muller leaned his tanned elbow on the window ledge of his truck and grinned at her. He had three other kids jammed into the cab, a boy and two girls, though Bonnie was too terrified to identify them. She saw nothing but masses of hair and faded denim, heard the other boy's deep cracking voice and the shrill laughter of the girls.

"Nice day," Jody said conversationally, letting his truck creep along beside Bonnie as she trudged doggedly toward her house.

"Yeah," Bonnie agreed, wishing desperately that he would go away.

She loved Jody Muller, adored him with every fiber of her being. Bonnie spent hundreds of hours thinking about the way his hair grew all dark and curly around his ears, and his eyebrows slanted upward like he was always asking a question. In the darkness of her room she fantasized endlessly about this boy, four years older than herself, who lived just a few miles down the road.

She dreamed about holding hands with him, walking in some misty place that was green and full of flowers. In her dreams, Bonnie wore a lacy white dress that swirled around her legs, and she carried a big white hat. She tossed her hair and laughed in the sunlight, graceful and beautiful and slim.

In her dreams, Bonnie was always slim. But reality was a far cry from her fantasies. In her daydreams Bonnie had wonderful, witty things to say, and Jody always gazed at her with a kind of stunned adoration, like the guys in the rock music videos looking at their girls. When she actually encountered Jody, though, ran into him in town or at school or on the road like this, she was miserably embarrassed and tongue-tied, especially if he had other people with him.

"Hey, kid, do you know where you're going?" Jody asked, his truck still inching along beside her.

"Sure I do," Bonnie muttered, her plump face flaming. "I'm going home."

"Up there? Is that where you live?" he asked in an exaggerated questioning tone.

Bonnie glanced at him quickly, then looked away, wondering what he was getting at. Of course he knew where she lived. They'd been neighbors most of their lives.

"Hey, kid?" he needled her. "I said, is that where you live?"

"Yes," Bonnie said desperately.

"Oh. I was just checking, see? You know why?"

Bonnie was silent, suddenly dreading his next words.

"Hey, you know *why?*"

"No," she said in a low, choked voice.

"Well, 'cause I heard an elephant escaped from the circus last night, an' I thought you might be it."

He gunned the motor and they roared off in a swirl of dust, laughing rowdily and leaving Bonnie staring after them, trembling with humiliation, so anguished that she couldn't even cry.

LEAH SAT VERY STILL in the front seat of Paul Temple's little car, gazing out the window in amazement. The world went spinning by, dazzling in its brightness and color after the quiet, gray safety of the hospital.

There was so much to see that she didn't even know where to turn her eyes. Masses of people thronged the streets, cars snarled and seemed constantly on the verge of crashing into one another, and neon signs flashed and sparkled, even in the midday sunshine. The whole world looked bright and dangerous, crowded with movement and color and hard-edged brilliance that left no room for her.

Leah was silent, huddled in a soft jacket of cream leather, clutching the ends of her belt with tense fingers as she stared out the window.

She felt Paul's eyes turn to her occasionally, rest on her in cold speculation, but she couldn't even acknowledge him. She was too frightened and miserable.

More than anything, Leah longed to go back to the hospital, the only environment she'd ever known. She wanted to creep into her darkened room and pull the covers over her head. She wanted to see Doris and the others moving quietly around, looking after her and keeping the dangerous world away.

But it was a little better when they left the city and skimmed out along a curving tree-lined rural highway. This place was less bewildering, more quiet and peaceful. Occasionally the trees thinned so that Leah, peering anxiously out the window, was able to see fields lying rich and golden in the sunlight, pastures where cattle grazed and a massive band of white-capped mountains glistening far away in the sunlight.

They topped a rise and pulled through an open gate, dipping down into a spacious valley along a creek bed where a set of buildings lay clean and orderly in the spring sunshine. Leah could see that there were two houses on the property. One was a small square bungalow, neatly kept and bounded by a white picket fence. Farther back, beyond a wide sweep of lawn and shrubbery, another house nestled in the trees, a big sprawling structure of stone and cedar and smoked glass.

Leah gazed at the house for a moment without recognition of any kind, then looked at a nearby pasture where several horses grazed quietly.

She glanced over at the golden-haired man who gripped the wheel in strong brown hands. His jaw was taut, his face cold and unrevealing. They hadn't exchanged a word since leaving the hospital, but there was a question that Leah badly needed to ask.

"Doris said...you weren't a farmer," she ventured finally in a small voice. "But there's...horses and cattle here..."

Paul Temple parked on the circular driveway, then turned to look at her. Leah saw with a sudden chill that his hazel eyes were dark with anger.

"Look, Leah," he said sharply, "just give it a rest, would you? We're all alone here, and there's no need to keep up this charade, okay? It's so damned embarrassing, watching you do this. Can't you understand how demeaning it is for both of us?"

She was silent, trying to understand what he meant. She really wanted to know why he kept livestock if he was a businessman, as Doris had told her, or if there was something she didn't know about him. Maybe people did both things. Maybe the livestock were like pets.

Leah frowned in confusion, searching her crowded memory, trying to recall whether people kept big animals as pets, or only little ones.

"Come on," Paul said impatiently. "Bob's waiting to put the car away."

Leah nodded and got out, standing hesitantly by the car and smiling at a stocky fair-haired man in a denim jacket and cap. The man nodded to her with quiet courtesy and took her suitcase from the trunk of the car.

"Hello, Mrs. Temple. Nice to see you home again."

"Thank you. You're Bob, aren't you?"

The man exchanged a quick glance with Paul, then nodded again, his face expressionless. "That's right, ma'am. I'm Bob McBride."

"And Anna? That's your wife, isn't it?"

Another quick glance, but this time Paul couldn't contain his irritation. He turned and started toward the house, grasping Leah's elbow and drawing her firmly along beside him.

Inside, there were too many impressions to take in all at once. Leah had a confused sense of spaciousness and beauty, of soft misty green and gold and silvery blue—colors that seemed to bring the outside world indoors. Her senses were assailed by richness and density: deep, soft carpets and shimmering silken fabrics, graceful shapes and colors as exquisite as rainbows.

Paul stopped abruptly in the middle of a big high-windowed room, setting down the leather overnight case and gesturing to her. "You can take this to your room," he said. "I'll see you at dinner."

Leah nodded, anxious not to annoy him further. She hesitated as he turned to leave, then forced herself to say his name for the first time.

"Paul?" she ventured timidly.

"Yes?" He turned and looked over his shoulder.

"I'm sorry," Leah began in that same shy, halting voice. "I don't want to bother you any more, but I...I don't know where to go. I don't know where I'm supposed to put my things."

He gave her a long intent glance, and a touch of uncertainty flickered in his remarkable eyes. Finally he nodded. "Come on," he said curtly, leading her down a carpeted hallway, pausing by a set of double paneled doors, which he opened.

Leah stepped into the room and gasped. The place behind the doors was so beautiful, so richly appealing that she couldn't take it all in. The colors were deep and jewellike, emerald green and maroon, amber and cream, combining to create a gracious splendor that took her breath away.

A huge canopied bed covered in green silk stood near French doors leading to a shaded terrace. Leah saw a carved rosewood desk, a maroon velvet couch, broad glistening dressers and mirrors, oil paintings in carved gold frames and a gleaming white-and-gold bathroom through an open door. "Oh," she breathed at last, forgetting her shyness and turning to gaze up at him. "Oh, Paul, it's just so beautiful."

Paul gave a brief, harsh laugh. "Now, isn't that strange?" he said coldly. "Last I heard, you were planning to rip this place apart and redecorate the whole thing in art deco."

She stared at him, unable to comprehend what he was saying. With another curt nod he turned and strode off down the hallway. Leah stood and gazed after him, watching as his tall frame was swallowed up in the luxurious depths of the house.

When he was gone she felt relieved, much more safe and comfortable. But she also felt strangely wistful and bereft, as if the very fact of his beautiful male presence filled some deep need in her, something even more pressing than the need for food and sleep.

She wandered around the luxurious room, touching objects as she went, picking them up and setting them down again. The room was full of such lovely things: small graceful ornaments, glistening tubes and bottles on shining crystal trays, framed pictures supported by little gold stands and hardcover books in shelves above the desk.

Leah shrugged out of her leather jacket and hesitated, then opened a mirrored door and gasped again. The closet inside wasn't at all like the one at the hospital. It was a whole little room, big enough to contain an armchair and a stereo unit, with racks and racks of hangers and shelves crowded with clothes. She saw dresses, fur coats, folded sweaters, dozens of shoes lined up in neat rows, glamorous wide-brimmed hats and gloves and scarves in colorful banks.

"It's like a store," Leah murmured aloud, too amazed to contain herself. "Who *wears* all this?"

She hung the jacket beside several others and lingered a moment, fingering the silk and leather and soft fur, but soon the roomful of clothes began to oppress her. Her battered body started to ache again, to throb wearily at the strangeness of everything. She shivered and closed the door on all that opulence, then wandered over to the wide mullioned window and sank onto the window seat, gazing out at the spring afternoon.

The terrace and yard were dotted with early tulips and sky-blue hyacinths, though the trees were not yet in leaf. At the edge of the big yard two girls were working, gathering dried twigs and withered brown leaves that drifted along the fence, cleaning dead shrubbery from the flower beds and piling everything in a huge stack beyond the fence.

The girls were both young, but one was plump and round like Doris while the other was thin. The round one had shining golden hair hanging down her back, glistening in the sunlight, and the other had carroty curls tucked into an old baseball cap.

They seemed to be fighting as they worked. Leah watched, fascinated by the uneven rhythm of their actions. She was intrigued by the way they raked doggedly at the dead vegetation for a while, then paused to exchange some brief, furious conversation before returning to their separate tasks. A woman came around the corner of the house, tall and brisk, with the same wiry frame and bright red hair as the thinner girl. She stood, her hands on her hips, saying something that Leah couldn't hear. The girls listened, their heads lowered, and both nodded reluctantly. They watched with interest as the woman moved forward, rummaged in her jacket pockets and did something in the huge mound of leaves and rubbish, then stepped back again.

Flames flickered and soared high in the air, shimmering in the afternoon light. The two girls laughed and capered around the fire, then returned to their task, their anger apparently forgotten. After the red-haired woman left they made a game of what they were doing, standing close to the fire with armfuls of trash, shouting and laughing as they dumped more vegetation on the pile and watched the orange flames leap high in response.

Leah gazed at the small tableau, her throat tight. She longed to go outside and ask the girls if she could help. It looked so pleasant out there with the sun glowing, the bright flames leaping, the two children laughing.

She moved closer to the window, drawing the silken curtain aside and leaning forward eagerly. The red-haired girl caught sight of her behind the curtain and said something to the other, and they both stared briefly in her direction. Then they turned their backs to her and quietly went on with their work, all the fun and horseplay abruptly halted.

Chilled, Leah let the curtain fall and moved over to sit on the bed, feeling unbearably lonely. She sat quietly with her hands folded in her lap, wondering when dinner would be, how she'd ever manage to find the dining room in such a vast house, who would be there and what it would be like.

She gazed around, trying to think what to do, how to fill in the hours that stretched ahead of her in this luxurious, unfamiliar place.

Suddenly Leah felt a dreadful flood of homesickness, an unbearable yearning for Doris, Dr. Holcross and the placid hospital routine.

She thought about this strange place the grim, golden-haired man had brought her to, about the wary coldness in all these people's eyes when they looked at her, Paul and Bob and the two girls. Leah's misery increased, became more than she could endure. Hot tears gathered in her eyes and trickled slowly down her cheeks, dropping unheeded onto her folded hands.

"HE TOOK HER HOME TODAY, just after lunch."

"Yeah? How'd you know that?"

"I got my sources." The man who was speaking jabbed his fork into a greasy mound of French fries, swirled them through an unsavory mixture of ketchup and congealed gravy and stuffed them into his mouth, a trickle of gravy running down his chin.

"So?" the man across the table asked, looking with covert fascination at the brown stain on the other's stubbled jaw.

"So what?"

"So, how'd she look? Is she okay? Will she go ahead with it, Joe?"

The man named Joe ate another mouthful of fries, drank gustily from his water glass and wiped his chin with a paper napkin. Then he leaned back and extended his booted feet beneath the table.

"She got a bad knock on the noggin, Tim," he said at last. "She was beat up pretty bad, so I hear, can't even remember her own name right now. I got a cousin who works as a chambermaid at the hospital," he added. "She hears stuff and passes it on when I want her to."

Tim was younger and slighter than his companion, with a round face and childlike blue eyes that shifted uneasily when he spoke. "What's she like?" he said finally.

"My cousin? She's kinda fat, about—"

"No, I mean Leah Temple."

"Oh, her. She's a looker, let me tell you, kid. But she's one tough broad. Hard as nails. I never seen her before that night when a mutual friend set up this little deal for us."

"She was talking to you that night, wasn't she?" Tim asked. "The night she got beat up?"

"Just before. She come down there to meet me, left her friends a couple streets away waiting for her in the car while we made our business arrangements. Some friends," Joe added, his coarse, heavy jowls quivering with scorn.

"Did they take off?"

"They must of. I come out of that greasy spoon a few minutes later an' heard her screaming in the alley, called the cops from a pay phone an' took off myself. I don't know who jumped her, but I sure didn't wanna be involved in anything like that."

"Funny you even called the cops. I never thought you did any favors for pigs, Joe."

The older man looked at his companion with weary distaste. "God, Tim, you are just so dumb. You know that?"

Tim looked offended and sipped at his coffee in silence.

"The reason I called the cops," Joe said with heavy, careful emphasis, like someone addressing a child, "was because I didn't want her killed, Timmy. She's worth half a million to me, you know."

"*If* we do the job."

"What's this 'we'?" Joe asked, leaning forward and whispering harshly. "*I'm* the triggerman, Timmy. I'm the one that makes the plans, does the contact, takes all the risks. You drive the car, that's all. Don't give me this 'we' crap, okay?"

"Okay, Joe," the other said meekly, frightened by his friend's vehemence. "You said she can't remember anything. You mean like amnesia, sort of?"

"Yeah. Like that. Apparently the doctors don't think it's gonna last very long, though, this amnesia."

"But...will she still go through with it, do you think?"

"Sure she will. Believe me, that chick wants her husband dead. She really does. She even wants it done sooner than we thought."

"How soon?"

"Before summer. He's divorcing her, see? She got the papers served on her just a few days before she came down to see me."

Tim frowned, his face tense with the effort of concentration. "But if he's divorcing her..."

"Yeah?" Joe prompted, taking a noisy sip of coffee.

"Then wouldn't he already have her written out of his will and all that stuff? What does she stand to gain by having him killed?"

"A few million dollars, if I get the job done quick enough."

"How? Where would she get all that money if he's dead?"

"From stocks that he won't have time to transfer. See, Timmy, these rich people, they move their money around all the time to save taxes. Apparently this Temple guy, he put a bunch of stock in his wife's name to split taxes. She found out that he's moving it back into his company since he's planning to divorce her. But she says it'll take him a few months, and if she can get him iced soon enough she'll hold on to all that money. A hell of a lot more than she'd get in a divorce settlement."

Tim whistled silently.

"Funny thing, though," Joe added, picking his teeth reflectively with a sharpened matchstick.

"What's funny?"

"She was talking about the money, but you know what? I got the idea that wasn't the only reason she wanted the job done. Maybe not even the main reason. She really hates the guy, but I don't know why."

"Maybe she doesn't know either," Tim said thoughtfully. "Women are like that sometimes."

"Yeah, sure," Joe said with heavy irony. "Listen to the world-class expert on women."

Another couple came into the shabby restaurant and sat down at a nearby table, unloading a whining baby from a snowsuit and fitting him into a food-splattered high chair.

"So, when do you do it?" Tim asked, leaning forward intently.

Joe frowned at his companion and jerked his head warningly toward the young couple. "In a few weeks," he muttered. "I gotta get in touch with her to make the final arrangements. Don't worry, kid, I'll let you know when I need you."

"What if she forgot about the plan, too?"

"I'll remind her."

"But if he took her home..." Tim paused, his eyes widening. "Maybe they made up, Joe. What if he changes his mind about divorcing her, and then she decides she doesn't want him iced, after all?"

"What about it?"

"She's *seen* you, Joe. She knows who you are."

"So? She's not likely to talk about me, now, is she? Tell folks about our little business deal?"

"But what if she's scared off by all this," Tim persisted, "and she doesn't want to go ahead with the job?"

"Then she'll die, instead. People don't mess with me," Joe said with a matter-of-fact viciousness that made the younger man stiffen in his chair, gazing at his companion in appalled silence.

"How will you know?" Tim asked finally. "How will you know if she's planning to weasel out on you?"

"You'll tell me, Timmy," the older man said softly.

"Me?"

"Yeah, you. See, this deal, it's worth a whole lot to us," Joe said, leaning forward earnestly. "So you're going to work, Timmy. You're getting a summer job tending livestock down there on Paul Temple's little farm, and you're gonna be keeping an eye on our Mrs. Temple. First sign she shows of remembering things and maybe backing out on me, she gets the bullet instead of her husband. But," Joe added calmly, "I don't expect no problems, Timmy. Not from that broad."

"Can you trust her? Are you sure she's gonna pay the balance when the job's done?"

"Oh, I'm sure," Joe said with a humorless smile, his stubbly face suddenly slack and vicious, his pale eyes glistening. "That little lady don't know what pain is right now. Not the way she'll find out if she tries to stiff *me,* I can tell you that."

Tim shivered and cast a nervous glance at the young couple, who were absorbed in their crying baby.

"Sounds real good, Joe," he said, levering himself out of the booth. "Say, can you drop me off downtown? I gotta go see a guy about my car loan."

They abandoned their sticky coffee cups, tossed some bills on the table and clattered out, climbing into a battered gray van parked at the curb.

The van was rusted and dented in places, crudely lettered on both sides with a sign reading Triple A Carpet Cleaning.

Tim sat in the torn, dusty passenger seat, staring out through a smeared side window. "So you get in touch with her," he said finally, "we go ahead with the job, she pays you for it...."

"An' she's a free woman," Joe said, unable to conceal his gloating triumph. "An' me'n' you, Timmy, are living like rich men down in Puerto Vallarta."

Tim nodded, his weak face lighting at the prospect. "You'll do it just great, Joe," he said. "Mrs. Temple's gonna be a rich widow before she knows it."

CHAPTER FOUR

PAUL TEMPLE SAT ALONE at the head of the oval dining table and gazed at the arched doorway. He was torn by indecision and filled with a helpless frustrated anger that made him feel almost sick.

Wearily he sipped his dinner wine, thinking about the strange woman he'd brought back to this house just a few hours earlier. He remembered her wide, frightened eyes and trembling hands, her air of startled awe when she looked around the big house, her timid questioning of Bob McBride.

Was Leah really that accomplished an actress?

His wife was certainly a polished liar, brazen and audacious even when caught in outright deceit. But this act was something new. Paul had never seen her look so innocent, so shy and anxious and uncertain. In fact, he wouldn't have thought her capable of those emotions. Even when Leah was at her best, in one of her rare moods of gentleness and laughter, she still had a latent air of arrogant confidence, a casual assurance of her own power that gave her personality an edge both threatening and dangerously appealing.

Paul frowned and crumbled a breadstick in tense fingers, thinking about her devastating attractiveness, fighting his own emotions. He realized miserably that he was still terribly vulnerable to her. Even though he despised Leah Temple, he remained somehow captivated by the woman's physical beauty and by the unspoken promises that he knew she couldn't fulfill, promises of womanly sweetness and sexual warmth that were nothing but a hollow mockery of reality.

Still, he hungered for that sweet, hidden image of her, yearned for the tantalizing, elusive woman who had never materialized and never would....

"Damn!" Paul muttered aloud, glancing at his watch and gazing at the door again.

Leah had won this round.

She'd done it to him all over again, he thought miserably. He'd served her with divorce papers, fully expecting to be free of her by now. Tonight she should have been gone from his house with all her bright, seductive clothes and coarse friends and mocking cruelty, all the troubling and disturbing aspects of her turbulent personality that had kept his life turned upside down for five long years.

More than anything, Paul Temple craved peace and serenity. He wanted her gone, wanted to be alone, wanted time to heal and put himself back together. Instead, here he was right back in the middle of Leah's squalid personal drama, playing the role she'd created for him, jumping obediently through hoops and doing everything she expected him to do, while she laughed in triumph behind those lovely golden-brown eyes....

He turned his gaze back to the table and saw a shadow fall across it. Paul looked up, then gazed in stunned silence.

Leah stood awkwardly in the doorway, her eyes enormous in a pale face twisted with anxiety. "I'm sorry," she said in a low voice. "Is it really late? I...I

couldn't find the dining room, and there was nobody
to ask...."

Couldn't find the dining room...

Paul felt a hot flare of irritation, quickly subdued
by his shock at the way she looked. She'd brushed her
short boyish hair and wore almost no makeup, just a
touch of pale pink lipstick. He realized that except for
those recent visits in the hospital he couldn't recall
seeing her face without its bright artificial look, all
skillfully shadowed and contoured and glossed.

Her slenderness and awkward stance, and the pale-
ness of her cheeks with their fading bruises, gave her
a look of exquisite vulnerability. Paul swallowed hard,
staring at her slim form behind the mass of spring
flowers at the center of the table.

She wore a full-skirted dress of simple white cotton, beautifully embroidered with masses of tiny white
flowers around the neck and hem. It was belted with
a circlet of gold that matched her low-heeled sandals.
Her bruised arms looked thin and fragile against the
soft whiteness of the dress, especially her left arm with
its heavy bandage.

Paul stared at the dress, swallowing hard, more
confused and upset than ever.

This white cotton gown was a gift he'd bought for
her years ago on one of his frequent trips to the Middle East. He remembered how lovingly he'd chosen it
at the elegant boutique in Cairo, back in the hopeful
early days of their marriage when he was still trying to
woo her with presents and gentleness.

"God! What do you think I am?" she'd jeered
when she unwrapped the delicate white garment.
"Heidi? Rebecca of Sunnybrook Farm? You sure
don't know your wife very well, do you, Paul?"

"I guess I don't," he'd replied grimly, hurt by her scornful amusement. "But I'm learning fast, Leah."

The unhappy memory faded. He watched as she seated herself opposite him, looking around uncertainly at the banks of cutlery and glassware.

"I've never seen you wear that dress before," he said abruptly.

Leah glanced up at him, her pale cheeks tinted delicately with alarm. "Is it...isn't it all right?" she asked timidly. "I didn't know what I was supposed to wear for dinner, but Doris said—"

"It's fine," he said, annoyed with himself for letting this woman upset his careful equilibrium. "It's just that I never thought you liked it much. You always said that dress wasn't your style."

She sipped at her water glass, her flush deepening. "I don't...I don't like those other clothes," she murmured finally.

"What other clothes?"

"In the closet. I don't like them. They all look so..." She paused, searching for words.

Paul watched her grimly, a bitter smile twisting his lips. Leah Temple's wardrobe was certainly inappropriate for someone pretending innocence, he mused. His wife deliberately selected clothes that were tight, flashy and calculated to be alluring, to catch and hold the eye of every man in the room.

Always advertising something she wasn't able to deliver, Paul thought. She made herself look so sexy and enticing that every man who met her was shaken with desire. But in bed she was either aloof or coldly deliberate. There was no sexual warmth or tenderness to Leah, just a brittle mockery that made a man feel clumsy and inept...

"What about the clothes?" he said harshly, shaking his head to dispel the troubling memory of himself and this woman in bed together. "Leah, you've spent a small fortune on the stuff in that closet. Now you're saying you don't like any of it? I suppose next you'll be telling me that you want to go to Paris and buy a whole new wardrobe this spring."

She turned pale and fell silent abruptly, toying with her fork and avoiding his eyes.

Heinz, the cook, came hurrying into the room at that moment, breaking the awkward silence with his bustling plumpness and jovial good humor.

"Mrs. Temple, welcome home," he said briskly. "Very nice to see you again. Very, very nice."

Leah nodded uncertainly, glancing at Paul with a look of childlike appeal.

Oh, I see. She doesn't know who this is, Paul thought with wry sarcasm. *Now I'm supposed to introduce Heinz, who's been here ten years longer than her, for God's sake, and explain who he is.*

Paul's anger flared once more. He resented his wife terribly for persisting with this ridiculous charade and putting him in such a miserably embarrassing position.

Heinz waited calmly, his white bib apron straining over his ample stomach, his bald head cocked to one side as he looked at his employer.

"Mrs. Temple doesn't recognize you, Heinz," Paul said without expression. "She seems to be suffering a temporary form of memory loss."

Heinz inclined his shining pink head gently in Leah's direction as if their relationship had never been anything but cordial, although Paul had overheard a few screaming arguments between them in the past.

Heinz abhorred any interference in his kitchen, and
Leah couldn't abide a personality that refused to yield
to her wishes, so it was inevitable that she and Heinz
would clash on occasion.

"I'm very sorry to hear that, Mrs. Temple," Heinz
said quietly. "I hope that you will be well soon."

"Thank you," she whispered, looking nervously at
the little man's clean white apron. "You're . . . you do
the cooking?"

"Every bit of it," Heinz said, apparently unruffled
by this bizarre question. "And for tonight," he added
briskly, rubbing his plump, reddened hands together,
"I have a nice vichyssoise, and a small roast of lamb
with mint sauce and parsleyed new potatoes. That
sounds good, no?"

Leah gazed up at him, then cast another anxious
glance in Paul's direction.

"Yes, Heinz," Paul said at last, surprising himself
by taking pity on her. "That sounds excellent. I'm sure
Mrs. Temple will enjoy your cooking after a week of
hospital food."

There was another awkward silence while Heinz
hurried out, leaving the two of them alone together.
Leah toyed with her salad fork, frowning thoughtfully and avoiding her husband's eyes. "What's vichyssoise?" she asked finally, looking over at him with
the clear, questioning eyes of a child.

Paul made a quick gesture of frustration and then
paused, struck by something in her face. Leah was
gazing directly at him with an expression he'd never
seen, a look so clear and candid that he was shaken all
over again. There was no curl to her lip, no smoldering, enigmatic depths in her eyes, and no scorn or se-

duction in them, either. She just wanted to know what the word meant.

"It's a kind of soup," Paul said gently. "It's creamy, made of puréed onions and potatoes, and Heinz usually serves it cold."

"Cold *soup?*" Leah asked in disbelief. "In the hospital, people always got really upset if their soup was cold."

Paul grinned. "People tend to get upset about hospital food in general," he told her. "But vichyssoise is supposed to be cold. Actually, it's one of your favorites," he added, sipping his wine and watching her closely. "That's probably why Heinz made it tonight."

"I can't *remember,*" she said in despair, pressing her fingers to her bruised head as if her hands could somehow restore its proper functioning. "I just can't remember what I like and don't like. But I do know that I don't like turnips," she added with a fleeting grin, the first time Paul had seen her smile since the accident.

In spite of himself he smiled back, touched by her unexpected warmth. "How do you know that, Leah?"

"I spat them out," she confessed. "The very first time they brought me food, I was so hungry I wanted to eat everything. I took a big mouthful of turnips and spat them right back onto the plate, and Doris had to clean them up. It was awful."

Again Paul returned her smile automatically, but he was deeply unsettled by this little story.

Painfully conscious of her own impoverished background, his wife had always lacked confidence in social situations and was careful to avoid anything that might put her at a disadvantage. As her husband, Paul had gained some inkling over the years of how hard she struggled to be accepted, how she used her wit and determination to fit herself into his milieu and appear as polished and gracious as the women around her.

He just couldn't imagine the old Leah Temple telling such a story on herself, deliberately confessing to a situation where she'd behaved in a graceless, unsophisticated manner. It was more likely that she'd quickly cover up such a gaffe, and then harbor a bitter, unreasonable grudge against any person who had happened to witness her faux pas.

For the first time, Paul found himself beginning reluctantly to believe that his wife's memory loss was genuine. He felt a stirring of despair, wondering just how far his responsibilities extended. Although he despised this woman, was he now obligated to take care of her until she recovered her senses? And how long would that be?

Heinz brought in the bowls of soup and watched carefully while Leah sampled hers, beaming when she exclaimed in delight at the delicious flavor.

The cook departed for the kitchen, still smiling, and Paul watched his wife in grim silence. She was eating the chilled creamy liquid with childlike enthusiasm, glancing up at Paul occasionally with a warm sparkle that made his heart lurch briefly, then steady itself.

Dammit, I can't let this happen, he told himself with growing misery. *I can't let her get to me again. I've served the divorce papers, the lawyers are already working on terms, and this is my chance to get rid of her and be free. I can't let her win this one, too, just by wandering around all wide-eyed and helpless....*

"Do I like lamb?" she asked in a small voice, setting her soupspoon carefully in the bowl and giving him an anxious, appealing glance.

"I beg your pardon?"

"Lamb," she repeated. "Do I like it, too?"

He was silent, staring at her across the table, his gaze level and cool.

"It just seems..." Her cheeks turned pink again and she moved uneasily in the high-backed chair. "I mean, lambs are just babies, aren't they? They're all little and fluffy, and they bounce around, and the idea of *eating* them, it seems kind of..." She fell silent, obviously distressed by his gaze, and plucked nervously at the edges of her linen place mat.

"Yes, Leah," Paul said wearily as the silence lengthened and grew uncomfortable. "Yes, you've always liked lamb. You like it more than beef, as a matter of fact. You've always said it's more tender."

"I...I see," she whispered, avoiding his eyes again, studying the banks of flowers in front of her while the misty spring twilight deepened beyond the windows and a solitary owl began to call from the trees along the creek.

RAIN SLASHED AND POUNDED against the weathered sides of the old barn, drumming with a regular crashing beat that made the interior feel cosy and soothing. Leah nestled on the piled straw tossed in one corner of the big dim space, sniffing the mingled scents of hay and horse, loving the feeling of privacy and safety.

She'd discovered that she was much more comfortable out here in the barn than she was in the big house, despite its luxury and beauty. The rooms of the house were filled with mocking ghosts, with haunting reminders of her lost past and the woman she used to be, and Leah was frightened by them.

She hugged her knees and rested her chin on them with a brooding expression, thinking about the woman who had so recently occupied her beautiful suite of rooms, the person who, in some mysterious fashion, was herself.

What was she like, really, this woman named Leah Temple? The mirror told her nothing, just gave her a reflection of a sad, beautiful face and a slim, curving body that was completely unfamiliar. The most effective mirrors were the eyes of the people around her who looked at her with dislike, suspicion, mockery or cool politeness.

All of them, from Heinz the cook and Bob McBride down to little Allie, had their own special looks for Leah, and none of them were loving. Not even gentle Anna was able to make her face and voice really warm when she spoke to her mistress.

She must have been so awful, Leah thought in despair. She must have been mean and cruel to everybody, even those sweet little girls. Automatically she corrected herself, forced herself to say "I" rather than "she." Because the woman who'd lived inside her body and mind all these years wasn't someone else. It was her, Leah, even though she no longer had the slightest memory of that life. She was still responsible for the things she'd done and the hurts she'd inflicted on others, and the thought made her tremble with anguish.

Nervously, she opened the little book on her knee and held it toward a dim ray of light from the smeared

window so she could read the powerful, blunt handwriting.

"I just *hate* the bastard!" the book read. "I hate
him more every day. Who the hell does he think he is,
acting so god-awful high-and-mighty, like I'm not
even good enough for him to touch? Sometimes I'd
really like to kill him...."

Leah shivered and closed the book quickly, dropping it back into her jacket pocket as if it burnt her
fingers.

She had found this little leather-bound diary in her
underwear drawer and had slowly come to understand what it was. These pages carried a message to
her from the woman she really was, but Leah could
hardly bear to read them. They were so full of anger
and pain, so vicious and harsh in their judgments.
Everybody appeared in the diary, all the people on the
farm as well as strangers that Leah had no memory of.
And they were all ridiculed, jeered and mocked by that
strong black handwriting, even "scraggly little Allie
and the fat kid."

But the worst of the anger seemed to be reserved for
Paul Temple, a bitter cold fury that Leah couldn't begin to understand. Why did she ... again Leah paused
and corrected herself. *Why did I hate him so much?
What did he do to make me so angry?*

The diary gave no clue to that question, and Leah
couldn't find any inside her own mind or experience.
Paul Temple was generally cool and distant with her
but still unfailingly courteous and helpful when she
asked him for information, automatically considerate
of her comfort.

And sometimes when he forgot to be careful and
chuckled at something she said, or glanced over at her

with a look of warm surprise in those striking hazel eyes, Leah's heart would turn over and then begin to pound in a most alarming fashion.

She was distressed at such times to discover that she wanted to touch him, to lay her hand on his broad chest or run her fingers over that hard, tanned cheek, those sculpted lips. . . .

Leah shivered and hugged herself again, thinking about love and physical attraction. The very first day she arrived at the farm, she'd discovered the spacious library and had begun to read with voracious energy, knowing that she had to learn how people felt and thought about life.

The books were a great help, supplying her with hundreds of vicarious experiences to replace the ones her memory had somehow lost. But almost all the books seemed to be intensely preoccupied with physical love between men and women.

Apparently it was a wonderful feeling, this closeness between two people that excluded the rest of the world. The characters in those stories would do anything for their passion. They were willing to work and struggle and sacrifice, even steal or kill to win and hold the person they loved.

In the books, the love stories usually ended happily. On the final page the lovers were together, locked in each other's arms with a wonderful future ahead of them. But real life seemed to be so different, Leah thought sadly. In reality there were all kinds of chasms that separated people, problems that just didn't seem solvable, hatred and resentment and painful misunderstanding.

She thought of herself and Paul Temple sitting opposite each other at the big dining table every night, trying to maintain polite conversation in between long, awkward silences. The air of mistrust and tension was almost palpable. Leah would huddle in the chair, full of questions she didn't dare voice because she knew how much it irritated him whenever she asked questions.

Leah understood now that Paul thought she'd made up the memory loss for some reason of her own, and he obviously believed she was fully capable of such deceitfulness.

She gazed bleakly at the row of mangers opposite her, wondering why anybody would ever pretend to have lost her memory. Why would a person want to feign such a helpless and desolate feeling? What could possibly be the purpose of that kind of pretense?

Leah wanted so desperately to recover her personal memories that she felt she'd do anything anybody asked of her, just to get her life back. Even if it turned out to have been a really awful life, Leah thought miserably, at least she'd *know*…she could face it and think about the things she'd done, try to understand herself and make things better, somehow.

But instead she just continued to drift endlessly in a hollow, echoing void, a sort of vast, empty plain that was without landmarks or guidelines, but still fraught with dreadful hidden perils. Leah fumbled and wandered over this emptiness with no memories to sustain her and nobody to help, nobody to care or offer guidance, the loneliest woman in all the world.

The thought of her loneliness made her so sad that she felt like crying again. She struggled against the feeling; she hated giving way to misery. But a few tears spilled out despite herself and began to trickle down her cheeks.

Suddenly she paused, sniffling, and lifted her head when she heard a noise nearby.

Remembering her first frightening nights in the strange bedroom, Leah recognized this as the muffled sound of somebody really crying, sobbing in broken-hearted abandon. She caught her breath, dashed a hand across her wet face and crept out of her nest of straw, brushing at her jacket and jeans and edging toward the source of the sound.

The sobs were coming from behind a closed tack-room door, constructed of heavy planks with a handle made from a horseshoe. Leah paused, her eyes wide, her face pale and tense, staring at the handle. At last she reached down, pulled on the cold metal hoop and swung the door open, then stared in alarm. Bonnie McBride was inside the little room, sitting on a pile of sacks and crying with noisy, shuddering misery. Her bright golden hair was matted all around her face and her plump, pretty features were streaked with makeup, mascara and eye shadow and blusher, all smeared and wet with tears.

As she cried, her chubby hands scrabbled automatically in a small pile of papers and boxes that spilled over the sacks and onto the floor. Leah saw chocolate-bar wrappers, tinfoil packaging for small iced cakes and a cardboard carton of the kind that doughnuts were sold in.

Scattered amongst the debris of Bonnie's secret feast were other things as well: golden tubes of lipstick, little crystal bottles of perfume, dainty hinged cases full of pressed powders and miniature brushes.

They looked exactly like the things that littered the desk and dresser tops in her own room, Leah thought in surprise. In fact, some of them even had the same designs worked into the glass-and-plastic cases. A big hand mirror lay on the floor nearby, half-hidden by trailing edges of burlap. Apparently Bonnie had been absorbed in eating and making up her face when misery had overwhelmed her and she'd begun to cry so desperately.

Leah stood uncertainly, wondering what to do. Her heart ached for the child's obvious pain but she didn't understand the problem, didn't have the slightest idea what to say.

While Leah hesitated Bonnie looked up, her face bloated and patchy. The girl's reddened eyes widened with panic, and she began to sob again.

"Don't tell my mom!" she wailed. "Please don't tell my mom! I'll pay for them," she went on in a choked voice, her words tumbling frantically over themselves. "I'll pay for everything out of my allowance. If you can just wait till Friday, and please don't tell my parents—"

"Tell them what?" Leah asked, genuinely puzzled. "Don't they allow you to use makeup, Bonnie?"

Bonnie stared. She was silent a moment, and then apparently yielded to some kind of overpowering emotion, heaving her fat body recklessly erect and staring up at Leah with hot defiance.

"You think you're so smart!" she shouted, her rage and pain plainly evident. "Pretending you don't remember stuff and all that, laughing at everybody all the time. Just because you're pretty and... and slim, and you have all these nice things, you think you can be so mean to everybody else. I hate you!"

Leah stood quietly, stunned by the girl's outburst, wondering what she'd done to make Bonnie hate her so much.

"Pretending you don't know where I got these things," Bonnie went on bitterly, clearly unable to stop now that she'd begun. "You're just playing with me, aren't you? Just the way Ginger plays with a poor little mouse after she catches it. You're mean, all right. You like to see people get hurt. You'll go tell my parents and get me into all kinds of trouble, and laugh about it, won't you? *Won't* you?"

"Bonnie, I—"

"Well, I don't care! You hear me? I don't care one bit what you do, you mean witch. Because maybe *I'm* going to do something pretty soon, and then nobody will be able to hurt me anymore. You'll all be sorry. Wait and see."

Chills ran up and down Leah's spine, prickling at the nape of her neck. She stared at the girl's swollen, unhappy face where the anger was already ebbing, replaced by a look of bleak despair that was not at all childlike in its intensity.

"Bonnie..." Leah began helplessly, appalled by the child's words and manner.

"Wait and see," Bonnie repeated in a choked voice, kicking at the scattered cosmetics and food wrappers, stamping them underfoot with her sneakers. Leah reached out for her but Bonnie broke away and ran, swaying awkwardly as she pounded through the barn and out into the chill spring rain.

Leah looked in troubled silence at the doorway where Bonnie had disappeared, then bent slowly and picked up the debris on the floor, depositing it in a big trash can by one of the doors. She stared down at the bright bits of foil and plastic glimmering in the depths of the barrel; she was still shaken and distressed by Bonnie's final words.

Should she tell somebody? Bonnie had accused Leah of wanting to get the girl into trouble, of planning to go and tell her parents what she'd been doing. Leah hated the thought of telling them about the incident, because that would just prove to Bonnie that her suspicions had been justified.

But she was also terrified by the look of despair in the child's eyes, and her veiled threats to "do something."

Leah shook her head, frowning and biting her lip. The problem was, she just didn't know how people were supposed to behave in a situation like this. Leah had no store of experience to draw on; she had to rely on her own, often faltering judgment.

"Hello, Mrs. Temple," a husky voice said nearby, startling her.

"Hello," Leah said hesitantly, turning to see a young man who stood near the box stalls with a power saw dangling from one hand and a loop of electrical cord in the other. He was blond and slender, of medium height, with a pitted complexion and childlike blue eyes that shifted nervously as he looked at her.

"Nice rain, isn't it?" the young man offered, hefting the power saw and lifting the cord up higher on his shoulder. "Gonna make everything come real green, this rain."

"Yes," she murmured, looking awkwardly down at the dusty floorboards, agonizing over this situation that had become so wearily familiar to her. Leah hadn't the slightest knowledge of who this young man was, his name or position on the farm, anything about him. She didn't know what had happened between them in the past or what their present relationship might be, and she had no idea how to respond to him.

But she was relieved to see that his face was not hostile. Unlike most of the people on the farm, he looked at her with a gaze that contained nothing but mild curiosity. His expression reminded her of the accepting, friendly attitude she'd encountered at the hospital, where people were unaffected by prior opinions of her or past experiences with her.

"I haven't really met you yet," he said. "I just started working here a few days ago. My name's Tim Connor."

"Hello, Tim," Leah said, smiling at him, feeling an absurd surge of relief. It was so nice to find a new person, someone who was just starting fresh like herself. In a strange way she felt closer to the young man named Tim than she did to anybody else in this unfamiliar new world.

"It's nice to meet you," she murmured, shaking his outstretched hand. "Do you like working here?"

He shrugged. "It's okay. Better than living on a welfare cheque."

Leah frowned, trying to recall what a welfare cheque was, and looked up to find Tim examining her closely in the dimness of the big barn.

"I heard," he began awkwardly, "that you got hurt a while ago. Some kind of accident?"

Leah nodded, giving him a shy, nervous smile. "I'm almost better now," she said. "All the bruises are fading, and they even took the bandage off my arm yesterday."

"That's good." The young man hesitated, shifting on his booted feet, and then looked at her again and cleared his throat.

"Bob said . . . he said something about your head getting hurt, somehow? That you kinda lost your memory?"

Leah tensed. She hated anybody talking about her memory loss, hated the feeling that everybody knew about her struggle and confusion.

"Oh, that's getting a lot better, too," she lied with a childlike attempt at dignity. "I'm remembering a lot of things now. I'm almost back to normal."

"Yeah?" the young man said with interest. "Is that right?"

"Yes," Leah said. She gave him a quick, nervous smile, then murmured a goodbye and moved hastily off before he could prolong the conversation.

At the entrance to the barn she paused to pull her hood up over her short hair, then plunged out into the rain, still aware of the young man's pale eyes resting on her with thoughtful speculation.

CHAPTER FIVE

KEN HOLCROSS LEANED BACK in his swivel chair and studied the beautiful, withdrawn face of the woman in front of him.

She lay on a leather divan with her hands folded quietly, her slender body clad in a creamy-white suit and blue silk shirt. Her eyes were closed; her thick dark eyelashes cast a shadowy fan onto her pale cheeks. The lovely curving mouth was childlike in its softness.

"Leah," the doctor murmured gently. "Leah, can you hear me?"

"Yes," she said in a thick, sleepy voice.

"Good. Now, Leah, you've been traveling back, haven't you? Way, way back?"

"Yes," she whispered.

"That's very good. How old are you now, Leah?"

"I'm four," she said in a piping treble, holding up a slim ringed hand with the thumb tucked against her palm. "I'm just four."

The doctor glanced at her intently, his eyes lighting with interest behind the glasses. This was the furthest back she'd ever allowed herself to be taken. He had no idea what to expect.

"Where are you, Leah? Is it a nice room?"

She shook her head with a violent, childlike motion. "No," she whimpered. "Not nice. I'm scared."

She hugged her arms to her chest and looked troubled.

"Where is it, Leah?" the doctor repeated patiently.

"Don't know. It's a place. The lady brought me here."

"What lady brought you here?"

"The lady who came to our house. Mommy didn't come home and I was crying and the lady came and took me away."

"Why didn't your mommy come home?"

"The lady said she ran away. She said mommy doesn't want me anymore. Mommy ran away, and then I had to come to the place."

Ken Holcross scribbled hasty notes on the pad in front of him and looked at the woman's unhappy face for a moment.

"Are you all alone at the place, Leah?"

"No," she said with a brief, shining smile, hugging herself again. "I have my dolly."

"Do you love your dolly, Leah?"

The elegantly dressed woman rocked on the divan, smiling and hugging an invisible object. "Love my dolly," she sang tenderly in her husky child's voice. "Love my dolly, love my dolly...." Suddenly her face crumpled and tears spilled down her cheeks.

"Leah? What is it?"

"They took my dolly!" she wailed, sitting tensely erect and gripping the chair arms with taut, anguished fingers. "They took my dolly!"

"Who took your dolly?"

"The lady and the other lady. They said my dolly was too dirty. They took her away. I want my dolly," she sobbed, curling up and crying with heartbroken abandon. "I want my dolly, I want my dolly, I want my dolly...."

Despite years of professional practice, during which he'd probably witnessed more horrors than anyone could imagine, Ken Holcross still found himself outraged by this scene. He'd encountered these people too many times before, the kind of unthinking officials who'd take away an abandoned child's only source of comfort because it didn't meet certain standards of cleanliness.

But his sympathy and indignation weren't what Leah Temple needed at this point. He composed himself and murmured soothingly to the distraught woman. "Let's leave the place, Leah, shall we? Let's leave now and go forward."

She gulped and nodded obediently. "Leave now," she echoed in her child's voice.

"That's right. Just wander forward, Leah, and stop wherever you like."

Skillfully he led her through some fragments of the story that he already knew: a succession of foster homes and bewildered confusion, a little girl's fear and dashed hopes and growing alienation. The memories seemed mostly intact, but still as curiously random and disordered as they'd been since the accident.

Gradually she began to tense again, gripping the sides of the divan and pulling herself a little more erect, her face wary.

The doctor tensed as well, knowing that they were edging toward dangerous ground but convinced his patient was ready.

"Leah? How old are you now?"

"I'm eleven," she said in a voice that was beginning to alter, to take on a more mature depth and timbre. "I was eleven in the fall, and now it's spring and I've come to a new place."

"Is it a nice place, Leah?"

She shrugged, her face noncommittal. "It's okay. There's other kids here. There's a little baby named Tommy, and he's nice."

"Who else is there?"

"There's the mother and father, and me and the baby, and a little girl who's retarded, and Allan."

Again the slim fingers tightened and flexed.

"Who's Allan, Leah?"

"He's their kid. I mean, he's the only one who's really theirs. Me and the baby and the little girl, we're all foster kids, but Allan is theirs. He's sixteen."

"Do you like him, Leah?"

"He's really cute," Leah said with a girlish smile that stabbed unexpectedly at the doctor's heart. "He's tall and he has this really black hair, and he plays basketball. He has a jacket with leather sleeves and his name on it."

Her face blanched suddenly in alarm, and she began to shiver.

"Leah? What is it?"

"We're alone," she whispered. "Me and Allan. They took the little kids to the clinic and we're alone in the house."

"Why does that frighten you?"

"Allan is . . . he's acting really weird. He's scaring me. He won't stop—" Suddenly the woman on the lounge began to scream, heartrending, childlike cries of pain and anguish. The doctor watched her impassively, though his gray eyes were gentle with compassion behind the thick lenses of his glasses.

"Oh," Leah moaned. "Oh, it hurts! Oh, it's so awful, it's so awful, it's so awful. . . ." At last she subsided, huddling and whimpering on the divan, her slender body looking broken and fragile.

"Leah, it's all right. It's all right. You can move forward now if you like, to get past the pain."

Her face cleared, then turned blank and cold. The beautiful lips were curled slightly. She lay back comfortably, and tossed her head with an air of brittle nonchalance.

"Leah," the doctor murmured, looking at her with interest, "where are you now?"

"On the street. I'm on the street. I ran away. That son of a bitch will never touch me again. He kept hurting me all those months but I put a stop to it, that's for damn sure."

"Did you tell his parents what he did?"

"How could I?" she asked in that same flat, bitter tone. "They think he's just the cat's ass. They wouldn't believe their little darling would behave like that. If I told them, they'd punish *me,* not him. So I stabbed him in the leg with his goddamn little jackknife and then I ran away. I wish to hell I'd killed him."

"What are you doing on the street? How do you live?"

"I get by," she said coldly.

"How? You're only eleven years old, and all on your own."

"I'm twelve now, and I'm real smart. I run errands, carry packages for people, do all kinds of stuff. I get by."

"Are you a prostitute?"

"No!" she shouted with sudden violent passion. "Nobody's ever going to do that to me again! Never, never, never..."

Her hands shook with emotion and her face crumpled. "I wish I'd killed him," she whispered. "He deserves to die, treating me that way when he never cared a bit about me. I really want to kill him. I want him to die for hurting me."

Dr. Holcross looked up quickly, alarmed by the woman's twisted face, her cold angry mouth and the voice that sounded so mature now, not childlike at all.

"Who, Leah?" he asked, leaning forward tensely. "Who do you want to kill for hurting you?"

"Him," she muttered darkly. "That son of a bitch who treats me like dirt, who does...who does *that* to me, and then just walks away. I hate him. I hate him so much."

"Leah," the doctor repeated patiently, "who is it that you hate? Is it Allan? The boy who forced himself on you?"

"Yes," she whispered, relaxing against the pillows again. "And the other one," she added unexpectedly. "The other one, too. I wish *both* of them were dead."

Ken Holcross shivered as a strange cold breeze touched the nape of his neck.

He'd been Leah's therapist for a long time. He knew that despite her bold, seductive behavior prior to the accident, Leah Temple had only had sexual relations with two men in her entire life. One of them was the brutal teenaged boy who'd abused her for several months in that long-ago foster home.

And the other was her husband, Paul Temple.

"HOW DO YOU FEEL NOW, Leah?" The doctor gazed at his patient who faced him across the cluttered expanse of his broad teak desk. She was fully conscious and had left the divan, returning to the padded swivel chair opposite the therapist.

"Wonderful," Leah said with a smile. "I feel just wonderful. Light as air, and not a care in the world. Is it always like that?"

"You mean the posthypnotic state?"

Leah nodded.

The doctor smiled at her, his pink face gentle as he considered her question. "Not always. This is our first full-length session in the month since your accident, Leah, and it was most productive. But there were times in the past when you seemed to find the experience quite unsettling. Often you continued to be upset even after it was over."

She looked at him with wide eyes. Holcross waited, thinking about some of those earlier sessions and recalling that Leah herself had deliberately chosen to suspend treatment just a few weeks prior to her accident.

"Look, doc, this crap isn't getting me anywhere," she'd told him rudely. "Let's just skip it, okay? My head must be shrunk as small as it can get by now. I don't think you're helping me. To tell the truth, I don't think I *need* help. I'm just fine."

And with those words, and a defiant toss of her streaked mane, Leah Temple had turned on her slim spike heels and marched out of his office and his life. He hadn't seen her again until she turned up in the hospital a month ago, a broken, confused woman without an identity.

Ken Holcross had wondered at the time, and he wondered now, what her motives had been for suspending her therapy so abruptly. It was almost as if she had something to hide, and had cause to fear the probing hypnotic sessions that bared her soul and hidden thoughts. . . .

"Did I remember things?" she was asking with an anxious look. "Just now, I mean. Did I remember things about my life when I was hypnotized?"

"Yes, Leah, you did," the doctor said quietly. "You told me a few things I hadn't heard before, in fact."

"What kind of things?"

He gazed at her beautiful golden-brown eyes, touched by their shy eagerness. "Well," he began, "for instance, you told me something about a doll you had, back when you were just four years old. Apparently you really loved that doll."

"Did I?" Leah smiled wistfully. "I wish I could remember. I'd give anything to be able to remember something like that, any simple little thing about my past."

She paused, thinking deeply, her fingers tracing the fine topstitching of her cream skirt. "Why is it, Dr. Holcross," she asked finally, "that I can remember those things under hypnosis but not when I'm conscious?"

"They're different kinds of memories, Leah. You see, memory is like a big storage cupboard with a lot of locked doors and different keys that work in different locks. You apparently have the key to general memory, but not to personal memory. When you're under hypnosis," he added, "you're able to bypass that door altogether."

"And peek in the window?" she suggested, her face sparkling briefly.

"Sort of," the doctor agreed, smiling back at her, intrigued by the remarkable change in her personality since the memory loss. She was like another woman, he mused, entirely different from the bold, combative woman he remembered. What a fascinating, baffling mystery it was, this whole business of human personality....

"Leah," he said casually after a moment's silence, "I see that you're wearing your rings again."

"Two of them," she said, holding up her slim hands and displaying the heavy gold rings set with sapphires and diamonds. "Do you like them?"

"They're very pretty. You have such beautiful hands, and the rings look nice on them."

Leah flushed at this praise and once again gave him a tentative smile that stabbed right through his professional detachment to his very soul.

"There are so many rings in the jewel case," she murmured. "It seems a shame not to wear them. It's fun to look at them and see how they sparkle in the light, and pick the ones that will look nice with what I'm wearing."

"You still aren't wearing your engagement ring, though," the doctor said, watching her from the corner of his eye as he reached for a pencil.

Leah tensed. "Which one is my engagement ring?"

"I believe it's a very large square-cut emerald surrounded by diamonds."

"I don't think there's a ring like that in the case," Leah said after a few moments of frowning concentration. "I wonder where it is?"

"Maybe it's stored somewhere else, Leah. I'm sure it's very valuable. Perhaps it's kept in a safety vault of some kind."

"I should ask Paul," Leah said, settling back in her chair. "Maybe he'd like that," she added with a shy smile.

"What, Leah? What would he like?"

"If I wore my engagement ring," Leah murmured, so low that the doctor could hardly hear her words as she gazed down at her hands. "Paul might be pleased if I wore the ring and showed that I like it."

"Are you and Paul getting along better these days?"

"A little. We talk more now, and sometimes we even laugh together. And yesterday at dinner he said I looked prettier than he'd ever seen me," she added with a timid smile, her eyes shining.

Leah glanced up at the doctor, then dropped her eyes quickly, her cheeks flushing a delicate pink.

Doctor Holcross studied her bent head with its boyish haircut and the trembling fingers gripped together in her lap. He opened his mouth to speak, but was interrupted by a brisk knock and the sudden opening of the outer door.

"Sorry," Paul Temple said, stepping inside. "Am I interrupting? Mary said you were finished and I could just walk in."

Leah jerked her head up and gazed breathlessly at her husband, her eyes alight, her lips parted.

Ken Holcross turned away from thoughtful contemplation of his patient to smile politely at the young man who seemed to fill the consultation room. Paul was dressed for business today, in flannel slacks and a well-cut tweed jacket that rested easily on his broad shoulders. His tall body was taut and graceful, his smooth golden head gleaming softly under the banks of concealed lights.

"Hello, Leah," Paul said, smiling at his wife who still gazed speechlessly up at him. "How did it go today?"

"The doctor thinks...he said it was all right," Leah replied awkwardly. "He said I remembered some new things."

Paul turned to Ken Holcross, a look of inquiry on his face. "Did she, Ken?"

Ken Holcross nodded, returning the young man's gaze with calm steadiness, wondering what Paul Temple was really thinking. Did he still believe his wife was faking this condition? Or had her helpless bewilderment finally aroused his sympathy and compassion?

"Yes," Ken said, nodding thoughtfully. "Leah went back further than she ever has, all the way to the age of four, in fact. She recalled some significant memories of that period."

"But no carryover?" Paul asked quickly, glancing at his wife and then back at the doctor. "No recollection of anything after you brought her out of it?"

"I'm afraid not. But," Ken added, seeing Leah's unhappy face, "it's just a matter of time, you know. I'm convinced that her condition has no physiological basis any longer, and it's almost certain to improve. In fact, I expect small recoveries of memory to start occurring anytime."

Leah brightened and looked at him hopefully. "Really?"

"Really," the doctor assured her.

"Did you hear that, Paul?" Leah said with a delighted smile. "Did you hear that? Ken thinks I'm going to start getting better soon!"

Paul Temple looked at his wife in silence. Dr. Holcross, watching keenly with his trained eyes, saw a whole gamut of emotions crowding that handsome face... alarm, concern, fear, tension, sympathy.

And finally, a strange kind of reluctant tenderness.

The therapist nodded to himself, recognizing the answer to his question. Paul Temple had come to accept the reality of his wife's condition. And the doctor suspected that along with that acceptance something else was growing, something that Ken Holcross found much more disturbing.

"Yes, Leah," Paul said at last. "I heard. Come on now," he added. "We'd better go or we'll be late. Our reservations are for six o' clock, remember?"

"We're having Chinese food," Leah confided to the doctor with another sparkling smile. "I just *love* Chinese food," she added blissfully. "I had it for the very first time last week, and ever since I've been begging Paul to take me again."

"Nagging 'round the clock," Paul agreed cheerfully, taking his wife's arm as she crossed the room to stand beside him. "You'd think prawns and Peking duck and chop suey were just about the end of the rainbow," he added in a husky voice, looking down at the shining head near his shoulder.

This time he couldn't hide his teasing smile or the softness in his face and voice.

Ken Holcross got to his feet and watched them leave, then sank into his desk chair again, flipping automatically through a big appointment book.

Finally he leaned back and stared at the ceiling, thinking about Leah Temple's eager smile, the warm light in her husband's eyes, and the harsh voice he'd listened to just half an hour earlier in this very office, a voice that had said, "I *hate* him," and had expressed a wish that he were dead.

Again he reflected on the mystery of the human personality. Leah Temple's case was certainly powerful evidence for the impact of childhood experiences on the shaping of personality. Freed by this bout of temporary amnesia from the crippling burden of her memories, Leah had become another person entirely.

But was the trusting, happy woman who had just left his office the genuine Leah Temple? Was this really the woman she would have been if she hadn't been forced to create the brittle shell that protected her from years of unbearable pain and suffering?

Perhaps this new Leah was just a temporary aberration, like the ones manufactured by people with multiple personality disorders. He would be able to tell only when her memories started to come back. Despite all his years of professional training, Ken Holcross realized that he had no idea what would happen at that point.

Leah Temple might revert completely to her old destructive patterns, build a new shell that would need to be even harsher because the pain would be so fresh and strong when it returned. And she might continue to equate her intimate relationship with her husband to that devastating first sexual encounter and despise him simply for being a man and wanting her body.

Dr. Holcross had always worried about this possibility, but now there was a disturbing new factor in the equation. For the first time the doctor had begun to suspect that Paul Temple, strangely enough, was in danger of falling in love with his wife.

"DO YOU WANT SOME of this, Leah?"

Leah peered suspiciously at the grayish mass on her husband's plate. "What is it?"

"Grilled squid. Try it."

"*Squid?*" Leah stared at him, appalled. "You mean like *octopus?*"

Paul grinned. "Much the same."

"People *eat* that?"

"All the time. It's quite an expensive delicacy."

Again she stared wonderingly at the seamed grayish meat.

Paul watched her, enjoying the play of light and shadow on her features, the almost-awed expression in her eyes, the look of buoyant innocence and delight on her face.

It was so much fun to see Leah discovering the world.

Paul realized that he had finally abandoned his initial suspicions about her memory loss. Even the most skillful actress in the world could not continue to play a part so convincingly, twenty-four hours a day. And the bored, restless woman that he remembered could never have manufactured this look of pure sweetness and clarity, this childlike zest for the smallest of pleasures.

Leah was still examining the squid with deep uneasiness, unaware of her husband's scrutiny. "What does it taste like?" she asked finally.

Paul considered her question. "It's really bland and sort of rubbery."

She shuddered. "I don't think so, Paul. But," she added shyly, "I'll take those last two prawns if you don't want them."

"I don't want them."

"Are you sure?" Leah asked with an anxious frown. "I don't want to be a pig, you know. I think I already had more than my share."

"I don't want them," Paul repeated staunchly. "Wouldn't eat them if you tied me up and forced them on me at gunpoint."

Leah giggled and watched happily as he spooned the last of the batter-coated shrimp onto her plate.

"Leah?"

"Mmm?" she asked, swallowing a healthy forkful of chow mein and sipping from her little painted tea-cup.

"Leah, did you have a good session with Ken?"

"I guess so. I wasn't conscious for most of it, you know. But I felt so good when he woke me up."

"Did he play the tapes for you? Did he let you listen to any of your memories?"

Leah shook her head. "He says it might be harmful for me to hear them like that, before I've started to recall them naturally. I guess he wants them to come back on their own."

She was silent a moment, the light from the Chinese lanterns overhead gleaming softly on the fine planes of her face.

"Paul..." she began shyly.

"Yes?"

"Paul, wouldn't it be wonderful if I started to remember things? Wouldn't it just be the most wonderful thing in the whole world to get some of my memories back?"

Paul looked at her shining eyes with a cautious expression. "You really want that badly, don't you, Leah?"

"Yes, I do. You just can't imagine—" She stopped abruptly, toying with the engraved silver tip of one of the chopsticks that she tried so hard, but with no success at all, to use properly.

"Can't imagine what?" Paul prompted her gently.

"How it feels to be so...disconnected. I'm not *tied* to anything," Leah said with sudden despair. "It's like there's nothing anywhere to put my feet on. I'm just drifting like a leaf in the wind. And it's so terrifying because I don't have the slightest idea where I've been or where I'll land."

Paul's face twisted with sympathy as he reached out to squeeze her hand. "There's nothing to be afraid of, Leah," he said in a husky voice. "You're here with me, and I'll certainly see that you're looked after. Don't you know that?"

She returned his gaze steadily, with a look so direct and honest that it was difficult for him to meet it.

"Did you hate me?" she asked suddenly, startling him.

"What do you mean, Leah?"

"Before," she said, dropping her eyes and gazing at her plate, her hands gripped tensely in the folds of her linen napkin. "I know that I must have been a terrible person," she went on in a small, tight voice. "I can see by the way the girls look at me, and even Anna and Heinz.... I must have been awful. I wonder what I was like to you, Paul. Did you hate me, too?"

Again she looked up at him, and he moved awkwardly under her gaze. "We had some bad times," he admitted cautiously.

"But what were they like?" she asked him, with agonized appeal. "What did I *do,* Paul? What kind of person was I? What sort of things did I say to you?"

Paul hesitated, stabbed by a vivid mental image of this woman standing in the middle of her bedroom just a month or two ago, wearing a skimpy bra and panties, throwing books and makeup bottles at him and screaming abuse. He remembered her voice, harsh and thick with rage, and the words she shouted, a stream of profanity so shockingly coarse that it left him feeling sick and disgusted.

Paul Temple knew that his wife had suffered through an unhappy childhood, though he'd never been told any of the details. All she had ever told her husband was that she'd lost her parents at an early age and had grown up in a succession of foster homes.

Paul suspected, of course, that Ken Holcross knew much more about Leah's childhood experiences. But the good doctor honored the sanctity of the therapist-patient relationship, and never told Paul any of the things he learned during his lengthy therapy sessions with Leah.

Even now when she was suffering from the trauma of this memory loss, Ken wouldn't betray her confidence. He would tell Paul only that she was making progress and that he expected her personality to become more fully integrated as her memories began to return.

Paul thought about the doctor's cautiousness, keeping his eyes fixed on the delicate line of his wife's throat and lips. To his alarm he found himself battling a sudden desire to lean over the table and kiss that sweetly curving mouth.

He gripped the chopsticks in his tanned hands, struggling with the powerful urges that buffeted him.

The woman who sat across from him was growing more dear to him all the time, and she wasn't even aware of it. She had all of Leah's devastating physical beauty and sexual appeal, coupled with a shy, ingenuous sweetness and gaiety that was almost irresistible.

Lately Paul found himself having hot, anguished dreams about her in the loneliness of the night, and fighting when he was with her to keep from gathering her in his arms, tasting the richness of her lips, caressing the lovely body that he remembered with such painful vividness. . . .

"Paul?" she said, probing thoughtfully with a chopstick among the scattered remains of the chop suey, looking for the crisp water chestnuts that she especially loved.

"Yes, Leah?" Paul took himself firmly in hand, struggling to keep his voice calm and level.

He knew that his thoughts were unforgivable under the circumstances. Paul realized, in fact, that the doctor had tried to warn him about this very thing. Despite their turbulent shared history, this woman was like a child, trusting and innocent, wholly dependent on Paul to be honorable and considerate of her condition. He had no right even to contemplate the kind of things he was thinking.

Especially when just a few weeks earlier, his only thought had been to divorce her and get her out of his life completely.

"Ken mentioned my engagement ring today."

"Yes?"

"I didn't know which one it was," Leah said. "When he described it, I couldn't recall seeing it in the jewel case. Ken thought maybe you kept it in a safety vault or something."

Paul shook his head. "You've always looked after your own jewelry, Leah."

"Is there a concealed vault in my room somewhere? Hidden behind a picture or something, like they are in books?"

Paul grinned. "Not unless you had one installed without telling me."

Leah fell silent, looking troubled.

"Why, Leah?" Paul asked gently. "Why are you so concerned about that particular ring?"

"Because I just...I'd like to wear it," Leah said shyly, avoiding his eyes. "It's my engagement ring, the one you gave me, and I'd like to wear it."

Again Paul battled a surging desire to gather her in his arms and kiss her mouth, her throat and eyelids and breasts. "We'll find it, Leah," he told her, his voice steady and expressionless as he turned to signal the waiter for their bill. "The emerald must be somewhere in your room, or else it's in the safety deposit box at the bank. I'm sure we'll find it."

"WELL, WELL," JOE SAID genially, lifting his chipped coffee mug in a sarcastic gesture. "If it ain't Farmer Brown. Did you remember to scrape your boots real careful before you came in, Timmy?"

Tim grimaced without amusement and sank into the booth opposite the older man, who continued to study him with a sardonic grin.

"So," Joe asked, waving his empty mug at the harried waitress, "you like being a farmer?"

"It's okay," Timmy said shortly. "Black coffee, please," he added when the waitress arrived. "And a couple slices of toast."

"Okay?" Joe echoed. "You mean you *like* shoveling that stuff?"

"Lay off, okay?" Tim said wearily. "You wanted me to get the job and we both know why I'm there, so just lay off on the farmer jokes."

Joe leaned back in the booth, watching as the waitress filled their coffee mugs. "But it ain't so bad, right?" he persisted. "Living down there with the rich people and being a gentleman farmer?"

"I wouldn't know," Tim said shortly. "I'm just the hired hand. They treat me good," he added defensively. "The foreman, Bob McBride, he's a real nice guy."

"What about Temple? Is he a nice guy?"

"I never talk to him. I get my orders from Bob."

"I see. And how about the lady of the house, Timmy? You had a chance to talk to the sweet little lady?"

"Yeah," Tim said, sipping his coffee with a distant expression. "I talked to her. A couple times, in fact."

Joe leaned forward, his small eyes suddenly glittering with interest. "You did?" he murmured softly. "Well, that's good, Timmy boy. That's *real* good."

"She's pretty easy to talk to," Tim said. "She's not like you said at all. She seems real...real shy and quiet."

"Shy and quiet!" Joe echoed with a harsh burst of laughter, leaning back and extending his booted feet into the aisle. "God, Timmy, you're a great judge of women, ain't you? Shy and quiet," he repeated with a coarse chuckle, grinning privately. "Leah Temple. My God."

"Well, she did," Tim said defensively. "Like I said, I talked to her a couple times, once in the barn when it was raining and once on the road down by the creek. She likes to go for long walks."

"Does she now?" Joe inquired with heavy amusement. "Likely just slipping out to meet a boyfriend, that one. I sure can't picture her going for a walk to look at the little lambs and the butterflies."

"I don't know where she goes," Tim said weakly, his young face troubled and restless.

"So?"

"So what?"

"So what did she *say,* boy? You get any idea what our girl's mental condition is these days?"

"I asked her. She said she's fine."

"Fine?" Joe echoed blankly. "What's that supposed to mean?"

"Just what she says, I guess. I told her that Bob McBride said she'd had some trouble remembering things since her accident, and she said all that was pretty well over with. She said she was fine."

"Did she now?" Joe asked softly, his stubbled face warming with greedy interest. "Did she say that?"

"Yeah. She did."

"How long ago, Timmy?"

Tim shrugged. "At least a week ago. Maybe more, the first time I talked to her."

"Well, well, well," Joe murmured, sipping his coffee and gazing at the soggy toast that arrived in front of his companion.

"So what do you think?" Tim asked after a long silence, breaking open a plastic container of strawberry jam and spooning it onto the toast.

"I think we're home free, Timmy. I think we're on our way to Mexico with a bundle of cash."

Tim looked dubious, and his seatmate glanced at him sharply.

"What's the matter, kid?"

"I dunno," Tim said slowly, munching on the toast and wiping grease from his chin. "It's just that..."

"What, Timmy?" Joe prompted, his eyes glistening, his big body tense.

"I seen her with him a few times," Tim said awkwardly. "Her husband, I mean. They were walking outside, laughing and talking real friendly. I mean, it didn't look like..."

Joe relaxed and took another sip of coffee. "Hell, that don't mean a thing. She's just being smart, playing up to him and making sure nobody gets suspicious because she knows what's gonna happen to him pretty soon."

"How do you know? How can you be sure she didn't change her mind?"

The big man made a sudden impatient gesture. "Look," he said, "try not to be so dumb for once, you stupid kid. I told you all this before," he added with a heavy attempt at patience. "She knows who I am, Timmy. She knows how to get hold of me, and what I do for a living. If she'd changed her mind, don't you think the cops would have paid me a little visit by now? You think she wouldn't have sent them some kind of anonymous tip and had me put away, just to make sure I didn't go ahead with it? Use your head, Timmy."

Tim nodded slowly, sipping his coffee in reflective silence. "You're right, I guess," he said at last. "She's either gotta go through with it, or get hold of you and let you know she's changed her mind, or call the cops and turn you in. She doesn't have any other choices, does she?"

"She sure doesn't. But just to make you feel better, I'll go talk to her, okay? I'll drop in for a visit and make sure that we're still on the same wavelength, me and Mrs. Temple. Meantime," Joe added with elaborate casualness, "here's a little something in advance, kid, just to let you know this job is worth the trouble."

He shoved a wad of bills surreptitiously across the grimy table. The young man took them and gasped, then held the bills instinctively below the surface of the table, his blue eyes widening as he counted.

"Joe . . . hell, there's *five grand* in here."

"Damn right, Timmy," Joe said placidly. "And there's a hell of a lot more where that came from. This is just an advance."

"But where did you get that kind of money?"

"From our little lady friend, Timmy. From Leah Temple."

"I thought you said she didn't have any money yet."

"She didn't. But I told her I wanted a down payment just to show me she was serious about the job. She gave me a ring, said I could sell it wherever I liked and keep the cash."

"When did all this happen?"

"The night we made our little arrangement. The same night she got beat up. She brought the ring with her."

Tim looked at the wad of money in his hand, then at the grizzled, brutal face across the table. "Must have been some ring," he ventured finally.

"It sure was. A square green rock as big as my thumb. I took it to a fence I know out in Vancouver. He said it was worth a fortune if I could sell it legally, but I had to settle for his price."

"How much?" Tim asked in awe, his uneasiness obliterated by the surge of power that flowed through his whole body from that warm mass of bills. "How much did you get, Joe?"

"Twelve grand," Joe said briefly. "Can you believe it? For a goddamn little ring that she said she just didn't feel like wearing anymore."

Tim thought about the gentle face of the woman he'd met, her luminous eyes, her faltering, childlike manner and timid smile.

Joe was right, he decided. The woman was just a real good actress, pretending to be so shy and innocent when she owned rings worth thousands of dollars and made deals with hit men. She was a greedy rich bitch who wanted her husband dead, and they were going to help her get what she wanted.

Tim levered himself out of the booth and stood erect, grinning down at Joe as he stuffed the wad of bills into his hip pocket. Still grinning, he turned and strolled out of the restaurant with a bold, self-conscious swagger.

CHAPTER SIX

THE YELLOW SCHOOL BUS, crowded with noisy children and teenagers, pulled to a halt at the side of a dusty prairie road. The door opened and Bonnie McBride trudged down the steps, turning her back deliberately on her rowdy schoolmates as the bus lurched away.

She plowed miserably along the road leading to the farm, her blue backpack bright in the spring sunshine, her pretty hair shining. But there was nothing bright or shining about Bonnie's face on this warm afternoon in early May. Her soft, plump features were taut with suffering.

Bonnie was thinking about the miserable two hours she'd just spent, and a bitter resolve was growing in her mind.

Never again, Bonnie told herself, wiping tears from her eyes with the back of a shaking hand. Never again would she suffer through the agony of gym class and the annual checkup that involved a public recording of each girl's height and weight.

"Bonnie McBride!" the gym teacher had exclaimed in horror, examining the notations on the chart. "You've gained *thirty-two pounds* since last spring! Now Bonnie, you know this isn't good, dear," Mrs. Anderson went on, sounding shocked and concerned while the other girls snickered and whispered behind their hands.

Bonnie's face burned as she remembered the scene. She saw herself standing in front of everybody wearing nothing but gym shorts and a T-shirt while Mrs. Anderson held her weight chart out for everybody to see, and all the slim, coltlike girls in the class watched with avid fascination....

"Oh, *hell!*" Bonnie moaned aloud, shuddering with the anguish of the memory. "I can't stand any more," she whispered fiercely to the banks of brown-eyed sunflowers that lined the prairie road. "I just can't take it any longer. I never, ever want to see them again, any of them. This is the last Friday afternoon I'll ever walk home from that place."

She kicked aimlessly at the silent flowers, almost wishing that Allie was with her. Usually she and Allie walked home from the school bus together, fighting all the way. Allie was a constant irritant, but Bonnie realized that sometimes even her sister's maddening presence was better than being all alone with her thoughts.

But Allie was busy today, staying after school for a fifth-grade gymnastics competition that Bonnie had refused to watch. With her whip-thin, agile body, Allie was a wonderful athlete, skilled and fearless. Just watching her sister do flips and vaults made Bonnie feel heavy and awkward.

She paused at the side of the road and squatted on her plump haunches, removing her backpack and digging into its depths. The package of cake doughnuts was safe, all rich and promising beneath the shiny cellophane covering. Bonnie's mouth watered as she looked at them and her stomach rumbled with hunger.

But she packed the doughnuts away without touching them and got to her feet, shouldering the backpack once again and heading for home, her face grim with determination. The doughnuts had to remain unopened until tomorrow. They were going to be part of the ceremony, along with the pretty white dress from her recent church confirmation and the bottle of sleeping pills she'd pilfered carefully over the past few weeks from Leah Temple's medicine cabinet.

Bonnie had been a little surprised to find how easy it was to get the pills. Mrs. Temple didn't seem to use them much anymore, even though Anna went in and had all the prescriptions filled every week when she shopped for groceries. Anna probably thought Mrs. Temple was still taking the pills regularly. She didn't realize that Bonnie was helping herself, building up a stockpile of little blue tablets in the plastic cylinder hidden on a shelf in her closet.

Bonnie knew by now that she had enough pills to kill herself. The thought made her feel frightened and strangely peaceful, because this was the weekend she was finally going to do it. Tomorrow she was going to go into the tack room in the barn and spread out a blanket, then dress herself in the lovely, long white dress so she'd be pretty when they found her.

Bonnie sighed dreamily, picturing herself all pale and tragic and beautiful with her golden hair spread wide and her eyes closed in death. She wondered who would be the one to find her. Probably her father, since he went to the barn more often than her mother. But they'd all crowd in to see her, and everybody would hear how she'd died, and they'd all be sorry....

Jody Muller's truck whipped past in a swirl of dust and gravel. Bonnie tensed, but her young neighbor didn't stop. Usually Jody didn't bother her much when he was alone, just called something rude out the window and sailed on by.

"Oink, oink," he shouted now as he passed. "Hey, piggy, how's it going?"

Bonnie's pleasure at her death scene faded, replaced with another searing wave of misery. She quickened her steps, longing to get safely into the musty stillness of the tack room, to close the door on this vicious world, eat the whole pack of doughnuts, swallow her bottle of pills and leave the pain behind forever.

She trudged up the walk, pushed open the screen door and stepped into the kitchen of her home. Then she stopped in her tracks, stunned by the picture in front of her.

Anna bustled around the kitchen wearing a red gingham apron over jeans, her weathered cheeks pink with happiness. And Leah Temple sat at the table, sipping coffee and eating strawberry shortcake, smiling at Anna with shy friendliness.

Bonnie continued to gape at this astounding scene, her mouth open in amazement. She couldn't remember a single time in her whole life that Leah Temple had ever set foot in their house. The thought was almost unimaginable. And yet here she was, wearing faded jeans and a bronze-colored plaid shirt that matched her lovely eyes. Even in these casual clothes her body was exquisitely slim and graceful. Her creamy face glowed as she took another hefty forkful of cake and strawberries.

"Hello, Bonnie," she said with a gentle smile. "How was school?"

"It was...it was fine," Bonnie muttered, swallowing hard.

She cast her mother an eloquent glance and then vanished down the hall to deposit her backpack in her room, pausing to hide the doughnuts on her shelf next to the bottle of pills. When she came back into the kitchen Bonnie was further amazed to see that Ginger, their marmalade house cat, was actually curled smugly in Mrs. Temple's lap, being petted and fed occasional bits of cake. And Fluffy, their cocker spaniel, groveled at her feet, gazing up at her with mute adoration.

"Your mother says she'll teach me how to make this," Leah said, smiling at the plump girl who hesitated awkwardly beside the table. "I'd just love to learn how to cook. Heinz isn't always happy about having someone underfoot in his kitchen when he's busy," she added ruefully.

Bonnie struggled to find an answer, casting another glance of helpless appeal at her mother who was approaching with a steaming coffeepot.

"Would you like some shortcake, Bonnie?" Anna asked her daughter, just as casually as if the mistress of the estate dropped in every afternoon for tea.

"No, thanks, Mom. I'm not...I'm not real hungry," Bonnie lied, thinking that she would probably die on the spot if she had to sit and eat in front of Leah Temple. "I think I'll just go out and...and see if..." Her voice trailed away as she searched frantically for some excuse to get out of the kitchen and the house.

"Before you go, Bonnie," Leah said pleasantly, "I'd like to show you something. You, too, Anna."

Bonnie's mother approached the table, looking curiously at the flowered plastic bag that Leah Temple was lifting from beneath her chair.

Leah set the bag on the table and began to remove things from it: tubes of lipstick, brushes and compacts and packages of blusher and eye makeup.

Bonnie's heart began to thunder in alarm, and her cheeks turned white with fear. She bit her lip and glanced covertly at her mother, shivering with dread and a slow-growing outrage.

Leah Temple was going to tell her mother, after all. She was going to sit here in front of both of them and calmly expose Bonnie's thievery, let Anna know just what her daughter had done. And then, Bonnie thought bitterly, Leah would sit back and enjoy the fireworks. She'd watch Bonnie's humiliation and pain with the same cruel enjoyment she had always taken in other people's suffering.

She's just the same as always, Bonnie thought in despair. *She's just awful, and now Mom's gonna be so mad at me, and she'll say things and yell at me, and Mrs. Temple will watch and smile. . . .*

Hatred burned in her, so hot and strong that it was a moment before she really understood what their visitor was saying.

". . . And Doris told me they learn about it in school these days," Leah was saying to Anna with shy earnestness.

"In *school?*" Anna echoed with obvious disbelief. *"Makeup?"*

Leah nodded, catching Bonnie's eye briefly and then turning back to Anna. "Doris is the nurse at the hospital who was so nice to me. I call her every week or so to ask her things and let her know how I'm doing. She has a daughter just Bonnie's age."

Anna approached the table, still dubious, looking at the bright masses of metal and plastic and colored powder, the bottles and brushes and cylinders.

"So I was thinking," Leah continued awkwardly, "since Bonnie could probably use these things and I really don't have any idea what to do with them, that I should...that I should just give them to her. But first I wanted to make sure it was all right with you," she concluded, looking quickly up at Anna again.

Bonnie stared at both women, too astonished to speak, processing this information slowly in her mind.

Leah Temple was saying all this to protect Bonnie, not to get her into trouble. She'd actually thought of a way to give Bonnie most of her beautiful makeup, and give it in such a manner that her mother couldn't disapprove or forbid Bonnie to use it. The whole thing was just amazing.

Hope rose suddenly within her. Bonnie licked her lips and cast her mother a glance of desperate appeal.

Anna looked back at the girl, still doubtful. "Do you learn about makeup at school, Bonnie?"

"Sometimes," Bonnie said briefly.

She couldn't help glancing at Leah Temple when she said this. Leah's beautiful face sparkled with a look of impish mischief that made Bonnie feel like laughing out loud for the first time in weeks.

"Sometimes we study it in health class," Bonnie told her mother solemnly, looking away from those shining bronze eyes so she wouldn't start giggling. "They teach us all about grooming and makeup skills and everything, and the teacher said it would be really good if we had our own makeup to practice with."

"But . . . you're not wearing all this to school. Not at your age," Anna said firmly.

Bonnie braced herself to argue, then thought better of it, knowing it was foolhardy to press for further concessions. "Just at home," she agreed. "On weekends and stuff. Until high school, all right?" she added cautiously. "Then I can, right? All the high school girls wear makeup, Mom."

"We'll see," Anna said in a distracted fashion, turning back to Leah who was calmly finishing her shortcake. "Mrs. Temple, you mustn't give Bonnie all these expensive things. If she needs makeup for health class, we can buy her some at the store."

Bonnie's heart sank. She could imagine all too well the kind of cosmetics her mother would be likely to purchase. Pale pink lipstick and transparent blusher with a brand name like Little Miss Cosmetics.

But Leah shook her head firmly. "I want Bonnie to have these things. If she won't take them I'm just going to throw them all away, and that would be such a terrible waste, don't you think?"

Anna, who abhorred waste of any kind, nodded reluctant agreement and Bonnie's spirits rose again. She beamed at her mother, who nodded once more in a defeated fashion. "Bonnie, thank Mrs. Temple for such a generous gift."

"Thank you," Bonnie murmured, overcome with embarrassment and gratitude, completely unable to look at the woman's beautiful, smiling face.

"Oh, my," Anna said suddenly, looking at her watch. "It's after four o'clock. If I don't get some water in those chick brooders right away, the poor little things will be dying of thirst. Mrs. Temple, do you want to come along and help me with the chicks again?''

Bonnie gaped at her mother, who had just asked this astonishing question as if it were the most natural thing on earth.

But Mrs. Temple didn't seem at all surprised. ''Not this time, Anna,'' she said regretfully. ''Paul will be home soon, so I'd better get back to the house and start cleaning myself up. I'm just a terrible mess.''

Anna smiled. ''You look lovely,'' she said truthfully. ''Just lovely.'' Still smiling, she removed her gingham apron, took her old cardigan from a peg by the door and went outside, her movements as spare and brisk as always.

''Bonnie,'' she called back through the screen door, ''you take care of Mrs. Temple, now. See that she gets another cup of coffee if she wants one.''

Then she was gone, leaving Bonnie alone with the quiet woman across the table.

An awkward silence fell while Bonnie stood by the table feeling fat and clumsy, and Leah sipped the last of her coffee.

''That was...that was nice of you, to say all that stuff to my mom,'' Bonnie ventured finally in a muffled voice, her face flaming with embarrassment. ''Thanks, Mrs. Temple. I'm sorry I yelled at you like that the other day,'' she added painfully.

''I hope you like the makeup, Bonnie,'' Leah said with a gentle smile. She finished the last mouthful of her dessert, dislodged Ginger tenderly from her lap and got to her feet, patting Bonnie's arm as she passed.

Bonnie tensed nervously, overcome by a growing panicky knowledge that there was something else she needed to do.

"Mrs. Temple?" she said in a faltering tone when the woman reached the door.

Leah paused with one hand on the doorknob. "Yes, Bonnie? What is it?"

"Mrs. Temple...why are you giving me so much stuff?" Bonnie waved a plump hand at the shining array of cases and bottles. "This is almost all the stuff from your dresser. You won't have any left for yourself." Bonnie's face flamed and she cursed herself for her stupidity as soon as she'd spoken. Now Mrs. Temple would realize for sure that Bonnie had been snooping in her things.

But Leah Temple just shook her head with a small, rueful smile. "I really don't know what to do with any of these things, Bonnie. I look at them and they're all just a mystery to me. I have no memory at all of ever using makeup," she concluded, sounding a little sad and withdrawn.

"But I could show you," Bonnie said impulsively. "I know lots about it," she went on, warming to the idea, glancing up at the taller woman with shy eagerness. "I've been reading all kinds of books and magazines and practicing every chance I get. I can show you how to outline and contour, and how to use base and foundation and highlighter, and do your eyes...all that stuff."

Leah's face lit up with interest. "You could? Really?"

"Sure. I'd like to," Bonnie said recklessly, all her nervousness evaporating when she saw how excited Leah was.

"Well, I'd like it, too," Leah said with childlike enthusiasm. "It would be such fun to learn all that. And then I'll look prettier, won't I, when I get all dressed up and put my makeup on?"

"You used to look just gorgeous," Bonnie murmured, her face soft with memory. "When you wore your pretty dresses and had your face done, you were the most beautiful woman in all the world."

A hot wave of awkwardness washed over her as she realized what she'd just said, but Leah Temple only nodded and smiled wistfully. "When could you start teaching me, Bonnie?"

"How about tomorrow afternoon?" Bonnie suggested, forgetting completely that she had other plans for her Saturday afternoon. "I don't have to go to school. I could spend as much time as you liked."

Leah reached out to squeeze the girl's plump arm, laughing aloud in pleasure. "That's just wonderful, Bonnie. Come over any time after lunch, all right? Oh, and you'd better bring your makeup," she added with a teasing smile, "since I don't seem to have any of my own."

Bonnie grinned back at her. "We'll divide it up," she promised. "There's lots here for both of us."

"You're such a nice girl," Leah said, giving her an impulsive hug. "And you're so pretty, Bonnie, you know that? You're just the prettiest girl, with that beautiful hair and those blue eyes and your face just like a flower. I hope I look half as nice as you do when I've learned to put on my makeup!"

Thunderstruck, Bonnie stood in the doorway watching as Leah crossed the yard with quick, graceful steps. Then she turned back into the kitchen, by-

passed the strawberry shortcake with her eyes averted
and went slowly into her bedroom.

Still almost numb with amazement at all the incredible things that had just happened, Bonnie stood
on tiptoe and rummaged through the junk on the
closet shelf, removing Allie's old ant farm so she could
reach the doughnuts and the cylinder of blue pills.
Once she had them, she put the ant farm carefully
back into position.

She sat on the bed staring at the bottle of blue pills,
thinking deeply. Just an hour earlier these pills had
been like a magic ticket to a place where there would
be no more pain and humiliation. In fact, they had
represented Bonnie's only possible course of action.

But now she wasn't so sure. She remembered Leah
Temple's warm, smiling face, the absolute sincerity in
those lovely golden-brown eyes when she said,
"You're so pretty, Bonnie...."

The girl hesitated a long time. Finally she heaved her
plump body from the bed, crossed the room and hid
the pills away once again on the shelf.

Then she took the box of doughnuts and marched
into the bathroom, sitting on the edge of the tub and
opening the package with careful, deliberate motions.

The fragrance assailed her at once, so tempting that
her stomach rumbled and she felt almost faint with
hunger. But she set her jaw and lifted the first doughnut from its little nest. Then she slowly broke it into
pieces and dropped it into the toilet bowl.

One by one Bonnie consigned the doughnuts to
oblivion, flushing each away with a ceremonial so-
lemnity that would probably have been amusing to
anyone who was watching. But there was nothing

funny about the girl's taut face or the blazing determination in those pretty cornflower-blue eyes.

LEAH PAUSED BY A GATE at the end of the walk leading up to the big house. She leaned over to sniff at a mass of little white flowers adorning a shrub near the gatepost. The shrub had burst into bloom just a day or two earlier, and now it looked like a bride, gowned in shimmering white. Leah frowned, trying to remember what the flowers were called.

Sometimes this kind of information was readily available. Other times she would have to search for a long time to remember a familiar word like "puppy" or "fireplace."

The doctor had explained that the easiest words to remember would be those acquired by the rational, fact-processing part of her brain which was apparently unaffected by her condition.

But anything that involved strong personal experience or that had been learned on the basis of feeling or emotion would be more obscure and difficult to retrieve.

Leah shivered in the grip of a familiar dread and a great wave of sadness. There were frequently times like this when melancholy overcame her and she despaired at her condition and the lonely terror of her life. Things that other people took for granted were so difficult for Leah. Every experience was unfamiliar and possibly threatening, and each new day was like a mine field full of hazards that had to be negotiated with anxious caution.

There were compensations, of course. Leah understood that she took more pleasure in enjoyable experiences than other adults did. Everyone told her that,

Paul and Doris and Dr. Holcross, and they must know.

Simple things like the taste of food, the beauty of a sunset or the fragrance of a crackling wood fire on a rainy spring evening were enough to send her into transports of joy. Nothing was old or stale to Leah. Every experience was fresh and vivid, so stimulating to her newly awakened senses that her pleasure was often intense enough to cause pain. Especially when Paul sometimes took her arm as he walked beside her or laughed and gave her an impulsive hug when Leah exclaimed about something that appealed to her. The touch of those hard, tanned hands made Leah almost faint with happiness, and there were other surging emotions that she couldn't understand.

All she knew was that when Paul touched her she yearned to nestle against him, press closer and closer until his body was wrapped all around hers and his lips and hands were—

Leah shivered and hugged herself in the sudden crispness of the spring breeze. She gazed at the shimmering cloud of white flowers with a brooding expression.

Probably she hadn't forgotten what the flowers were called at all. It was much more likely that she'd never known. After all, she thought grimly, the Leah Temple that the world knew, the one Leah saw reflected in the eyes of everyone who'd been acquainted with her, *that* woman wouldn't have been likely to bother herself with the names of flowers, would she?

Still troubled, she opened the gate, then paused. A big gray van crept along the circular driveway until it lurched to a halt beside the gate where Leah stood.

Leah squinted at the dusty, battered vehicle, trying to make out the faded lettering on the side. Triple A Carpet Cleaning, it read.

A man alighted from the driver's side and walked around to gaze steadily at Leah as she hesitated on the walk. He was a big, beefy man with a coarse face, stubbled jowls and small glittering eyes that appraised her with interest. Leah shivered and gripped her elbows again, feeling uncomfortable under that cold, speculative gaze.

"Hi, Mrs. Temple. Remember me?"

Those agonizing words haunted her every day.

Remember, remember, remember... The syllables jangled a crazy, disjointed chorus inside her weary brain.

"Of course," Leah said nervously. "You're Mr.—"

"Joe's good enough," the big man said with a genial smile that never touched his eyes. "Just call me Joe, like always. Now, Mrs. Temple, you remember our little business arrangement, don't you?"

Leah tensed. This sort of thing happened all the time, conversations with strangers who expected her to remember plans and arrangements that had been made before her accident. They contacted her about jewelry to be picked up, plans for redecorating her bedroom, fittings for clothes.

Leah hated explaining that she'd lost all traces of memory. She hated the reactions of shock and sympathy she got from people, and more than anything, their ill-concealed fascination with her condition. Usually she just bluffed her way through these awkward encounters, pretended to be normal and hoped for the best.

Now she lifted her chin and nodded. "Of course," she said.

"Good. And you remember what we talked about last month?"

"Yes," Leah lied again.

"Well, that's real good. Now, we don't need to go into all the details because that's my job, looking after the details. I just wanted, you know...to make sure the job was still on."

Leah gazed at him, her mind working rapidly, wondering which carpets in the house needed to be cleaned. Everything always looked so spotless, but of course that was because of regular, meticulous care. Maybe it was the pale green carpet in the living room, where a piece of furniture had been moved, exposing a slightly darker rectangle along one wall....

"Mrs. Temple?"

"Yes," Leah said hastily. "You can go ahead, just as we planned."

The big man nodded. "And you'll pay me the price we agreed on, same terms, same conditions?"

"Certainly," Leah said, wondering what price they'd agreed on. But she wasn't particularly concerned, since the carpet cleaning had obviously been negotiated earlier.

The woman she'd been before the accident had been a shrewd bargainer, with a keen money sense that Leah apparently still retained. She knew what most things cost, and what they were worth, and Doris had taught her how to write cheques before she left the hospital.

At first Leah had found it a terrifying experience, signing her name and waiting to see what would happen, if it would work, if the recipient would actually be able to turn that piece of paper into real money. But gradually her nervousness had faded and now she wrote cheques quite calmly, paying for household services when Paul wasn't home and for clothes and personal supplies when he took her shopping.

"Okay, then. It'll be late next month just like we planned, since that's the earliest I can make my own arrangements. And you know what you have to do? You'll have things ready for me?"

Leah nodded, feeling another brief twinge of panic. What responsibilities did she have regarding preparations for carpet cleaning? Probably just to see that the furniture was safely out of the way, and all the plants were—

"Mrs. Temple?"

"Yes," Leah said, drawing a deep, ragged breath and shifting uncomfortably, wearied by the strange conversation. "Yes, everything will be ready."

"Good," the big man said softly. "That's real good, Mrs. Temple. It's a pleasure doing business with you. I'll be in touch after the job's done."

"Thank you," Leah murmured, longing for him to leave so she could escape into the house and run her bath, then find something pretty to wear for Paul when he got home.

The carpet-cleaning man turned and walked back toward his dusty van, then paused to look over his shoulder. "Hey, Mrs. Temple," he called.

"Yes?"

"I just wanted to say that this is a real good scam," the man said with an unpleasant tone of admiration. "This whole amnesia thing, it's a damned smart move. Even if they was to suspect something, they could never pin it on you when they all think you've lost your memory, could they?"

Leah stared at the man, shaken and appalled by his words.

What on earth did he mean? Who would be trying to "pin something" on her? She frowned, searching for the meaning of the phrase, but it eluded her as slang terms often did.

Still, she felt a deep welling of distress, and a looming sense of ominous danger that chilled her almost to the point of nausea.

But of course these feelings were irrational. Whoever he was, this man was coming next month to clean the carpets, nothing more. He might be rude, but he certainly posed no threat to Leah or the people she cared about.

Firmly she turned her back on him as he got into his battered van. She walked up the path to the house without looking back as the man drove slowly out of the yard.

CHAPTER SEVEN

PAUL TEMPLE SAT at the dining table the following evening, gazing across the flickering candles at his wife. He was dazzled by her beauty on this warm spring evening, hardly able to take his eyes off her.

Leah wore a pair of off-white silky slacks and a cream-colored dress sweater scattered with delicate seed pearls. The sweater was loose-fitting with a softly draped cowl neck, utterly different from the clothes his wife used to wear.

Paul often wondered where Leah found the clothes she wore these days. Most of them were garments he'd never seen before, tasteful, well-made clothes that made her look quietly elegant.

The woman he'd known just a month ago would never have chosen to wear an outfit like this. Leah's sweaters usually dipped low to expose her breasts and clung tightly to her body. In fact, when Paul thought about his wife's wardrobe, all the old suspicions flared again for an uncomfortable moment.

Could it really be an elaborate ruse, after all, this whole episode? Could she have planned the beating, the amnesia and the resulting personality transformation, orchestrated it all skillfully in advance, right down to the new wardrobe that would be in keeping with her changed image?

He shifted in his chair, hating the suspicious thoughts that filled his mind. This was the way it had always been with Leah; the powerful attraction was inevitably clouded by doubt and mistrust.

Leah, always sensitive to his moods, glanced at him across the table with a shy, anxious look, her eyes wide and nervous.

Paul looked at her with a sharp, indrawn breath.

God, but she was lovely, he thought. She'd lost a little weight since the accident, and her face looked almost ethereal. Her mouth was soft and gentle, and her eyes were...

Paul leaned forward to examine her more closely, while she shifted awkwardly under his intent gaze and glanced down at her plate in embarrassment.

"That's what's different about you tonight, Leah. You're wearing makeup."

He studied the skillful blending of colors around her eyes, the dense loveliness of her eyelashes.

Leah flushed and nodded, still unable to look up. "Does it look...does it look really terrible?" she asked. "Is it that obvious?"

"It looks beautiful," Paul said with sincerity. "Exquisite, in fact. It's really quite a professional job," he added casually, sipping his coffee. "I thought you said you couldn't remember how to put on makeup, Leah. Haven't you just been wearing lipstick since the accident?"

Leah nodded. "Bonnie did it," she said simply.

"Bonnie?" Paul asked, staring at her. "Bob and Anna's little girl? She made up your face like that?"

Leah nodded, becoming more animated when she saw that he was interested. "Bonnie's just fascinated with makeup. She knows all about shading and

blending and everything. She did it this afternoon,"
Leah added with the same childlike directness that
characterized all her conversation. "She's going to
teach me how to do it myself, but there's so much to
learn. It's really complicated, Paul."

"My God," he muttered, stunned by this information, still gazing at the beautiful shadowed face of the
woman who sat across the table. "Leah, did you..."
he began, then paused.

"Yes?"

"I was just wondering where you got all the clothes
you're wearing these days. Most of them are things I
can't remember seeing before. Have you bought them
since you were hurt?"

Leah shook her head. "There are so many clothes
in the closet. I just couldn't imagine going out and
buying more."

"But you said you didn't like those clothes. And
nowadays I don't ever see you wearing the things you
used to wear."

"I don't like the things on the hangers," Leah said.
"But there are boxes full of other clothes piled at the
back, and some of them I like. When I want something new to wear, I just get the boxes down and look
through them."

Paul nodded thoughtfully.

Possibly because of her deprived and rootless
childhood, Leah had always been a terrible hoarder.
She could seldom bear to part with anything that was
hers, even when she grew tired of it. Except for brief
irrational bursts of generosity when she'd give expensive things away on a whim to Anna or the girls or one
of her unsavory friends, Leah hung on to all her pos-
sessions with grim determination.

Paul assumed the boxes that she spoke of were probably stuffed with old clothes from the early years of their marriage. Those costly, beautiful items hadn't suited her increasingly flashy and seductive image, but obviously she still hadn't been able to dispose of them. Her explanation made sense, he thought. It all made perfect sense.

He felt a flood of relief, and realized with a brief chill that all this was beginning to matter terribly to him. He felt a powerful need to believe in this new, gentle Leah, to trust her completely and rid himself of his nagging doubts.

Because soon, very soon, he was going to—

"Paul?" Leah ventured timidly, interrupting his troubled thoughts. "May I ask you something?"

"Of course."

Heinz appeared at that moment to clear away the dessert dishes and offer more coffee.

Leah smiled up at him as she held out her cup. "It was just lovely, Heinz. I think that chocolate cake was the most wonderful thing I've ever tasted."

"My grandmother's recipe," Heinz said with pride, beaming at her. "A family secret."

"It was just wonderful," Leah repeated. "Wasn't it, Paul?"

"Yes, it was," Paul said, still gazing at her, loving the glow on her face and the warmth of her smile when she addressed the rotund cook.

He grinned at the way Heinz expanded under Leah's praise, then bustled from the room with his bald head high and his face shining.

"You know, you've made a real conquest there, Leah," Paul observed dryly. "I think our poor old

Heinz has fallen hopelessly in love with you over these past few weeks."

For some reason the words made her sad. Paul saw her lovely bronze eyes cloud over, her mouth droop. He gazed at her in concern.

"Leah?" he prompted her gently. "You were about to ask me something?"

"I was looking through my desk drawers today," she said, her eyes downcast so all he could see was the delicate line of her brow and cheek. "The carpet cleaning man stopped by yesterday to confirm an appointment, and I wanted to see if I could find some kind of contract that I'd made with him before my accident."

"Did you find it?"

"No, there was nothing."

Paul frowned. "You never mentioned having any carpets cleaned, Leah."

"Didn't I?"

"Not that I can recall."

Leah shrugged. "Oh, well, I guess it doesn't matter. He seems to know what he's doing, and it was all agreed on in advance, so it should be all right. That's not what I'm worried about."

"What are you worried about?" Paul asked gently.

"When I was looking through the desk I came across some papers I hadn't seen before. They'd been ripped into pieces and stuffed down the back of a drawer. I had to smooth them out and fit them together again before I could read them."

Paul tensed. "What were the papers about, Leah?"

"Divorce," she whispered, looking up at him briefly. He caught a fleeting impression of stricken eyes and soft trembling lips before she lowered her head again.

"Leah—"

"They were legal papers from you to me saying that you wanted to divorce me."

Paul drew a deep breath and clenched his hands, then forced himself to relax slowly as he considered his next words. He looked at the shy, vulnerable line of his wife's neck and her long, downcast eyelashes, the play of light and shadow on her cheeks.

"Leah," he began quietly, "things have been pretty terrible between us these past few years. You don't remember the way it was, but I'd just about reached the point where it was unbearable. I thought the relationship was destructive to both of us and it would be best to end it."

"I'm sorry," she whispered. "Paul, I'm just so sorry."

"How can you be sorry? You don't even remember the things you did. You shouldn't have to apologize for what you can't remember, should you?"

"But it was *me*, Paul," Leah said in despair, looking up at last to meet his eyes, her face pale with anguish. "It was *me*. Can't you understand? The person who did those things and behaved that way wasn't some...some stranger. It was the same person I am. I have to feel responsible for my own actions even if I can't remember them."

Paul shook his head. "I don't think so. You were different then. You were another woman entirely, Leah. I don't see how you can be held responsible for things that you have no memory of and wouldn't be likely to do now."

"That would be so nice to believe," Leah said wistfully. "But I just can't. It's not like being able to shift the responsibility onto another person. I was that person, and the people I hurt were hurt by me. If anybody's going to make things right, it has to be me. But," she added in despair, "I can't even remember the damage I did. How can I repair it?"

"Why not look on it as a clean slate?" Paul said gently.

"A clean slate?"

He smiled at her puzzled look, remembering that she often had difficulty recalling the meaning of slang expressions.

"A second chance. A new beginning," he explained. "You've been given a rare opportunity, Leah, something a lot of people would love to have. You've got a chance to leave the past behind you and to start over completely. Why don't you just accept it and stop agonizing over things you can't change?"

"Because," she whispered, giving him another stricken glance, "what's to stop it from happening all over again? What if I . . . I start to get better soon, like Ken says I will, and then I turn out to be just the same as I always was?"

Paul felt a chill of unease, realizing that Leah had just voiced his own fears with uncanny accuracy. This was the very possibility that haunted him every day, the thing that kept him from yielding to his own urges.

All the time he longed to take his wife in his arms and kiss her. He wanted to tell her how beautiful she was, use the gentleness and strength of his body to warm and comfort her and protect her from all the dangers and confusions of this unfamiliar world she found herself wandering in.

But what if it all started happening again? What if the gradual return of memory did indeed cause a reversion to her former personality and habits?

Paul knew absolutely that he couldn't bear it, couldn't survive the trauma of giving his love a second time to a cold, mocking woman who'd meet his tenderness with cruelty and obscenity.

"Do you think that's possible, Leah?" he asked quietly, watching her face as he spoke. "Do you believe that you'll... start to feel differently when you begin to remember things?"

"I don't *know,*" she murmured in despair. "But that's the person I was, Paul. I can see it in the faces of everyone around me, and read it in the diary I wrote.... Even Ken tells me things sometimes about what I was like. How can a little tap on the head change an entire personality? I guess I'm afraid all the time that I'll start turning back into what I was."

Paul nodded and sipped moodily at his coffee, unable to find an answer despite the look of pleading in her eyes.

"Is there something I should do?" Leah asked suddenly, her voice low and uncertain.

"Do? About what, Leah?"

"About those papers. About... about the divorce. Do you want me to... see a lawyer or something, or can I just tell you that it's all right to go ahead?"

Paul stared at her. "Go ahead?"

She nodded, shrugging awkwardly. "I don't want... don't want you to feel that you have to keep me here, Paul. I'm a lot better now, really I am. I could... live somewhere else. In town or something...maybe close to Doris. That'd be nice," she added wistfully, "to live close to Doris."

"Leah—" he protested.

"And I learn so quickly, Paul," she continued, warming to the idea. "If you just helped me out a little, just at first, pretty soon I could get a job somewhere and look after myself, and then you'd be—"

"Leah," Paul interrupted, hardly able to bear the ache in his heart. "Leah, look at me."

She glanced up at him silently. Her lips trembled and her eyelashes were damp with tears, but she tried to give him a reassuring smile. "It's all right, Paul. Truly it is."

"Leah, I don't want a divorce. All right? Let's not talk about it just now."

"But the papers said—"

Paul made an abrupt, almost angry gesture. "Those papers were delivered at a time when I was finding my home life unbearable. It's not unbearable now. In fact, I can't remember when..."

He fell silent, buffeted by surges of emotion that threatened to betray him.

"Can't remember?" Leah echoed with a misty, teasing smile, making a gallant effort to lighten the sudden tension in the room. "Is there actually something *you* can't remember, Paul?"

I can't remember when I've wanted anyone so much, he longed to say. *I can't remember when I've needed so badly to hold you and kiss you, to take you into bed with me and make love to you for hours and hours, until we both...*

He shook his head and gave her a casual, offhand smile. "I can't remember when I've spent so many weekends at home," he said lightly. "This is something new for me, Leah, being an at-home kind of family man like this."

"Really?" She glanced at him, her eyes wide with surprise. "Where did you used to go on weekends?"

"To my cabin. You used to hate my going there. You made jokes all the time about the hermit in his cave."

Paul's face shadowed briefly at the memory of those cruel taunts, but he forced himself to smile when he saw how upset his wife was by the reference.

"Don't worry, Leah," he said gently. "It's just a little log cabin I built on the property a few years ago, about a mile up in the cliffs and back in the trees."

Leah's face lost its tense, unhappy look and began to sparkle with interest. "Which way? Past the creek?"

Paul nodded. "You go over the footbridge behind the barn and then follow the path up into the trees."

"Oh," she said in delight. "Is that where that little path goes? I walked part way up one day, then turned back because it was getting late."

"Well, if you'd kept on, you'd have come out right at my cabin."

Leah was silent a moment, gazing wistfully out the window at the silvery twilight sky. "It must be so beautiful and quiet up there," she said finally.

"It really is. There's no phone or electricity, just a wood stove and kerosene lamps, and no people anywhere nearby. I always feel like the only man in the world when I'm at the cabin," he added, feeling almost shy. After all, Paul Temple was not accustomed to confiding in his wife.

But she was absorbed in thought, her face soft and dreamy. "What do you do up there? I mean, when you're there for the whole weekend?"

"I read, hike around in the cliffs, take pictures of wildlife...nothing too spectacular."

Paul fell silent, thinking about those healing weekends at his isolated retreat. For the past several years that peaceful haven had probably kept him sane.

"Did I ever see it?" Leah asked, avoiding his eyes.

Paul stared at her in disbelief. "It's a mile-long hike, mostly uphill, Leah. Not your style at all."

She flushed and toyed awkwardly with her napkin, then smoothed it and set it decisively on her plate.

"Well, I guess I'd better excuse myself," she said with a bright smile. "Bob thinks the old black cat has kittens hidden somewhere in the barn, and Allie promised she'd help me find them tonight if she gets her homework done in time. We can't wait to see what they look like. Allie says that last time she had kittens, two of them were—"

"Leah," Paul interrupted gently.

"Yes?"

"Would you like to see my cabin? Would you like me to take you there?"

Her eyes brightened but she turned aside with obvious reluctance and shook her head. "Paul, it's your private place. I wouldn't want to...to intrude on that."

"You can't intrude," Paul said reasonably. "You've been invited."

Still she hesitated, gazing longingly out again at the pastel swirl of clouds along the horizon.

"You'll need some jeans and a warm sweater," Paul said. "Do you have hiking boots? No, I guess you wouldn't," he answered himself with a wry smile.

"But the path's pretty good. You can wear sneakers. Go and change, and I'll tell Allie you'll see the kittens another time."

She turned to him, her face transformed, as joyous as that of a child being offered a rare treat. "You mean . . . right now? You'll take me right now?"

"Sure. Hurry up, before it gets dark."

"But, Paul, the sun's almost setting. . . ."

"We've got lots of daylight left. I'll take a flashlight just in case, but we should be home before it's full dark. Come on, Leah. I'd like you to see the cabin."

"Oh," she breathed, smiling at him in delight. Then she was gone, running down the hall with light, happy steps while Paul stood silently, gazing at the candles flickering on the table.

He pictured the cosy isolated cabin, the warm lamplight, the soft bed of stripped logs with its covering of warm, rough blankets.

And the stillness of the moonlight, and Leah in his arms . . .

Paul shivered and moved blindly out into the hallway, reflecting with a grim smile that there probably weren't many men who would be so nervous and breathless, so weak with passion and pure terror, simply at the prospect of being alone with their wives.

THE FOOTPATH WAS ROCKY and steep, so narrow in places that they had to climb in single file. Leah walked ahead, delighting in the piny fragrance, the soft, damp smells of twilight and the hushed chorus of birdsong from the tall trees lining the path.

She was also warmly conscious of the man walking behind her. She could hear his light, agile tread and feel his intent glance resting on her body as she moved. In spite of herself Leah kept thinking about those beautiful jeweled eyes, all green and brown and sapphire, set in a dense fringe of lashes, crinkling warmly when he smiled....

She shivered and hugged herself.

"Chilly, Leah?" Paul asked with quick solicitude, coming abreast of her and dropping a casual arm around her shoulders.

Leah shook her head. "I'm fine. It's a lovely evening, Paul."

She rested against him for a moment, feeling a blissful pleasure in the breadth and warmth and safety of him, the clean, pleasant smell of his clothes and his skin.

But when his arm tightened a little and his golden head dipped closer to hers, Leah pulled away and started blindly up along the path once more, chattering in a bright, determined manner about Bonnie and Allie, about chicks and kittens and flowers, about the books she was reading and all the small pleasures that occupied her days.

"Do any of your friends still call you these days?" Paul asked casually from behind her.

Leah shook her head. "Only Doris. I didn't like any of those other people who called," she added with childlike simplicity. "I kept telling them I wasn't feeling well and making excuses, and they've quit calling me now."

"Good," Paul said briefly. "None of those people were any good for you, Leah. And judging from what I saw, they weren't really the kind of people who'd make loyal friends."

But they were my friends, Leah thought. *They were the kind of people I chose to spend my time with.* She shook her head again, as if to clear it of the disgust and self-loathing that was growing in her day by day as she learned more about her past life and behavior.

"Well, we're just about there," Paul said cheerfully over her shoulder, unaware of her brooding thoughts. "Wait a minute, Leah."

He reached out to hold her elbow and then moved up beside her, dropping his arm around her shoulder once more and leading her through a screen of undergrowth into a small clearing.

"Oh," Leah breathed, gazing at the little log cabin nestled beneath towering pines.

The rustic building looked as sweetly natural as if it had taken root and grown there in the wooded clearing, its weathered roof and sides blending in beautifully with the ground and trees, its small windows shining like molten gold in the waning twilight glow.

A handmade rocker sat on the porch looking off into the valley, and a chimney of fieldstone rose at one side, hinting at a cosy fireplace and welcoming hearth within.

"Do you like it?" Paul asked, grinning boyishly at her reaction.

"I love it," Leah said simply, her eyes shining. "I just love it. May I see inside?"

"Not until you've praised my handiwork. I built most of this with my own two hands, Leah. I even set the stones for the fireplace and whittled the rocker on the porch."

Leah smiled up at him. "It's just amazing, Paul. First you're a wealthy businessman, and then you're a farmer, and now a woodsman.... You're too hard to figure out. You keep confusing me.''

He smiled back at her, his face lighting with pleasure at her gentle, affectionate words. For a long moment they gazed at each other, until Paul finally turned away with an awkward gesture and led her up the path toward the little veranda and the broad hand-hewn door.

"My castle is at your disposal, my lady,'' he said with mock courtliness, turning a key in the padlock and holding the door open with a sweeping bow. "Mind you don't snag your skirts on the doorsill there.''

Leah giggled and stepped past him into the building, sniffing in pleasure at the mingled scents of pine and woodsmoke, of clean blankets and charcoal and dusty sunshine.

The cabin was a single room with a small loft above, in which she could dimly make out a brass bedstead and a bright patchwork quilt. On the ground level there was an ancient wood stove with a generous cooking surface, a rough handmade table and two chairs, an old easy chair covered with a Navaho blanket, and a wall of glass-fronted cabinets containing books, dishes, packaged food and photographic supplies.

The silence was profound. Time slowed as dusk gathered beyond the windows, soft and dense and richly peaceful. Leah felt an ageless sense of safety and absolute rightness, an understanding that this was the way life was meant to be.

"It's supposed to be like this, isn't it?'' she murmured aloud, hardly aware that she was voicing her thoughts.

"Like what, Leah?"

"Like this," she said shyly, waving her hand at the snug little building. "Natural and good and quiet, with no complications, and just a...a man and a woman together, peaceful..."

Her stumbling words trailed off into silence. She glanced up at Paul, frightened all at once by his intent look, the fierce light in his eyes when he gazed at her, the tension of his hard, tanned jaw with its faint dusting of golden stubble.

Leah gazed at him as he leaned toward her, gazed at his gleaming eyes and firm chin and finely molded lips. Suddenly her face went white with shock and she swayed a little on her feet, staring wordlessly.

A memory was brushing at the edges of her mind.

The image was dim and troubling, as blurred as an old photograph. It had something to do with this place, this isolated cabin in the woods...and Paul, all alone here....

"Leah," he was saying as he gazed at her in concern. "Leah, are you all right?"

"I remember..." she began hesitantly. Her voice trailed off and she stared out the little square window.

"You remember?" Paul asked tensely. "What, Leah? what do you remember?"

"I don't know. This place. Something about this place, and you being here."

"But you couldn't be remembering this place. You've never been here before."

"Couldn't I have walked up here one day when you were at work?"

Paul shook his head. "That's really hard to picture. You never used to walk anywhere, Leah. And you couldn't have gotten inside, anyway, because the door is always padlocked and I have the only key."

"But I feel like I remember..." She shook her head in confusion. "It's an image of you in this cabin, Paul. And there's something else. There's another person in the memory, but he's all shadowed."

"There's never anybody else up here, Leah. I always come here alone. Solitude is the whole idea of the place."

"But I can *see* the other person," Leah went on slowly, hardly aware that he had spoken. She pressed her fingers to her forehead. "I think it's..." She fell abruptly silent, glancing up at Paul with a troubled look.

"Who?" he asked gently. "Who is it?"

"It's the carpet-cleaning man. The one I talked to yesterday. The memory has something to do with him and you and this cabin."

Paul relaxed and laughed. "Leah, its just déjà vu. Some recent experiences have gotten jumbled in your mind, that's all. I've never even seen the carpet-cleaning man, and he's certainly never been to this cabin."

"Déjà vu?" Leah echoed.

"Everybody experiences it now and then, even people without memory problems."

"But what is it?"

"It's a strange feeling, actually," Paul said, holding out a chair by the hearth for her and seating himself opposite, leaning forward earnestly. "Something is happening to you, and all the while it's going on you have the strongest feeling that it's happened before, even though you can't quite capture the memory. But you feel that you can remember the exact words that are being said. Sometimes you even have the impression you know what's coming next because you've been through it all before."

Leah gave him a thoughtful glance. "I feel that way a lot of the time, but I thought it was probably because I'd actually had similar experiences and just couldn't remember them."

"That might well be," Paul said. "But there's a difference between memory and experience, Leah. Also between memory and imagination. This business with the cabin and me and the carpet-cleaning man, that's just something your brain has assembled from a group of random impressions. It's not a memory."

Her face shadowed. "I was so excited," she murmured, trying to smile. "I really hoped I was remembering something. It felt like I was, Paul."

"You'll remember," he said, reaching out to take her hands in a comforting grasp. "Ken keeps saying it'll happen soon, Leah, and I have a lot of confidence in him. I believe your memories will start coming back."

"I hope so." Leah was silent a moment, gazing at the darkening window above the little table.

"What are you thinking now?" Paul asked, studying her profile.

"Just . . . how strange it all is."

"What's strange?"

"I don't know. Life, I guess." Leah turned back to him with a brief smile.

"What do you mean?" Paul asked gently, releasing her hands and leaning back in the chair.

Leah frowned, searching for words.

"This place," she said finally, waving her hand at the silent, rustic cabin, then turning back to gaze at his intent face. "It's all so *real*, Paul. And so are you. You've been coming here for years. You had a whole life up here where you lived and ate and slept and did things. Right?"

He nodded, watching her closely as she spoke.

"And you remember it," Leah went on slowly. "You remember all the things you did here, and what the weather was like, and the animals you saw, all those things. Don't you?"

Again he nodded.

"And while you were here," Leah continued, waving her hand toward the window, "I was down there living my own life, too. I was doing things and talking to people and eating and sleeping, just like you were, but I have no memory of it so it's like I didn't exist at all, not the way you did. Do our lives only exist if we can remember them?"

Paul shook his head. "No. They exist because they happened, Leah. Our memories can't create reality. They can only reflect it."

"I feel almost invisible," Leah said with another sad little smile. "I feel as if a puff of wind could blow me away, because there's nothing to me—nothing to give me shape or substance. I'm completely transparent."

"Leah, I don't think you realize..." Paul fell silent, still looking at her with that same serious expression.

"Don't realize what?" she asked, both warmed and troubled by the intensity of his gaze.

"I don't think you realize just how much shape and substance you have now, Leah. You may feel transparent and invisible, but in my opinion you're more complex and interesting than you've ever been. You think more deeply, express yourself with more eloquence, and get far more involved with the people and things around you. In many ways you're a much more real person now than you were before, even though your memories are gone.''

For some reason his words made Leah feel ridiculously happy, almost as light as air. She couldn't stay in the chair, could hardly keep her feet on the rough plank floors as she got up and hurried across the room to gaze out the window. She stared at the darkening woods, biting her lip and blinking back tears.

''Leah?'' Paul asked, moving up behind her and dropping an arm around her trembling shoulders. ''Are you all right?''

''I'm just so happy,'' she murmured, standing close beside him. ''Paul, I'm so happy to hear you say that I'm like a real person and not just a . . . a puff of air, or something.''

''Leah, my God . . .'' His arm tightened around her and his head dipped lower, so near that she could feel his cheek brushing her hair, his lips moving softly against her forehead.

Leah turned blindly and nestled against him. Suddenly she was assailed by a fierce, disturbing hunger, a need that she didn't understand and was afraid to analyze. She wanted only to be close to him, wrapped up in him and drowned in him. She wanted to be lost inside him, swallowed up in a world where there was nothing but his mouth and hands and the big golden warmth of him and this strange sweet feeling that was washing over her in surging waves.

He drew her into his arms and his mouth quested lower, soothing and slow, caressing her brow, her eyelids, her cheeks and throat, finally resting on her lips with a firm, gentle pressure.

Leah gasped and trembled, troubled by her own lack of control, almost overcome by these feelings that she couldn't remember or understand. Her knees felt weak and shaky, her heart thundered against his chest, and her cheeks were hot. She wanted to stop, tear herself from his arms and run and hide from him before anything else happened.

But her mouth and hands betrayed her own wishes. Her fingers kept reaching up to stroke his hair, touching his neck and ears and shoulders, loving the feeling of him. And her mouth opened against his, warm and seeking, thrilling at the wild sweetness of the kiss that went on and on and on...

Panic mounted within Leah, a fear that she was doing something wrong, something that would make him despise her later. She whimpered and stiffened in his arms, and Paul released her immediately, gazing down at her with a worried look.

"Leah?" he whispered huskily. "Is something the matter?"

She shook her head, hiding her face from him, feeling clumsy and ashamed. "I'm sorry, Paul," she whispered. "I didn't mean to..."

"Didn't mean to what?"

"To...to do anything wrong," she said with child-like anguish.

"This isn't wrong, Leah," Paul murmured softly, taking her into his arms again. But this time there was no urgency in his embrace, just a comforting tenderness as if he were cuddling a frightened child. "People do this all the time. Especially people who are married to each other."

NO RISK, NO OBLIGATION TO BUY...NOW OR EVER!

GUARANTEED

PLAY "ROLL A DOUBLE" AND GET AS MANY AS FIVE FREE GIFTS!

HERE'S HOW TO PLAY:

1. Peel off label from front cover. Place it in space provided at right. With a coin, carefully scratch off the silver dice. This makes you eligible to receive two or more free books, and possibly another gift, depending on what is revealed beneath the scratch-off area.

2. Send back this card and you'll receive brand-new Harlequin Superromance® novels. These books have a cover price of $3.50 each, but they are yours to keep absolutely free.

3. There's no catch. You're under no obligation to buy anything. We charge nothing – ZERO – for your first shipment. And you don't have to make any minimum number of purchases – not even one!

4. The fact is thousands of readers enjoy receiving books by mail from the Harlequin Reader Service® before they're available in stores. They like the convenience of home delivery and they love our discount prices!

5. We hope that after receiving your free books you'll want to remain a subscriber. But the choice is yours – to continue or cancel, anytime at all! So why not take us up on our invitation, with no risk of any kind. You'll be glad you did!

NOT ACTUAL SIZE

You'll look like a million dollars when you wear this lovely necklace! Its cobra-link chain is a generous 18" long, and the multi-faceted Austrian crystal sparkles like a diamond!

THE HARLEQUIN READER SERVICE®: HERE'S HOW IT WORKS

Accepting free books puts you under no obligation to buy anything. You may keep the books and gift and return the shipping statement marked "cancel." If you do not cancel, about a month later we will send you 4 additional novels, and bill you just $2.71 each plus 25¢ delivery and applicable sales tax, if any.* That's the complete price, and – compared to cover prices of $3.50 each – quite a bargain! You may cancel at any time, but if you choose to continue, every month we'll send you 4 more books, which you may either purchase at the discount price...or return at our expense and cancel your subscription.

*Terms and prices subject to change without notice. Sales tax applicable in N.Y.

BUSINESS REPLY MAIL

FIRST CLASS MAIL   PERMIT NO. 717   BUFFALO, NY

POSTAGE WILL BE PAID BY ADDRESSEE

HARLEQUIN READER SERVICE
3010 WALDEN AVE
PO BOX 1867
BUFFALO NY 14240-9952

NO POSTAGE
NECESSARY
IF MAILED
IN THE
UNITED STATES

"Did we?" Leah asked awkwardly, her face hidden against his shirt front.

"What? Did we hold each other like this? Kiss each other?"

"Yes."

"Not lately," Paul said briefly. Leah glanced up in time to see the sudden grim set of his jaw, the look of bitter memory in his eyes.

She shivered and bit her lip, fighting the urge to ask for more details. This was something she longed to know. For weeks she'd wanted to ask Paul if they ever did the things together that husbands and wives did in the books she read, things that Leah could barely imagine.

She didn't have even the slightest recollection of sexual experience. But sometimes at night she had dreams of naked bodies, of thrusting strength and flowing sweetness and a joy so intense that she woke gasping, then lay in the darkness and stared at the ceiling for hours with a troubled ache in her heart and body that almost made her cry....

"Come on, Leah," Paul was saying, his voice quiet and remote. "We'd better start for home before it's too dark to see the path."

Leah nodded and followed him outside, watching as he secured the door. Then she fell into step beside him, moving quietly across the clearing and into the hushed twilight stillness of the woods.

CHAPTER EIGHT

BONNIE POUNDED ALONG the dusty road leading to the farm. Her arms swung in jerky motions, her knees buckled a little with each running stride and her breath came in noisy, ragged gasps. Fatigue pounded in her chest and sang in her ears until she yearned for relief. She wanted nothing in all the world but an end to this breathless pain, a chance to sink into the cool weeds lining the road and lie on her back for about an hour doing nothing at all.

"Just a little more," she panted aloud, willing herself to continue. "I'll count to fifty, then I'll stop. One, two, three..."

At last the farm buildings loomed out of the dusk and Bonnie slowed to a walk, then stood gasping noisily as she leaned against the mailbox to catch her breath.

When she started walking again her whole body felt rubbery and her legs were as weak and as hard to control as mounds of jelly. But she noted that it didn't take her as long to catch her breath now, and her thighs no longer burned quite as much from the effort of running.

Bonnie glanced down at her plump legs in the navy blue sweatpants. Hope surged within her, warming her and making her forget the agonizing pain of the two miles she'd just run.

Probably it was her imagination but she thought maybe her thighs looked a little slimmer, not quite as fat and loose. Cautiously she ran her hands over her upper legs, hardly daring to believe what she sensed. After all, it had only been a week since she'd started, but still . . .

Bonnie drew a deep breath, paused to compose herself, then slipped through a gap in the hedge and trudged toward the little bungalow with a fair imitation of her old listless manner.

A major part of her overall plan was this careful concealment of her actions. For some reason it was vitally important to Bonnie to keep what she was doing to herself until her weight loss became so spectacular that she couldn't hide it any longer. She had a superstitious dread of people talking about her diet, watching and commenting on her progress, even offering encouragement.

Just now, Bonnie wanted to be all alone with her pain.

She sighed with relief to see that nobody was around. Her mother was probably out tending the chicks, her father was down in the stable with one of the horses who was having difficulty foaling, and she knew where Allie would be. Allie and Mrs. Temple had finally managed to find the batch of kittens in the barn, and they went out almost every evening to play with them.

Normally Bonnie would have felt some jealousy over this, especially when she saw Allie and Mrs. Temple laughing together as they cuddled the plump, tumbling kittens, or lay in the straw of the loft teasing them with bits of yarn and soft toys.

But just now, Bonnie liked having everybody concentrating on other things. Besides, she still got lots of attention from Mrs. Temple. They had their makeup sessions almost every day after school, long, blissful interludes when Bonnie was allowed to enter Mrs. Temple's beautiful bedroom, sit with her at the mirrored dressing table and apply colors and creams to that lovely smiling face.

She cherished these private times with the mistress of the estate. Mrs. Temple was really, truly, a different person from before. She talked to Bonnie as spontaneously and happily as another teenager, and she took a genuine interest in the things Bonnie did at school, what her life was like and what she thought about things.

There was something so comforting about Mrs. Temple's shy smile and gentle voice.

Best of all, she kept saying how pretty Bonnie was, how sweet and generous to teach her how to use makeup so she could look her best at night when her husband came home for dinner....

Bonnie smiled, still thinking about Mrs. Temple. The beautiful woman was feeling a lot better these days, and she seemed happier and more relaxed with every week that passed. Sometimes she even teased Bonnie gently or made little jokes that cracked both of them up.

It was so much fun being with her, saving up things to tell her and thinking of stories to entertain her. The surprising warmth of their friendship actually kept Bonnie from thinking about food all the time, made it easier for her to resist the powerful cravings that gripped her so viciously, especially during the really bad time in the late afternoon when she first got home from school and knew that she'd have to wait a couple of hours for supper.

Bonnie hurried into the bathroom, stripped off her sweatshirt to splash water on her hot face and shoulders, and looked longingly at the scale in the corner. She'd promised herself that she'd just get weighed once a week, and she had to wait another two hours for it to be exactly a week since last time. But she felt so hollow and hungry, and besides, it was already Friday evening. A couple of hours couldn't make any difference.

Holding her breath with anticipation, Bonnie moved the scale into the precise spot on the linoleum floor where it registered an optimum weight, then took off her sneakers and sweatpants.

Her plump young body trembled with nervousness and dread as she stepped into position, closed her eyes briefly in a silent prayer, then opened them and stared down at her feet in stunned disbelief.

Six pounds! She'd lost six pounds since last Friday evening!

Bonnie's heart soared. She wanted to sing and dance, to shout aloud, to rush out and go for another two-mile run. But most of all she wanted to find Mrs. Temple and give her a big hug, though she knew she wouldn't because she was far too shy to touch the woman unless they were having one of their makeup sessions.

Nevertheless Bonnie felt an urgent need to look into those smiling golden eyes, see Mrs. Temple's gentle face and hear her soft voice and bubbling laughter.

Bonnie hurried into her room and tossed her sweaty clothes into the hamper, dressing herself in jeans and a T-shirt.

The jeans definitely fit looser. They were easier to zip, and they didn't strain at the seams as much as they always had. Bonnie almost laughed aloud in delight and triumph. If it felt this good to lose the first six pounds, just think how wonderful it would be to lose all *thirty-seven* of them!

But not all the weight would be this easy to lose, Bonnie reminded herself firmly.

Bonnie knew all about dieting. She'd read a dozen books on the subject and probably a hundred magazine articles. She knew that the initial weight loss was mostly fluid, that you reached frustrating plateaus where you didn't lose any weight no matter how hard you tried, that calorie counting needed to be supplemented with an exercise program in order to be effective, and that the whole process always went much, much slower than you wanted it to.

Still, this initial progress was definitely encouraging.

Singing under her breath, Bonnie rummaged through the cluttered upper shelf of her closet, burrowing into the secret place behind the ant farm where she kept the things she wanted to conceal. The vial of blue pills was still there, but Bonnie hardly noticed them, just brushed them aside to remove a red plastic folder with a big leering Garfield on the front.

A fierce hand-lettered sign neatly attached to the cover read Personal and Confidential! Property of Bonnie McBride and NOBODY ELSE. Do Not Open on Pain of Death.

She climbed onto her bed, opening the folder and studied the contents gravely. Most of the pages were elaborate ruled charts with spaces for check marks and daily notations, following long lists of instructions that bristled with asterisks and underlining.

No eating between meals. Exercise *at least* half an hour each day. Eat *slowly* and chew *every* mouthful at least ten times. *No* chocolate bars, just apples and oranges. Drink at least *eight* glasses of water each day..."

The list went on and on. Bonnie pondered the separate charts, nibbling her pencil as she checked off items.

The final chart was the really important one, and filling it out required some ceremony. Bonnie heaved herself from the bed, went to the kitchen and poured herself a glass of skim milk. She took three carrot sticks and a stalk of celery from the fridge, lined them up precisely on one of her mother's best flowered plates, then carried her treat back into the bedroom and shut the door.

Smiling with triumph she recorded her new weight in the box indicated, and entered the six-pound weight loss in the loss column as she sipped dreamily at her glass of milk. Finally she lay back on the mound of stuffed toys that cluttered her bed, munching carrot sticks and examining the full-page drawing at the back of the folder.

This was a surprisingly skilled, hand-drawn likeness showing a slim and shapely Bonnie in a brief two-piece bathing suit, standing on a beach and staring haughtily across the water.

Bonnie gazed at the picture and sighed in bliss, thinking how lovely it would be to escape this ugly, confining flesh, to have a body that was slim and quick and graceful, like Mrs. Temple's.... At last she cleared away all traces of her little snack, then paused to glare sternly at her stomach, which still rumbled with hunger. She took a jacket and left the house, heading off into the murmuring twilight to look for Allie and Mrs. Temple.

LIKE BONNIE, PAUL TEMPLE was also in search of his wife, but he didn't have as clear an idea where to find her.

He emerged from his house, hesitated at the gate near the mass of flowering spirea, and looked around at the silent farmyard. He frowned, wondering where Leah might have gone and how she filled her time when he wasn't home.

This past week had been a frantically busy one at the plant, concluding in a business trip to Chicago. Paul had hardly seen Leah since the night they walked up to the cabin together, and he was surprised at how much he missed her.

When his plane landed in the early evening Paul didn't even go to the office, just jumped into his car and headed for home. As he drove he thought about her smiling, gentle face, the childlike glow of her eyes, the shy delicacy of her curving body in his arms. By the time he arrived at the farm he'd found himself almost running up the walk to his house, as eager and lovestruck as an adolescent boy. But the house was silent and strangely dim, as if Leah's presence was the magic ingredient necessary to make the place come alive. So Paul had changed his clothes and headed back outside, looking for the woman who had begun, in some troubling and unfathomable way, to be the light of his life.

Anna passed by, carrying a couple of brimming metal pails and smiling at him with unusual warmth.

"Hello, Anna," Paul said. "It's a nice evening, isn't it?"

"Just lovely," Anna agreed, pausing to set the pails down at her feet. "I caught some rainwater in the barrels by the barn," she explained as Paul looked at her burden. "I'm taking them over to water my flower boxes. The plants love rainwater."

"Let me carry them to the house for you," Paul offered.

Anna looked shocked, then embarrassed. "Oh, I don't think so, Mr. Temple," she murmured, so awkwardly that Paul didn't press his offer.

"I'm looking for my wife," he said. "Any idea where she might be, Anna?"

Anna smiled, her weathered face lighting with affection. "Last I saw, she and Allie were heading for the barn."

"The barn?" Paul echoed. "What are they doing over there?"

"They finally found that batch of kittens they've been looking for. Allie and Mrs. Temple spend hours playing with those kittens."

Paul grinned. "I see. Well, do you think they'd mind an intruder?"

Anna smiled back at him, bending to lift her pails again. "I don't think so, Mr. Temple. I don't think they'd mind at all."

Still grinning, Paul swung off across the yard and into the barn, pausing to nod at the young man who worked near the front doors. He was slight and fair with a pocked face and a tense, furtive manner. But Paul noted that he was working hard, shoveling huge forkfuls of straw and manure onto a wheelbarrow.

"Good evening," Paul said pleasantly. "It's Tim, isn't it? I don't think I've had a chance to speak with you since Bob hired you."

The young man glanced up, badly startled, his face looking more cautious and frightened than ever.

Paul returned his gaze in silence, a little surprised by the man's reaction. He watched while Tim licked his lips and gave a jerky nod.

"Hello, Mr. Temple. I was just . . . just finishing up here," he added with a vague wave of his hand.

"I see. Well, it's Friday night, Tim, and it looks like you've done a pretty good job. Why don't you knock off and enjoy the rest of the evening? That can be finished tomorrow, can't it?"

The young man shrugged awkwardly and nodded, his face lowered.

Paul hesitated, looking curiously at those hunched shoulders. "By the way, Tim," he said casually, "do you have any idea where my wife is?"

"Up there," the farmhand murmured, indicating the wooden ladder leading to the hayloft. "She's in the loft with the kids. They spend a lot of time up there," he added, his face twisting in a brief smile.

Paul smiled back, thinking that everybody on the farm seemed to know his wife's habits. He nodded to the young man, crossed the barn and began to climb the ladder. Soon his head and shoulders emerged through the trapdoor leading to the loft. Paul paused, blinking, while his eyes adjusted slowly to the dim light. Once they had, he took a moment to enjoy the pleasant sight that greeted him.

Sunset's fading glow spilled through a big window at the front of the loft, spreading a wash of pale pink over tumbled mounds of straw. The air was rich and heavy with the scents of summer, earth, sunshine and warm, lazy days. Dust motes danced in the beams of light that made the piled straw glisten like drifts of gold.

At one side of the loft Leah lay on the straw with a young girl on each side of her, laughing softly as she rested her chin on her folded hands and watched a tumbling, furry mass of kittens.

Paul gazed at the three of them, who were not yet aware of his presence. The girls were sprawled on their stomachs beside Leah's slim, shapely form. One of them was thin and wiry with coppery hair glinting in the light. The other's body was soft and plump, her hair a rich, spilling mass of gold like the gleaming straw all around her. Allie had one arm thrown casually over Leah's shoulders, and her carroty curls were close to Leah's boyish, light brown head.

"See, Mrs. Temple?" she was saying. "See Huey? His eyes are finally open now, too. He was almost a week later than the others."

"And they're *blue*," Leah said, enchanted. "I didn't think cats had blue eyes."

"Siamese cats do," Allie said absently. "Do you know what Siamese cats are?"

Paul could see Leah's frowning expression, the sudden tension of her shoulders that always showed she was struggling with her memory. "They're white and brown, aren't they? Some kind of special breed?"

"Yeah," Allie said with a dismissive wave of her small hand. "Sissy cats that live in town and wear diamond collars and stuff. Huey's eyes won't stay blue, though. They'll turn green or brown or yellow."

"Just like Paul's," Leah murmured in such a fond, dreamy tone that Paul had to restrain himself from crossing the room in a few swift strides and seizing her in his arms.

"Huey?" Bonnie echoed. "That's his name?"

"Yeah," Allie said. "And the little gray one, that's Lewis, and this orange-and-white one is News."

Bonnie chuckled. "You're crazy, Allie. You should've let Mrs. Temple name them."

"*She* wanted to call them Meg and Jo and Amy, like the Little Women," Allie said with scorn. "She just finished reading the book."

"What's wrong with that?" Bonnie asked loyally. "I think those are really nice names."

"These kittens are *boys*," Allie said, staring at her sister in disbelief. "All three of them."

"Oh."

"I didn't know they were boys at first," Leah interjected placidly, shifting on the straw so Lewis could climb onto her arm. "Allie showed me how you can tell. The boys have these little furry bumps down here, see?" she added with intense interest, turning Lewis upside down like a display in a biology class.

Unable to contain himself any longer, Paul laughed aloud. All three of them turned to look at him.

Leah was the first to react to his presence. Her face lighted with joy and her eyes shone like golden stars in the dimness of the hayloft as she watched him hoist himself through the trapdoor and stand erect on the plank flooring of the loft.

"Paul!" she exclaimed, jumping to her feet, still holding Lewis, using her free hand to brush straw from her jeans and shirt before she hurried toward him. "I didn't know you were coming home so early!"

She hesitated awkwardly, clearly longing to fling her arms around him but overcome by shyness. Paul noted with a grin that she was also somewhat hampered by Lewis, who clung frantically to her shirt and emitted piteous yowls of terror.

"Poor baby," Leah murmured, patting the kitten's plump, trembling body with a gentle hand. "Poor little baby, he's so scared."

Paul's throat constricted and his mouth went dry with sudden longing as he watched the womanly tenderness of his wife's actions. He'd dreamed this scene a thousand times: coming home to a gentle, sweet woman with a newborn in her arms and a welcoming smile on her face....

"This is Lewis," Leah said with a smile, offering the kitten for inspection. "He's the smallest."

"Huey, Lewis and the News," Paul echoed with a grin. "I was eavesdropping."

"Allie named them."

"I thought so," Paul said gravely, unable to take his eyes from Leah's face, with its shining, gentle smile, glowing eyes and delicate cheeks and mouth.

"Did you...did you get everything finished?" Leah ventured, glancing up at him as she cuddled the fat gray kitten under her chin. "I know there were a lot of problems this week, weren't there?"

"A lot of problems," Paul agreed, smiling down at her. "I just got off the plane from Chicago and came straight home. If there are any more problems at the office, they can damned well wait till Monday. I'm ready for my weekend."

Leah smiled in delight. "Oh, good! Did you Paul?" she added after a moment. "Because just gave me a cold supper in the kitchen a hour ago, but I'm sure he could find somethi

"Don't worry, Leah. I had dinner on the plane. Heinz fed you in the *kitchen?*" Paul added in amazement.

Leah nodded, walking over to return Lewis to the furry warmth of his brothers in their little nest of straw.

"It seems kind of silly to eat all alone in the big dining room when you're not home. It's more fun to eat in the kitchen with Heinz. Sometimes he shows me how to cook things, or talks about his family and what it was like when he was a little boy growing up in Germany. They had a pond with swans on it," she added, with one of those shining, innocent smiles that always brought a lump to Paul's throat.

"Last night Mrs. Temple ate supper at our place," Allie volunteered, glancing up at Paul with a cheerful grin. "We had barbecued short ribs and home fries."

"It was delicious," Leah said. "Anna made her extra-special, secret barbecue sauce."

Paul nodded gravely. "And what did Heinz do with himself for the evening while you were dining out?"

"He took his girlfriend into the city for dinner," Leah said, smiling as the orange kitten called News leaped straight up into the air and landed stiff-legged in the straw, pursuing a wandering beetle with a great deal more energy than precision.

"Heinz has a *girlfriend?*"

Leah nodded. "She drives the mail truck. Heinz always goes down for the mail in the morning so he can visit with her, even though he hates walking. He says she's just a little apple dumpling."

Paul threw his head back and shouted with laughter, dropping an arm around his wife's slim shoulders in a brief, powerful embrace, then watching with loving fondness as she followed the two little girls down the ladder into the lower floor of the barn.

Suddenly the worries and tensions of the week fell away and he felt rich with well-being, full of contentment and pleasure, deeply happy to be at home and surrounded by warmth and laughter. He descended the ladder partway and dropped lightly to his feet, turning to smile at Leah who stood alone near the box stalls waiting for him. "Where are your little friends?" he asked.

"They were in a hurry to get home and turn on the television. Their favorite music videos start at seven-thirty."

"I see. And how about you, Leah?" Paul whispered huskily, gazing down at his wife with a sudden hungry intensity, fighting the urge to gather her into his arms and kiss her shy, curving mouth. "Are you in a big hurry to get anywhere?"

She shook her head gravely. "I just want to spend the evening with you and hear all about what you did this week."

Paul turned away abruptly to examine a new supply of alfalfa bales stacked near the door, trying to hide his emotions from her.

Leah no longer had any memory or understanding of how to flirt, how to manage subtle, mocking interchanges and simmering sexual tension. She said what she was thinking and looked directly into a person's eyes with all the candor and sweetness of a child.

In recent years Paul had grown bitterly weary of sparring and bantering with his wife; the subtle erotic messages that were so arousing were ultimately disappointing. He was both charmed and discomfitted by this straightforward innocent who spoke her mind with such honesty.

I just want to spend the evening with you.... Paul clenched his fists briefly, then forced himself to relax and turn back to her. "Well, I'm completely at your disposal, Leah. What would you like to do? Shall we walk down by the creek a little?"

Leah nodded eagerly. "Could we go up along the other bank to the garden and pick some rhubarb? Heinz said that if I picked the rhubarb he'd make a pie out of it tomorrow."

"Well, that's a powerful motivation," Paul said cheerfully. "Heinz's rhubarb pie is one of the foods they serve in heaven."

Leah giggled. "I can't remember. Heinz says it's one of your favorites, but he thinks I didn't used to like it very much."

Paul fell into step beside her, strolling across the dusky farmyard. "That's true, but it doesn't always mean anything," he said. "Even your tastes have changed, Leah. There are foods you used to love that you're not crazy about now, and vice versa."

"I know. Isn't that strange? Dr. Holcross says that a lot of our tastes in food and things are tied up with our memories."

"So if somebody had a bad experience while eating rhubarb pie he might hate it for the rest of his life, even though it was a food he'd normally like?"

"Something like that." Leah paused to watch as a bird swooped overhead, the setting sun glistening on its sharply angled wings. "That's a nighthawk. They sleep on the tree branches all day long, stretched out just like kittens," Leah told her husband. "Bob showed me one that lives over in the big poplar by the windmill. At night he comes to life and flies around catching bugs."

"How does he catch them?" Paul asked, knowing the answer but enjoying the animation of her face as she spoke.

"Like this," Leah said promptly, opening her mouth very wide and flapping her arms. "They just open their beaks as wide as they'll go and fly around swallowing whatever comes into their path."

Paul looked down at her and chuckled, thinking how adorable she looked with her mouth open in solemn imitation of the nighthawk. "Be careful, Leah," he told her gravely. "*You* don't want to catch any bugs in there, do you?"

She looked alarmed and closed her mouth promptly, then gave him an awkward little smile and started across the small footbridge that spanned the creek.

"Was your week really awful?" she asked with sympathy. "You looked so tired on Wednesday night when you told me you had to leave for Chicago the very next day."

"It was a tough week. But very profitable," Paul added. "We landed a major supply contract we've been working on for months, and another one with a Japanese company that just came to us out of the blue."

"Is that good?"

"Really good," Paul said solemnly. "In fact, I can probably afford to buy you a nice present, Leah. What would you like?"

She paused on the bridge, glancing up at him and then down at the swirling brown water, her face thoughtful. "I have everything in the world," she said finally. "There's nothing I could possibly want."

"Clothes, jewelry, something for your room?"

Leah shook her head. "I'd like..." she began shyly, then stopped.

"What, Leah?" Paul said, watching her curiously. "What would you like?"

She gave him another diffident smile, then looked quickly down at the water again. "Last time I talked to Doris, she was telling me about her son. He's fourteen, Paul, and he's a real whiz at hockey. He wants to go to a camp this summer where they get all kinds of professional training, but Doris and her husband can't afford to pay the fees. I'd really like to give her the money so he can go."

Paul placed a gentle arm around his wife's shoulders. "How much will it cost?"

"Seven hundred dollars," Leah said, casting him a timid glance.

Paul nodded gravely, then frowned. "Doris would never accept that kind of money from you, Leah. You know she wouldn't."

"I know. But I was talking to Anna about it, and she said maybe you could...sort of sponsor him, you know, through your business? Then Doris and her husband wouldn't mind if..." Her voice trailed off awkwardly.

Paul hugged her in delight. "What a good idea, Leah! Of course, that's how we'll do it. I'm really grateful to Doris," he added, still holding his wife, loving the feel of her slender body curving against his in the mellow stillness of the spring twilight. "She's been a good friend to you since your accident, hasn't she? She's certainly shown you kindness above and beyond the call of duty.''

''Yes,'' Leah murmured, resting comfortably against him. ''She really has.''

She smiled, obviously thinking about the pleasure of helping her friend's young son as she snuggled happily in Paul's embrace. He drew his breath in sharply, wondering if she had the slightest idea how her nearness affected him, how her innocent warmth set his body throbbing with aching waves of need.

''So, Leah,'' he said with forced casualness, turning to lead her off again toward the garden area on the other side of the creek, ''how was *your* week? What did you do to keep yourself occupied while I was gone?''

She began to chatter about the small events of her days, the triumphs and challenges, all the things she'd learned and seen and done.

Paul paused at the edge of the garden and drew her down beside him on an old bench beside the apple tree, listening with pleasure to her ingenuous recounting of her actions and thoughts.

She was such a strange bundle of contradictions, this wife of his. In the time he'd spent talking with her since her memory loss, Leah had surprised him by disclosing a brilliant mind, so quick and incisive that she could often see the answers to problems at a glance. A couple of times in the past month she'd even helped Paul with business concerns by listening carefully and then making suggestions that were both wildly innovative and breathtaking in their simplicity. But she was still shy and awkward in her dealings with other people, conscious of the gaps in her experience and nervous about her lack of worldly knowledge.

And always, highlighting everything, was the amazing freshness of her outlook, the buoyant delight and pleasure she took in the world and all the new experiences it offered.

"Any more memories?" Paul asked casually, taking her hand and playing idly with her fingers. "Has anything else come back to you?"

Leah frowned, gazing down at their linked hands. "I don't know," she said slowly. "Sometimes I have really jumbled impressions of things, you know, and at first I'll think they're memories. But they must be just what you said, Paul. They must be things my brain is organizing and manufacturing on the spot, then presenting as if they were memories."

"Like what?"

Leah continued to look at their two hands joined on the rough wooden surface of the bench. "Like my ring," she said finally. "The emerald that we looked for, you know, and couldn't ever find?"

She glanced up at her husband, who nodded.

"Well, I had a memory about it the other day, or thought I did. I saw myself very clearly giving it to somebody, just handing it over and knowing I'd never see it again."

"That's pretty hard to picture, Leah. You wouldn't have been likely to give away a piece of jewelry that expensive."

"I know," she said with a brooding expression.

"Who were you giving it to?"

She peeped up at him with a sparkling rueful smile. "The carpet-cleaning man," she confessed.

Paul threw his head back and laughed. "*Again?* My God, that guy has certainly made a profound impact on you, hasn't he, Leah? Maybe I should be jealous,'' he added with a teasing grin.

Leah smiled back at him, then shook her head and shuddered. ''I don't think so, Paul. He was really an ugly man. Not like you at *all*,'' she added with a frank glance of admiration at her husband's handsome face and big athletic body.

Paul put his arm around her again and drew her close to him. He cuddled her tenderly, resting his chin on her shining hair, thinking in despair that no man in the world could continue to resist someone as utterly adorable as this innocent, delightful woman who was his wife.

CHAPTER NINE

LEAH STOOD in her white-and-gold bathroom gazing thoughtfully at the vast wall mirror. But she was hardly conscious of the image reflected there: a slim body in a transparent yellow nightgown.

As she stared at her reflection Leah thought wistfully about Paul, recalling the warm, friendly feeling she'd experienced earlier when they'd walked to the garden, and the fun they'd had picking and stripping the rhubarb stems. Later they'd sat together in the library, laughed and talked for more than an hour over their coffee and cake, watched a couple of shows on television, and then he'd held her and kissed her gently before they parted at last to go to their separate bedrooms.

Leah hugged herself and shivered, remembering that kiss.

Since the night at the cabin Paul had kissed her quite often. But it was a casual kind of affectionate gesture, much like the spontaneous caresses Anna would occasionally bestow on one of her daughters in the midst of a busy day.

Leah knew that she hungered for something more, but she had only a dim awareness of what she wanted. She knew that her yearnings had to do uniquely with Paul, with the breadth of his shoulders, the lines of his cheek and forehead, the way his hair grew silky and soft along the nape of his neck and how his jaw glistened at twilight with that golden stubble of beard. Whenever Leah thought about her husband she ached inside, was troubled by dark, muddled longings that had nothing to do with gentleness. Her dreams were filled with silky blackness and naked skin, with hard muscles, seeking lips, fiery warmth and a kind of straining closeness that she could hardly imagine with her conscious mind.

Still, these disjointed yearnings always made her feel breathless and confused, damp and warm and unsettled.

Most of all she felt lonely. Somehow it didn't seem right, the way they enjoyed each other's company so much, then when bedtime came, Paul retired to his room and she went to hers, where she lay awake for hours staring at the ceiling and thinking about him.

"Paul..." Leah whispered, gazing at her reflected image with parted lips and wide, troubled eyes. "Paul, I just feel so lonely."

She imagined herself going and knocking on his door, pictured the way he'd smile a welcome and draw her inside, close the door behind them and lead her to his bed, take her under the covers with him and put his strong arms around her....

Leah moaned with sudden anguish and hurried out of the bathroom. She wandered across her darkened bedroom to linger restlessly near the French doors and gaze at the moonlit terrace.

The evening was mild and sweet, unusually warm for May. A full moon rode just above the treetops, high and pure and serene, spilling radiance onto the sleeping earth. Crickets sang in a sweet piping chorus against the muffled counterpoint of the bullfrogs down by the creek booming their mating song.

Leah watched as fireflies flitted in and out of the trees, dancing in pairs, while two nighthawks swooped and dived overhead in a joyous aerial ballet, the moonlight glistening on their wings. In her loneliness it seemed to Leah that all the world was busily mating.

Leah stepped through the French doors, her whole being aching with the need that she couldn't understand. She moved to the centre of the terrace and paused in the moonlight, her slim arms and throat burnished with a wash of silver, her yellow nightgown drifting around her like the petals of a tall, lovely flower.

The cadences of the night and of her own body moved and surged within her. She began to dance alone on the silvered terrace, lifting her arms to the starry sky, dipping and swaying on the rough flagstones, moved by rhythms so ancient and powerful that her body obeyed without question.

She was a swirling moonlit nymph in her transparent robes of misty gold, so absorbed in her dance that she didn't see Paul come padding softly out of his room and stand watching her, wasn't even aware of him leaning against a pillar to gaze at her shapely, swaying form with an expression of hungry intensity. She was lost in the starry darkness and the music that throbbed within her, the rhythms of love and longing that surged and sang in her blood.

Suddenly there was a break in her rhythm, an awareness of looming warmth and hardness. Leah gasped abruptly and stopped dancing. She saw Paul beside her in the moonlight, wearing only a pair of

jeans. His broad chest was covered with a dense mat
of curly hair that glittered silver in the pale, slanting
light, and his muscles rippled and flexed as he leaned
toward her, holding out his arms.

He was gazing at her with eyes so intent and full of
emotion that they looked black. His jaw was tense and
hard, his big body taut when he reached for her.

Leah's arms fell slowly to her sides as she stared up
at him, her lips parted, her breath fast and uneven.

"Paul..." she whispered.

Then she was in his arms, crushed in his powerful
embrace so tightly that she ached with a wild, sweet
pain. His lips were moving forcefully over her face,
her forehead, her throat and eyelids and mouth, and
there was no gentleness at all in his kisses, just a driving, mounting urgency. Leah gasped, so lost in her
tumultuous emotions that she was like a woman on the
verge of drowning.

"Paul," she whispered in sudden panic. "Paul, I
don't know what to do. I don't know how to..."

His arms relaxed. He moved to cover her mouth
softly with his, running his hands slowly over her back
and her rounded hips.

"I know, Leah," he murmured against her face. "I
know you don't, sweetheart. Do you think you can
trust me not to hurt you?"

Leah hesitated for a moment, then nodded. "Yes,"
she said simply.

Even more than her confusion and her fear of what
was happening, Leah was terrified that he might let her
go, give her another of those distant, polite smiles and
send her back to her lonely room with her heart and
soul on fire. She strained against him and lifted her

mouth to his, kissing him in an innocent frenzy of need.

"Don't go away, Paul," she whispered. "Please keep holding me. Kiss me again, Paul. I like it. I'm just...I'm just a little scared, that's all."

"Oh, Leah," he said, his voice husky and broken. "Oh, Leah, you're so beautiful. You're just the most beautiful woman...."

He bent his head to kiss her neck and throat, slipping a hand inside the lacy bodice of the yellow nightgown to cup her breast and raise it to his lips. Leah stiffened for a moment in shock and alarm, then yielded to an almost unbearable tide of pleasure as she felt the softness of his hands and mouth against her skin, felt her body begin to tingle and shiver in response to his caress.

"Oh," she murmured, leaning back in his arms, her throat arched, her eyes closed in ecstasy. "Oh, Paul, that feels so good."

Paul Temple swept his wife up in his arms as lightly as a drift of thistledown and moved across the terrace toward the house, pausing to kiss her face and throat as he walked.

Leah nestled against him, loving the feeling of being completely in his power, knowing that whatever happened next would be his decision, not hers. In fact, Leah had only a vague concept of what was likely to happen next, and she was afraid to think about it very much. The only thing she knew for certain was that she didn't ever want him to stop holding her like this, not as long as she lived.

Paul hesitated near the doors, still holding her close in his arms, and gazed down thoughtfully at her as if he could read her thoughts. "Do you trust me, Leah?"

he asked softly. "Are you sure that you want this as much as I do?"

"Yes," she whispered, meeting his eyes directly, her face quiet and serious. "I don't want to be alone anymore."

He kissed her tenderly and edged the door open, moving through it into a broad, darkened room.

"Where are we?" Leah asked as he carried her across a shining hardwood floor and set her gently on a wide bed that looked dark and strange to her.

"In my room," he whispered. "Is that all right, Leah?"

"I've never been in here," Leah said, gazing around at the silvered darkness. "Have I?"

"I don't think so," Paul said with a sudden edge to his voice. "Back in the days when we still did this, it was always me going to your room, Leah. Hat in hand like a beggar boy."

She frowned, feeling ill at ease with this reference to a shared past that she had no memory of. Paul caught the flicker of unhappiness and bent to kiss her again, holding her tenderly in his arms.

"It was a different time, Leah," he murmured. "Like a million years ago. I can hardly remember those days myself."

She relaxed and glanced up at him. "Why did you have your hat?"

"My hat?" he asked blankly.

"You said that when you came to my room you had your hat in your hand."

Paul stared at her a moment, then leaned back and chuckled. "I keep forgetting that you have trouble with slang, don't you? It's just an expression, Leah. 'Hat in hand' implies begging or submission."

"Oh," she said thoughtfully.

Leah was silent, pondering the mysteries and intricacies of language, and the infinitely deeper complexities of the world that it reflected. For a moment she felt frightened and insecure, completely out of her depth here in this strange darkened bedroom with a man who seemed so different, somehow...hard-edged and intense....

"Leah?" Paul asked gently.

He was sitting on the bed, close to her but not touching her, his eyes questioning and full of concern.

Leah looked up at him and tried to smile, meeting his gaze with childlike candor. "Maybe I'm a little scared, after all," she confessed.

"Why?" he asked, reaching out to cup her cheek and chin in his hand. "What are you scared of, Leah? Is it me?"

She shook her head, frowning thoughtfully. "Not you," she said. "I could never be afraid of you, Paul. I know how kind and understanding you are. I guess it's just that..." She paused, her cheeks flushing warmly in the darkness.

"What?" Paul murmured, still touching her face, running his thumb gently over her earlobe.

"I know that there's...something people do," Leah said, stumbling awkwardly over the words. "I've read lots of books about it and I know what it's...it's supposed to be like, but I've never..." She paused to correct herself. "I have no memory of doing it myself, Paul. I might not be...able to do it right, and then you'll be disappointed in me."

"Disappointed in you," he echoed softly, gazing at her with burning intensity. "My God, Leah, how could you ever think that?"

She glanced up at him, her face shy and pleading. "Paul..."

"Don't worry, Leah," he murmured, drawing her into his arms and pulling her gently down on the bed with him. "Don't worry, sweetheart. This doesn't take any kind of talent. All it takes is sweetness and warmth, and you've got lots of that, darling. You've got all kinds of sweetness...."

Leah shivered as he lifted the nightgown gently over her head and tossed it aside. His lips moved over her face and throat again, and his hands began to explore her body with more purpose. She was stunned by the feelings he roused in her, the tumultuous waves of need that surged through her.

But even more, Leah was amazed by the emotions she seemed able to induce in her powerful, confident husband. She'd never imagined that Paul could be like this, shaken and murmuring with tenderness, so hungry for her body and so intensely concentrated on her that he was oblivious to the rest of the world.

Leah realized with a little thrill of surprise that she wanted nothing more than to satisfy this man's needs, to fill him so full of love and happiness that there would be no place inside him still unfulfilled. She watched as he tugged off his jeans and shorts and cast them aside. Then she moved purposefully over his long, still form, seeking and exploring, loving him instinctively with her hands and mouth and body.

He was so hard and firm, so powerful under her hands and yet so completely in her power. Leah heard him gasp with startled pleasure, arching and moaning beneath her. She smiled as she reached up to kiss his mouth.

"You like this, don't you?" she whispered, snuggling happily beside him. "And this?"

"Leah . . . oh, my heavens, where did you . . ."

"You know, it sounds strange but in one of the books I read," Leah whispered, "the lady did this. . . ."

Her hands and lips moved slowly, sending her husband into another transport of ecstasy that rendered him briefly incoherent.

When he was able to speak again, Paul gathered his wife into his arms and drew her up beside him. "That's where you learned to do all these things, Leah?" he asked in a ragged, husky voice. "From reading books?"

Leah nodded innocently against his broad chest. "They do this all the time in books," she said. "But, you know," she added thoughtfully, "I thought it would be harder."

"What?" he asked with a chuckle.

"Sex," Leah said with an earnest glance at him, wondering why he was laughing. "I thought it would be a lot more complicated. This is easy, Paul. It's really fun, isn't it?"

He laughed again, a joyous, masculine burst of merriment that drew a warm cloak of happiness all around their two naked bodies on the wide bed.

"Yes, Leah, it's really fun. And only parts of it are hard," he told her solemnly.

"What parts?"

"Oh, Leah . . ."

He drew her into his arms and rolled her gently onto her back, caressing her with slow, feathery strokes that took her breath away, lifted her out of herself and left her burning with a need she couldn't understand.

"Is this hard?" he whispered in a gentle, teasing tone.

He moved above her, settling himself and lowering his body into hers. He was warm, silky smooth and full of power, so thrilling and satisfying that Leah gasped with wondering pleasure.

"Oh, Paul...I never knew..."

"Relax, sweetheart. Just relax. It gets better...."

He moved within her, his rhythms powerful and infinitely tender, carrying her on a slow, drifting tide of liquid gold that ebbed and flowed like the ocean. Gradually his tempo increased, the waves rose higher and the sun burned brighter....

Leah lost all consciousness of herself, of Paul, of her early anxieties and even her earnest desire to bring him pleasure. All she knew was happiness and rich abandon, a drifting, soaring, sweeping ecstasy that carried her out of the crashing waves into the sun and beyond the stars to a throbbing world of sweetness and warmth and gentle darkness.

She lay trembling and shivering in her husband's arms, marveling at the gentle contractions of her body that seemed to match the rhythms of all the universe and set her at peace with herself and the world. Paul shuddered with his own release, his smooth golden head next to hers, his big shoulders taut as he held her.

Leah laughed softly and hugged him, lost and transported with adoration, so deeply in love with the man in her arms that she could hardly tell where her body ended and his began. They were as close as two people could be, and she wanted this closeness never to end because she simply couldn't imagine a life without him.

He stirred and murmured something, then kissed her neck and throat, still breathing in ragged gasps. Leah cuddled him and gazed at the dim expanse of ceiling.

Suddenly, as soft and gentle as a breath of wind, a memory drifted into her mind.

Leah stiffened, then relaxed, understanding that this was a genuine memory and it was pleasant. She was very small, sitting on a patch of grass. The recollection was so vivid that she could feel the warm grass prickling her bare legs, smell the flowers nearby and hear the gentle buzzing of insects. She held a doll in her arms, the most wonderful thing she'd ever seen. The doll's soft, smiling face aroused the same feelings of tender adoration in that far-off little girl that Leah now felt for Paul's golden head and big, quivering body in her arms.

She smiled, loving the warmth of her memory, examining it with the startled delight of a child being given some rare and marvelous toy.

This was a real memory. It wasn't fading or getting jumbled and threatening like the other ones always did. The image of the grass, the summer day, the beautiful doll, was like Paul's lovemaking. It was a gift that had been given to her by some powerful and benevolent fate, and it was hers to keep as long as she lived.

Leah smiled again and moved luxuriously in her husband's embrace.

"I love you, Paul," she whispered. "I just love you so much."

KEN HOLCROSS LEANED BACK in his chair and glanced up with thoughtful interest at the tall, golden-haired man walking into his consultation room.

"Paul," he said, "I was afraid Mary had made some kind of mistake when she booked this appointment for you instead of Leah."

"No, she didn't. I need to talk to you, Ken. Leah will probably come to see you later in the week." Paul seated himself opposite the doctor and leaned back in the padded leather chair.

The white-haired doctor neatened some papers on his desk and hunted briefly for a pen, his sharp trained eye taking in all the details of his visitor's appearance. Paul Temple was casually dressed in pleated cotton slacks and a white polo shirt and loafers, but he still had a commanding air. There was a look of wealth in his slim gold wristwatch, his soft leather shoes and his finely barbered head. And there was power in his sculpted mouth, the arrogant lift of his head, the level hazel eyes that regarded the doctor calmly across the desk.

But, Ken noted with his usual keen observation, there was something else as well, something he hadn't been accustomed to seeing in Paul Temple. He caught a fleeting hint of uncertainty, an expression at the back of those remarkable eyes that was strangely awkward and cautious.

"Is something the matter, Paul?" the doctor asked casually, leaning back and regarding his visitor. "Any new developments in Leah's condition?"

"A couple," Paul said, turning aside to gaze at a small oil painting on the opposite wall, his jaw suddenly taut. "She's started remembering a few things, just the way you said she would."

Ken Holcross leaned forward, his gray eyes lighting with interest. "She has? What kind of memories?"

Paul described the confused recollections that involved the mysterious carpet-cleaning man who had, for some reason, made such a profound impact on Leah's consciousness.

Ken shook his head and made a couple of notations on his desk pad. "I'd tend to agree with you, Paul. I don't think those can be classified as memories. They're more like random impressions or fabrications, although the mind is a strange thing and Leah's case is certainly unusual. You say she had no prior dealings of any kind with this carpet man?"

"Well, not exactly. She must have talked to him earlier because an appointment's been made to have the carpets cleaned sometime next month. But she has no record of their transaction and no memory of the details. She just keeps having these little random memories that seem to involve him in an irrational way."

"I see." Ken frowned thoughtfully. "Probably it's just because he's one of the few people outside her own sheltered world that she's encountered since the accident."

"That's what I told her. But that's not the important thing, Ken. She's also started having some actual memories, things that she recognizes as very early childhood experiences."

The doctor's round face brightened. "Now, that's more like it. Describe these memories, Paul."

Paul told him about Leah's memory of her doll, and another image she'd had the next morning of plunging into deep, swirling water and being held up in a woman's arms. The woman wore a blue bathing suit, and she was laughing in the sunshine.

"How old was Leah in this second flash of memory? About the same age as when she held the doll?"

"I think so," Paul said. "She had the impression that she was maybe slightly older and bigger, but she didn't know why she felt that."

"Well, she's probably right. I don't suppose you'd be familiar with Ribot's theory of memory, Paul?"

The younger man frowned. "I'm not sure." He gave the doctor a brief grin. "I've been reading a lot about memory and amnesia since Leah's accident, but things are so busy at the office these days it feels like my own memory suffers sometimes."

The doctor smiled. "Ribot's theory postulates that true amnesia victims recover their lost memories in strict chronological order, from the most distant to the most recent. These childhood memories you describe would certainly be consistent with that theory."

Paul nodded, his face thoughtful.

Ken watched the other man, taking in the tension in those broad shoulders, the way Paul's tanned hands gripped the chair arms and his brilliant hazel eyes gazed unseeingly at the oil painting.

"Paul?" he said gently. "Is there something specific that seems to trigger these memories for Leah? Anything that her recollections seem to have in common?"

The big golden-haired man moved awkwardly in his chair, meeting the doctor's eyes briefly and then looking away again. "They seem to follow... moments of intimacy," he said in a low voice.

"Intimacy?" Ken looked up, suddenly alert. "What kind of intimacy? With whom?"

"Physical intimacy," Paul said dryly. "With me, Ken. I'm her husband, remember?"

"You're sleeping with her again," the doctor said without expression.

Paul nodded slowly and cast the other man a brief enigmatic look that was half challenging, half pleading. "Ken, I tried. God only knows how hard I tried. But I don't think there's a man on this earth who could keep resisting a wife like Leah, not the way she is now. She's just so..."

He fell silent, gazing down at his clenched hands.

"I know, Paul," the doctor said quietly. "I know exactly what you mean. I've been afraid of this," he added. "I've seen it coming for some time, but short of taking her out of your home and putting her into some other kind of accommodation, I didn't know how to prevent it."

"Is it so bad?" Paul asked, looking up again, his eyes full of pain. "Am I just a real bastard to be taking advantage of her innocence, Ken? Will she be hurt because of me?"

"That depends."

"On what?"

"On a number of things, Paul." The doctor hesitated, his bland face troubled. "Leah has a complicated sexual history. Her life was—"

"I know she was promiscuous," Paul interrupted in a low, tight voice. "I hated it so much, all the time. Toward the end I couldn't even stand to touch her because of the way she behaved. But now she's—"

"She wasn't, Paul," the doctor interrupted quietly. "She wasn't, at all."

Paul threw his head up and stared at the other man. "What do you mean? She wasn't what?"

"She wasn't promiscuous. In fact, during the course of your entire marriage Leah was never sexually involved with any other man."

Paul stared, his face white with shock, his eyes widening. "I don't believe it," he said finally. "The way she dressed and behaved, and the kind of men who hung around..."

"She was wild and provocative, she dressed seductively and she led men on without mercy. But she never actually slept with them."

Paul shook his head in confusion. "You must be mistaken, Ken. I just can't believe that."

"I'm not mistaken," the doctor said with a brief, humorless smile. "People do tend to tell the truth under hypnosis, you know. Leah had a lot of negative behavior patterns, but she wasn't promiscuous."

"Then why did she behave that way?"

Ken's face clouded and his manner grew cautious. "I'm afraid there are limits to how much of this I can ethically discuss with you, Paul, even though you're her husband."

"I know that," Paul said with an imploring note in his voice. "But, Ken, if you could just help me to understand...."

The doctor hesitated, then began to speak again, his voice detached and professional. "Leah has been badly scarred by certain sexual experiences in the past, situations where she felt powerless and completely victimized. I would speculate that her seductive behavior gave her a kind of power that she found rewarding and enjoyable, even though she knew it was often a dangerous game to play."

"Oh, yes. Leah always liked danger," Paul said bitterly.

"Yes, she did. She was fully aware that it's risky for a woman to lead a man on and make sexual promises that she doesn't intend to keep. But the pleasure for Leah was in the sexual game itself, not the consummation of it. Leah always maintained power and control by holding her body and emotions in reserve, no matter what promises her behavior implied."

"I know. She did that with me," Paul said.

Ken gave him another sharp glance but said nothing, waiting while his visitor pondered what he'd just been told.

"This beating she got," Paul asked unexpectedly. "Do you think that might have been part of it, Ken? Could it have been some guy who just got too frustrated by her teasing and decided to teach her a lesson?"

"It might have been. The police are certain that if they hadn't received the anonymous call letting them know the attack was in progress, she would have been much more severely injured. But I doubt that we'll ever know the truth about the beating, Paul. Women who live on the edge like Leah did are always in that kind of danger, from strangers and even from close acquaintances. It's unfortunate but true."

"Would you be able to find out under hypnosis, Ken? If you put her under and asked her, would you be able to find out what she was doing recently and who the guys were who attacked her?"

The doctor shook his head firmly. "I couldn't possibly risk it, Paul, not even under hypnosis. I prefer to take her back into her childhood and lead her forward in a slow, logical progression. Recovering recent memories before she's ready to deal with them could be dangerously traumatic to her."

"Why?"

"Because amnesia, particularly the kind Leah suffers from, isn't just a physical condition, Paul. In fact, it's almost always psychological in origin."

"That's what the books tell me. But what causes it, Ken?"

"Emotional pressure. The memory loss is something like an overloaded circuit blowing a fuse, to make a very simplistic analogy."

"So if life gets just unbearable, your mind wipes it all away to keep it from destroying you?"

"Something like that. Emotional breakdown is in the same category, a kind of general system shutdown that allows time to heal and regroup. But amnesia is a very specific response. Except in certain cases of physical trauma to the brain it occurs only in individuals who are under some kind of severe emotional pressure."

"I still don't understand," Paul said. "What kind of pressure was Leah under? She always did exactly what she wanted and to hell with the rest of the world. She was the least pressured person I've ever met, because she just didn't give a damn."

The doctor laced his fingers together on his desktop and regarded them intently. "That's the impression she tried to create, Paul, but it wasn't really accurate. Leah was always racked with terrible destructive anger over other people's reactions to her. Particularly yours."

"Mine?" Paul asked in surprise. "She couldn't care less how I reacted to her, Ken. In fact, she did her best to make me feel alienated and disgusted."

"Paul..." The doctor paused, thinking deeply, then lifted his eyes with sudden decision to gaze at the man across the desk. "Children are like that, Paul. Often they seem to reserve their very worst behavior for the people who matter the most. It's as if they're testing to find out if they'll still be loved no matter how they behave."

"But I couldn't go on loving her, not after the kind of things she did," Paul said in a low, anguished voice. "Nobody could, Ken. Most of the time I just wanted her to get the hell out of my life."

"I know. And she knew it, too. And she . . ."

"What, Ken? How did she react to that?"

The doctor looked up again, his round pleasant face full of concern. "I think she hated you for it, Paul. I believe she hated you because you weren't able to give her the kind of unconditional love she craved. What's more, I think the force of her anger and hatred was tearing her to pieces."

Paul leaned back and shook his head.

"And you must understand, Paul," the doctor continued steadily, "that those feelings toward you were dangerously compounded by her sexual attitudes. Leah's past experiences have conditioned her to feel hatred and contempt for men who desire her in a sexual way. She incites men to that desire and then despises them for expressing it. As the only man who's possessed her sexually in her adult life, you've become a very specific target for her negative emotions."

"My wife despises me," Paul said quietly, gazing at the doctor in stunned disbelief. "My God, Ken, don't you think I should have been told this earlier?"

"This is privileged information, Paul. I shouldn't even be telling you now, except that you need to know how much more complicated the problem could be—

come now that you and Leah have reestablished a sexual relationship.''

''That's why I came to see you today, to talk about what's happening. But, Ken . . .''

''Yes?''

''Ken, it doesn't seem complicated,'' Paul began with another pleading glance. ''It seems . . .'' He paused awkwardly.

''How does it seem, Paul?''

''It's just so sweet and natural,'' Paul said. ''She's a different woman altogether. She's warm, spontaneous, responsive, much more concerned with my pleasure than her own.''

''But she also finds the sex pleasurable?'' the doctor asked with interest.

''That's the really amazing thing. I can't remember her ever having a climax before, Ken. Now she comes to climax easily even though she's so innocent and the whole experience is new to her.''

The doctor nodded thoughtfully and made another note on his pad.

''I shouldn't say that she never responded,'' Paul added after a moment's silence, still gazing at the oil painting on the opposite wall. ''She wasn't terrible all the time, Ken. There were times when I got fleeting glimpses of a woman like Leah is now. Sometimes she was sweet and warm and playful, and I could never resist her when she was like that. But she always slipped back into that old foul-mouthed, bitter person. Especially if I was stupid enough to make any kind of sexual advance.''

Ken nodded again. ''That's consistent with her personality problems, Paul. Any prospect of physical intimacy with you would be likely to trigger the old memories and protective responses.''

"So the reason she's the way she is now...that's just because she's been freed of all those painful memories?''

"I believe so. It's unusual for amnesia to cause such a dramatic personality change, but as you said, Leah has been relieved of the constant need to remember and defend herself against pain. It's even possible that the woman you see now is the 'real' Leah Temple, whatever that means.''

"You mean the woman she would have become if she hadn't been so badly scarred by her childhood experiences?''

"Something like that.''

Paul gazed at the doctor, his jaw hardening. "So it's really true,'' he stated flatly. "When her memories start to come back she'll turn into a monster again.''

"That's probably a harsh and simplistic evaluation, Paul. But there's certainly a very real possibility that Leah's present state of mind won't be permanent. In fact...''

"What?'' Paul urged the other man, his face taut. "What are you telling me, Ken?''

"When her memories return,'' the doctor said reluctantly, "they could be more traumatic than ever because they will feel extremely fresh and vivid. It's hard to know how she'll react. She might need to build a shell even more brittle than her old one, just to protect herself.''

Paul shifted in his chair, gazing earnestly at the other man. "But won't it make some kind of difference?'' he asked finally. "This pleasant, relaxed time she's had playing with Bob and Anna's kids, laughing with me, enjoying the farm... Won't those things have some effect on her?"

"She probably won't even remember them," the doctor said bluntly. He cast a quick glance at Paul, then went on, lowering his eyes to study the pen in his hand.

"Leah's present condition is what we refer to as the 'fugue,' Paul. It's the amnesiac state wherein the person is fully functioning but has no personal memory. That's what's happened when you hear all the stories of people wandering off, getting reestablished and starting completely new lives and relationships. Of course those stories are usually overdramatized, since the fugue very seldom lasts long enough for all those events to take place."

"But when memory returns..." Paul began slowly.

"When memory returns the fugue state is often completely forgotten. It's most likely that once Leah recovers her personal memories she'll retain no recollection at all of this pleasant interlude. Her consciousness will stop with the beating last month and resume with the recovery of memory."

"Oh, *hell*," Paul muttered with a weary slump of his shoulders. He passed a hand over his eyes and sat quietly in his chair, staring at the wall.

"Unless..." the doctor began cautiously.

"Yes?" Paul asked, suddenly alert. "Unless what, Ken?"

"Unless her memories continue to return in a slow and regular fashion. If she can recover them slowly and integrate them into her present life, they might be less painful for her to deal with. She could also retain some consciousness of the fugue state, which would be the optimum circumstance."

"Why?"

"Because," Ken Holcross said gently, "I'm quite sure that this past month has been the happiest time of Leah's entire life."

"So what's your advice to me, Ken? What's your final word?"

"My final word?" The doctor hesitated, then gave the other man a level glance that contained a warning as well as sympathy and compassion. "My final word is the same thing I've told you before. Leah is and always has been a greatly troubled woman. Take care of her, be gentle with her, surround her with as much happiness and security as you possibly can."

"But?" Paul prompted, waiting tensely for the rest of the statement.

"But take care to protect yourself. Don't get emotionally involved if you can help it, because you're likely to be badly hurt and disappointed."

"I see," Paul said with a polite nod. "Thanks, Ken."

Ken Holcross watched in troubled silence as the young man got to his feet, his face bleak and remote, and walked quietly out of the consultation room.

CHAPTER TEN

RAIN PATTERED on the leaves overhead, then rustled softly through the trees and the dense undergrowth in warm streams of silver. The world was gray and still, locked in the hush of twilight and gathering dusk, fraught with a whisper of menacing beauty that lurked in the darkened woods beyond the rugged back-country trail.

Joe frowned through the smeared windows of his van, oblivious to the peaceful stillness of the rain-washed evening. He was thinking about weather, about the possibility of a late-spring downpour and what it might do to this road.

"We gotta make damn sure we rent a vehicle with four-wheel drive, Timmy," he said to the man beside him. "This place could be a real hellhole to get out of if the weather turns ugly."

Beside him Tim Connor said nothing, just gave a brief, moody nod and continued to stare at the rain falling through the trees.

Joe contemplated his partner for a moment, drumming his stained fingers thoughtfully on the steering wheel. "So how's it going, Timmy?" he said finally. "You got anything new to tell me?"

The younger man shook his head. "It's just the same as always," he said. "Like I been telling you for the past month. He comes home early, spends all his time with her, takes her out for long walks and drives in the car. They're together all the time."

"Still real lovey-dovey, like you said before?"

Tim nodded. "Same as always."

"Like what?"

"Well, like in the barn if he thinks nobody's looking he hugs and kisses her and stuff. And sometimes..."

"Yeah?" Joe asked when the younger man paused.

"Sometimes they go up to the hayloft to look at the kittens, but they spend a long time up there. God knows what they're doing."

Joe gave a wolfish grin. "Whyn't you climb up there and see?"

"Because Temple would probably kill me," Tim said coldly. "He may go to work in the city wearing a suit and tie, but he's still a big tough guy, Joe. I wouldn't want him mad at me."

"He's not gonna be a problem pretty soon," Joe said in a matter-of-fact tone. "He's gonna be dead. And we'll be rich."

Tim shifted uneasily on the cracked vinyl seat and his partner cast him a quick glance. "You ain't losing your nerve by any chance, Timmy boy?" he asked in a soft voice.

"No," Tim said abruptly, keeping his eyes averted. "I just..."

"What?"

"I dunno. It just doesn't feel right, somehow. You should see her, Joe. You only talked to her that once, but I see her almost every day. She doesn't act like a woman who's planning to have her husband blown away. She acts more like a little kid. And she looks at him all the time like he just hung the moon."

"Hell, she's a damn smart operator. When you hire someone to kill someone for you, Timmy, the charge is still murder one. And the spouse is always the prime suspect, and she knows it. The way she was acting before, they could of arrested her on suspicion just because of the way she treated him. But now she's being smart enough to cover her tracks and set a whole different pattern. It's a real good scam, this memory loss thing. I told her so, too."

"You did? When?"

"Last month when we finalized the deal." Joe looked sharply over at the younger man. "Look, Tim," he went on, "I don't need no babies or mama's boys on this job. You got a lot to do. You have to get the vehicle in position for me, keep me posted on what's going on down below, block the road after the job's done so we got some clear time to get outta here...all kinds of stuff. If you want out, tell me now so I can find somebody else who really wants to earn a couple hundred grand."

Tim's pitted face flushed, and he licked his lips at the mention of the money, turning to glance briefly at the older man before he shifted to look out the window again.

"I'll do it," he said. "I just want to know more details, that's all. It's getting real close, Joe. I want to know exactly how you're planning to do it."

Joe stared suspiciously. "You know most of the details already. Why do you want all this information, Timmy?"

"I just want to know what's involved," Tim said with a stubborn set to his weak face. "I want to know what I have to do, and when I'll be doing it, that's all."

"I already told you what you gotta do. I'll fill you in on the details when the time comes."

"And when's that?"

Joe hesitated, then relented. "Two weeks from to-night. It's a Saturday night, Tim. He'll be all alone up there at his little cabin."

"See," Tim said with a frown, "that's one of the things I don't like. Temple never goes to that cabin anymore. Bob says he used to spend every weekend up there, but he sure doesn't go there now. These days he spends every weekend with his wife."

Joe's stubbled jaw tightened and his eyes glittered. "He'll be there. She told me he would. She knows what we agreed on, and when I talked to her last time she promised she'd have everything ready. She knows she has to get him up to the cabin the last weekend in June and she will."

"And how do you know he'll be... I mean," Tim concluded lamely, "how will you get a clear shot at him? What if he stays inside all day and we're just sitting there? Bob says he reads all the time and works with cameras up there, stuff like that."

"He won't stay inside all day," Joe said with an-other coarse grin.

"How do you know?"

"Because there's no plumbing in that cabin, Timmy. And your Paul Temple may be an aristocrat with a few million bucks but he's still built the same as anybody else. First thing in the morning he's gotta get up and go outside to the outhouse, and that little walk will be the last one he ever makes. By the time any-body finds his body, we'll be long gone. And the way his wife's been all lovey-dovey lately, the cops won't have any suspicions. They'll figure he just caught a poacher's stray bullet in the woods. We'll be home free and so will she. She'll pay us our money as soon as the dust settles and we'll have no more worries for a long, long time."

Tim's face flickered when the other man finally stopped talking.

Joe caught the look and reached out suddenly to seize the young man's thin shoulder in a merciless grip. "Tell me, kid!" he hissed. "If you're losing your nerve, you goddamn well better *tell me,* or I'll wind up killing you, too."

Tim shifted awkwardly in the man's vicious grasp, his face crumpling. "I'm not, Joe," he said in a pleading tone. "Honest, I'm not. I really need that money. I don't have a chance of anything without it. I just...oh, God," he muttered under his breath. "I just wish the whole thing was over."

"Well, it will be. Two weeks from now, kid, it'll be all over and we'll be on our way to the good life. You believe me?"

Tim was silent, gazing at the soft cascades of rain.

"Hey, Timmy. You believe me?"

Tim turned to the other man, trying to smile. "Yeah. I believe you."

"Good boy. Now take off, and let me get outta here before I get stuck and have to spend the night."

Tim nodded and stepped from the vehicle, hunching his shoulders and pulling the hood of his rubber slicker up over his head. He stood watching in moody silence as Joe's gray van wheeled around and plunged down the rutted trail. Then he turned and plodded off into the driving rain, heading for the farm in the clearing below.

"HELLO? DORIS, is that you?"

"Sure is, honey. How've you been?"

Leah smiled at the warm voice booming over the telephone. Then suddenly she felt a surge of nausea and fought it down, frowning in concern. These waves of sickness—sudden bouts of overwhelming nausea that seemed to vanish as mysteriously as they arrived—had been coming over her regularly for the past few days.

She didn't want to tell Paul about the attacks because he'd think she was just trying to get out of the dinner party they were invited to on Wednesday. He knew she was afraid of the idea, terrified of meeting other people in a social setting for the first time. Especially people who'd known both of them before the accident.

But Leah realized that she had to go through with the dinner and other social events if she was ever going to be a proper wife to Paul. More than anything, she hated to disappoint him.

"Leah? Hey, are you all right, kid?"

"Yes, Doris," Leah said automatically, smiling at the telephone receiver. "I'm fine. I was just thinking about Paul," she added with her usual childlike candor. "About him being disappointed in me."

"Is he disappointed in you?"

"I don't know."

"Well, he's still treating you nice, isn't he? Better than at the beginning?"

"Oh, yes. He's much better than he was at the beginning, Doris. It's just that I never really know what to expect."

"Why?"

"Well," Leah said awkwardly, "sometimes he's really nice and...and tender," she added, flushing warmly as she remembered some of those moments of tenderness. "But other times it's like he...he remembers that he's not supposed to like me, or something. Then he stays away from me for a while, just goes off and locks a door somewhere and does things by himself."

"But he comes back?"

"Yes," Leah said, smiling privately once more, thinking how wonderful it always was when Paul returned to her from his self-imposed isolation. Sometimes he even seemed reluctant to come back but unable to help himself, like a man drawn by some irresistible force. For Leah that was best of all, the feeling that he couldn't bring himself to stay away from her very long.

"Oh, men are like that," Doris said comfortably. "Sometimes they just need a little time to themselves, and then they come back. Besides," she added, "it's a lot harder for your man, honey."

"Why?"

"Well, because he's just getting used to having a wife," Doris said gently. "I don't think the two of you spent much time together before, you know. This is something different for him. No wonder he's taking a little time to adjust."

"I suppose so," Leah said, suddenly gloomy.

"Any more memories?" Doris asked casually.

Leah nodded into the telephone. "They come back a little more all the time. I can remember a lot of things now about the orphanage and the first two foster homes I was in. And just yesterday and this morning I've started to remember some things about the early years of school.''

"Are they nice memories?"

"Not very," Leah said briefly. "I can remember feeling really unhappy because I couldn't be in the second-grade Christmas pageant."

"Why not?"

"There was nobody to make a costume for me," Leah said, wishing Doris would change the subject. At first she'd been so excited about the gradual return of her childhood memories. But most of those memories were so bleak and miserable, especially from an adult perspective, that now she chose not to dwell on them if she could help it.

"So what else is bothering you?" Doris asked after a brief silence.

"How can you always tell when something's bothering me?"

"Because you're not exactly the greatest person in the world at hiding your emotions. Now, Leah, what's bothering you?"

"We're invited to a dinner party on Wednesday night. At the home of the production superintendent at Paul's plant."

"I see. Pretty scary stuff, hey?" Doris asked with immediate understanding.

"Oh, Doris, I just..." Leah choked and fell silent, unable to continue.

"Look, kid, none of this sissy stuff. No crying or sniveling. You just listen to me, okay?"

"I'm listening," Leah said humbly.

"Now, you quit worrying about this party, Leah. You get that little friend of yours...what's her name? The kid who's so fantastic with the makeup?"

"Bonnie."

"Right. You get Bonnie to make your face up real nice the way she did last time you came to see me, and let her help you pick out a pretty dress from your closet, and you go to that party and have fun. Because you know what, Leah?"

"What?" Leah asked, almost in a whisper.

"You're not only going to be the most beautiful woman there, kid, you're going to be the nicest. And everybody will love you."

"But Doris...they're people who work for Paul. They all know me. From...from before. And I don't remember any of them. I don't know what to talk about."

"That's easy," Doris said cheerfully.

"It is?"

"Sure. Just talk about *them,* Leah. Don't think about yourself at all. Keep the attention focused on whoever you're talking to and keep asking questions about them. That way, they'll all think you're a brilliant conversationalist and a terrific person, besides."

"Really?" Leah asked hopefully.

"Works every time. Are you still taking your pills, Leah?"

"Which ones?" Leah asked cautiously, startled by the abrupt change of subject.

"All of them. Come on, Leah, we went over all the medications, remember? I told you which ones are for what, and you wrote it all down and promised you'd remember."

Leah hesitated, thinking about the welter of pills in her medicine cabinet, multicolored tablets and capsules in little vials, in aluminum foil and shiny plastic disks. Headache pills, sleeping pills, pills to control ovulation and fluid retention . . .

The truth was she'd forgotten Doris's careful instructions about the pills, mostly on purpose. Leah hated these reminders of her former life with all its problems and intense self-absorption. Besides, a couple of times during the traumatic early days she'd tried the headache remedies and sleeping pills, and they had made her feel so heavy and out of sorts that she had become frightened.

The truth was that for some time now Leah hadn't taken any pills at all and she felt much better. But of course she couldn't tell Doris that.

"Yes," she said, "I'm taking them, Doris."

"Regularly, according to the prescriptions?"

Leah took a deep breath, hating all these lies but seeing no way out now that she'd started. "Yes."

"Good girl. And your periods are regular?"

"Yes," Leah said with another brief frown, remembering the shock and discomfort of her first menstrual period. Even though Doris had told her what to expect, the experience had been deeply upsetting to her.

"You're sure?"

"Yes," Leah said, trying to remember when the next period was due. She'd had one just after she came home from the hospital, and then according to Doris there should have been another...but was it two weeks ago, or more? Or had it happened at all?

Doris was talking, interrupting Leah's troubled attempts at remembering. "...And you just wouldn't believe how happy he is. The kid's been swinging from the chandelier ever since your husband called."

"You mean Shane? Your son?"

"Leah," Doris said fondly, "where do you go when you wander off like that? Of course I mean Shane. He's so excited about this hockey school we can hardly keep his feet on the ground. That was just a wonderful thing the two of you did, working it out so he could go."

"It was Paul," Leah said with a smile. "He arranged it all through the business. He says it's really a good investment to sponsor Shane because he's going to be famous someday and he'll bring them all kinds of publicity."

"Well, he's sure a sweetie, your Paul is. You give him a big hug for all of us, Leah, you hear?"

"I will, " Leah promised, shivering at the memory of how it felt to hug Paul, to snuggle against his broad chest and feel his big arms tightening around her. "I will, Doris."

She chatted a little more and then hung up, all the troubled thoughts gone from her mind for the moment.

"WHAT'S THIS, BONNIE? Have we used it before?"

"It's bronzing gel," Bonnie said, casting a glance at the tube in Leah's hand before returning to her careful application of eyeliner. "I thought it'd be nice for something really special like this party. It makes your cheeks shine and gives your face some color."

"Oh," Leah said dubiously, and Bonnie gave a little private smile. She knew that her friend was terribly nervous about the party tonight. It made Bonnie love her even more, knowing that someone as beautiful as Leah could get just as worried and scared as Bonnie did before a school dance.

"And that shade will be really nice with the dress we picked out," she added, leaning back to study the eyeliner with a critical frown.

"Are you sure the dress is right, Bonnie?" Leah asked anxiously. "It looks kind of...I don't know," she said, her voice trailing off as she waved her hand at the shimmering pale gold dress that lay on the couch.

"It looks great," Bonnie said firmly, in much the same tone she often used with Allie. "What did you expect to wear? Blue jeans?"

"That would be nice," Leah ventured with a wistful smile. "I'd really be much more comfortable in blue jeans."

The girl sniffed in contempt, not deigning to answer, and picked up a mascara brush. "Okay, we're almost done. Come on."

Leah leaned forward obediently, opening her eyes very wide as she'd been taught, still clearly thinking about the dress. "But it *shines,* Bonnie. Will the other ladies be wearing shiny dresses?"

"Everybody's wearing shiny dresses this spring," Bonnie said with unyielding firmness. "I showed you that fashion magazine, remember?"

Leah nodded humbly, careful not to make any abrupt movements that might jar the girl's careful hand as she applied mascara.

"And it fits so nice," Bonnie said dreamily. "Leah, when you put that dress on, you look just like a fairy princess. And," she concluded, "it's not low-cut like most of those other gross things in your closet."

"I hate those low-cut dresses," Leah said with a grimace. "I feel so silly in them."

Bonnie held the brush for a moment and looked at Leah's worried face.

Over the past month or two their friendship had progressed to the point where Bonnie couldn't believe how comfortable she was in this gracious room. Leah was just like a best friend.

Bonnie had often dreamed of times like this. She'd pictured herself chatting with a girlfriend about clothes and makeup, teasing and joking while they got ready for a party. But that particular pleasure had never been Bonnie's because her weight gain had locked her into a lonely prison of flesh just when she should have been moving on to all the breathless excitement of adolescence.

Instead, her days and weekends had passed in miserable solitude. She had spent countless hours reading books and magazines instead of living. Now she was beginning to feel the excitement again, though most of it was still vicarious, through Leah.

Bonnie had never had as much fun as this. She loved making up Leah's beautiful face, rummaging casually through her glamorous wardrobe and chatting about colors and styles, lying on the bed and laughing while Leah sat cross-legged next to her and plied her with questions about everything under the sun.

In the old days she had been so formidable, this Leah Temple.

To Bonnie's childlike eyes their boss's wife had seemed impossibly distant and hard and glittery, as graceful and cruel as a cobra. But now she was bubbly and warm, childlike in her zest and innocence. And she trusted completely in her thirteen-year-old friend to help her with problems that other people in her world weren't even aware of.

Bonnie made a final deft sweep with the mascara, then leaned back to examine Leah's face and nodded. "Perfect. Now," she added, looking at a book open by her elbow, "what's the basic rule for the silverware?"

"Start at the outside and work in," Leah answered promptly. "The bigger spoon on the outside is for the soup, and the first fork on the other side is for the salad."

"What's the little tiny knife at the top?"

Leah frowned. "A butter knife?"

"Good," Bonnie said, smiling her approval. "But they probably won't have stuff like individual butter knives and oyster forks and stuff. The book says just real fancy people have all that."

Leah shivered and hugged her arms gloomily. "I hope not. I won't have a clue, Bonnie."

"Sure you will," Bonnie said with another encouraging smile. "You remember stuff really easy once you hear it. You learned all this in no time. Besides, if you're not sure what to do, remember what the book said?"

"Watch the hostess," Leah said obediently. "Do what she does."

"Good. And what kind of stuff do you talk about?"

"The weather," Leah began hesitantly, "and politics, and—"

"Them," Bonnie said, consulting the book again as she crossed the room to sprawl on the bed. "Ask about their kids and their holidays. Those are two things people love to talk about."

"That's just what Doris said. But, Bonnie, I'm supposed to *know* all these people. How can I ask them questions about their families?"

Bonnie nodded thoughtfully. "You're right. Better stick to holidays and stuff like that. And don't forget to say thank you all the time. Remember the movie?"

Leah grinned. "How *kind* of you to *let* me come," she intoned solemnly in a regal British accent, then collapsed in a fit of giggles beside Bonnie who lay chuckling on the bed.

When Bonnie was informed of the upcoming dinner party she had shyly asked Paul to bring home a video release of *My Fair Lady* for her and Leah to watch. The two of them had passed a rainy Sunday afternoon in Leah's room, eating popcorn and watching the movie with happy absorption, witnessing Eliza Doolittle's transformation from gawky flower vendor to elegant lady.

Leah, who had no memory of seeing a movie in her entire life, had been most enchanted by the love story, although she confided later to Bonnie that Paul was much more handsome than Rex Harrison.

Bonnie had been more interested in the miracle of change than the leading man, probably because of what was happening now to her own body.

She lay on the huge bed beside Leah, gazing up at the plaster scrollwork on the ceiling, and placed one hand wonderingly on her stomach beneath the bulky school sweatshirt.

Through a rigorous combination of diet and exercise Bonnie had lost almost twenty-six pounds. Sometimes she couldn't believe it had happened, that all that hated flesh had melted away and vanished, freeing her at last from her lonely isolation.

The whole world was different now that Bonnie was getting slim. Boys occasionally looked at her thoughtfully in the hallway, and once the popular girls had invited her to sit at their lunch table. Even the teachers were nicer to her. Bonnie grinned privately, thinking that school life was going to change a lot more when she finally mustered the courage to begin wearing smaller-size clothes. She was still ten pounds short of her goal and too shy to reveal her new shape, so she wore her same old baggy jogging pants and sweatshirts all the time.

But whether Bonnie was fat or not, Allie was still loud and rude to her, and her father was too busy with his work to do more than give her an approving smile every now and then. Anna, too, was strangely reluctant to comment on her daughter's changing appearance, though Bonnie knew that her mother was very much aware of what was going on.

Anna was just as scared as she was, Bonnie realized, but for different reasons. Her mother was afraid that if she praised Bonnie or even commented on the weight loss she might jinx things somehow and the pounds would start to creep back on again. Probably she was also afraid that Bonnie might get anorexia or something and keep losing weight until she looked like one of those pitiful skeleton people.

Bonnie knew there was no danger of that. She had her diet all planned; she was aware of exactly how much she wanted to lose and how to increase her calorie intake at that point to maintain a normal weight. She'd always known how to do it, but until Leah had come along she just hadn't been able to muster the willpower to do anything about her problem.

The funny thing was that Leah, who was the cause of everything, was the only one who hadn't really noticed Bonnie's weight loss. Of course, Leah couldn't remember her from before, and though Bonnie had still been heavy when Leah had first come back to the ranch, Bonnie figured Leah had probably been too traumatized to notice.

The girl rolled her head on the dark green bedspread and grinned at her friend, who was sitting cross-legged beside her, still murmuring, "How *kind* of you to let me *come*," while accepting an imaginary teacup with haughty grandeur.

"You're nuts," Bonnie told her fondly. "You're just nuts."

Leah grinned down at the girl and extended her little finger in an exaggerated manner. "I am not. I'm a very elegant, fashionable lady," she said with such an air of bravado that Bonnie felt like hugging her.

Suddenly Leah's lovely face turned ashen. She crawled hastily from the bed and rushed off toward her bathroom. Bonnie watched the door, frowning, wondering if Leah's mysterious bouts of illness were occurring just because of tension over the dinner party, or if they signified something more serious, possibly even something that Bonnie should tell her mother about.

She'd wait a few days until Leah had recovered from the stress of the party and then see if she was still feeling sick, Bonnie decided.

The girl watched with protective concern as the bathroom door opened and Leah wandered back into the room, pausing to glance wistfully at the gold dress laid out on the couch.

"Feeling better?" Bonnie asked cautiously.

Leah nodded, trying to smile. "Much better. Just a little scared, that's all."

"You'll be great, " Bonnie said with more heartiness than she felt. "Come on, let's finish your makeup and then it's time for you to get dressed."

She vaulted off the bed, marveling again at how slim and agile she felt, how much easier it was to move her body through space with all that weight gone.

Impulsively she bent to hug Leah, who was sitting at the dressing table gazing moodily at herself in the mirror. "I love you, Leah," Bonnie murmured, overcome with gratitude and warm affection. "You're just so nice. You know that?"

Leah looked up at the girl, her eyes softening. She returned the hug, squared her shoulders and took a deep breath.

"Okay," she said. "Come on, Bonnie. Let's see if you can make me look enough like a real person so I can get through this awful evening."

CHAPTER ELEVEN

PAUL LEANED AGAINST a tall rosewood armoire, gazing across the room at his wife's reflection in the mirrored dresser. Leah caught his eye in the mirror and smiled shyly back at him, then frowned in concentration as she unfastened one of her shimmering gold-and-diamond earrings.

Paul took in her slender body, the elegant, curved line of her back and hips in the clinging gold dress, the sweep of her downcast eyelashes as she placed the earrings carefully in their padded velvet case.

"You were wonderful, Leah," he said gently. "Just wonderful. I think every single person in the room fell in love with you."

She glanced up at him in surprise, flushing warmly at his words. "Oh, Paul. Really?" she asked in a low voice. "I was scared to ask you about it. I thought maybe I was just so..."

He looked with compassion at her taut face under the skillful makeup, and saw the dark fear in her eyes. So that was why she'd kept up such a bright, determined chatter all the way home from the dinner party. She'd been afraid to hear how she'd done, was terrified that he might be critical of her behavior or somehow disappointed in her.

"Leah, you were just so sweet. I don't see how anybody could possibly resist you. And the way you *looked* . . ."

Paul stopped abruptly, his throat tight with yearning, his body suddenly on fire as he gazed at her lovely face and womanly shape. Sometimes he could hardly grasp the wonder of it, the fact that this supremely desirable woman was actually his wife, his partner to have and hold.

"Leah . . ." he whispered, aching to take her into his arms.

But she seemed tired and distracted, was still frowning slightly as she examined herself in the mirror. While she unfastened the clasp on her necklace Paul looked around the room. With a little jolt of surprise he realized that this was the first time in months he'd actually been inside Leah's bedroom for more than just a brief exchange of words. They spent almost every night together now, but she always came to his room by some kind of unspoken agreement. Paul had found himself reluctant to come to her, to enter these opulent surroundings where he had known such bitter pain and disappointment.

But it was all gone now, he thought. That had truly been a different lifetime. And no matter what Ken Holcross might say, Leah was a completely different woman now, too. She wasn't going to revert to her former monstrous behavior. Paul was growing more certain of her all the time.

"She just seemed so anxious," Leah was saying as she crossed the room in her stockinged feet. "Paul, can you undo me, please?"

Paul unfastened the catch on her dress, pulled the zipper down with lingering care, then leaned forward to plant a hearty kiss on the nape of her neck. Leah giggled softly and pulled away from him, disappearing inside her dressing room.

"Who seemed anxious?" Paul called after her, removing his tie and stuffing it into his pocket, then undoing the top buttons on his shirt.

"That lady with the gray hair and the blue dress. Eleanor? Was that her name?" Leah's voice said from the other room. "She was so nice to talk to, but there was something really sad in her eyes."

"No wonder," Paul said briefly, sitting on the edge of the bed to remove his shoes and socks. He frowned at the socks abstractedly, then stuffed them into his other pocket and took the jacket off, hanging it over a dainty gilt chair near the dresser.

"Why?" Leah asked, reappearing in the doorway in a lacy nightgown of shell pink that hugged her breasts and drifted softly around her body.

"God, Leah," Paul whispered, gazing at her in awe. "You're just so damned beautiful."

Leah smiled, then shook her head at him. "Don't change the subject. Why is that lady unhappy?"

"Because," Paul said, unfastening his cuff links, "her husband's having an affair with his twenty-two-year-old secretary, and everybody knows it."

"Oh, Paul. That's awful!" Leah stared at him in horror for a moment. Then she shook her head and vanished into the bathroom.

Paul gazed through the open door at the frothy pink swirl of her nightgown, his mind drifting back to thoughts of Leah's recovery. She was gaining new bits of memory every day. According to the doctor, she was even able to recall incidents from her childhood that she hadn't consciously remembered before the accident.

Paul's face twisted with pain as he thought about Leah's early years. She told him with calm detachment about those days of childlike terror, of her own bitter sorrows and disappointments.

"I can remember a lot of it now, but I don't really feel as if it was *me,* Paul, suffering all those things," she'd told him earnestly. "It's more like watching some other poor little girl, wishing you could help her even though you know you can't."

But Paul ached to make it all up to her, to surround her with so much love and safety that she'd never feel such fear or rejection again in her life.

And he was growing more confident with each passing day that the trauma of Leah's childhood memories wouldn't begin once more to affect their life together. Thus far she had recalled her childhood almost in its entirety, all the way up to the age of ten or eleven, and the knowledge hadn't changed her a bit.

It was true that there seemed to be some kind of block after that age, and her life from the time of early adolescence was still hidden. But Paul was certain those years would come back in sequence exactly as Ken Holcross had predicted. And as for Ken's cautious warnings, well, that was just the professional therapist's customary approach to everything.

Leah wasn't going to revert to her old ways. With every new day she was sweeter and more playful. As she learned more about the world and gained in confidence and assurance, she actually seemed to grow more trusting, more able to give herself fully to their relationship. Paul's mouth went dry as he thought about their nights together, about her body in his arms and the soaring sweetness of their lovemaking, the laughter and rich, surging tenderness.

He smiled, remembering a little incident at the dinner party earlier in the evening. Leah had been sitting across from him between their host and one of the director's wives, people she wouldn't even have bothered with a few months ago. She was listening quietly and murmuring answers to their questions, smiling gravely when one of them made a joking remark.

Paul could tell that both of the older people were entranced by her, and he'd felt such a wave of pride and love as he watched her across the table. She'd lifted her head and caught his eye at that moment and a glance had passed between then, a look of tenderness and humor and warm understanding that had thrilled him to the core.

At that moment Paul Temple felt more truly married than he ever had in his life.

He smiled fondly at the memory and padded across the thick carpet in his bare feet, entering the white-and-gold bathroom and embracing Leah from behind as she stood at the mirror rubbing cream on her face.

She gasped and stiffened, clearly startled by his silent approach. Paul chuckled softly and cradled her tight in his arms, pressing himself against her slender back and leaning over her shoulder to kiss her throat and earlobe.

Leah continued to struggle. Paul held her closer, still laughing, delighted by the way she made everything into a game. He glanced over her shining, tousled head of hair and caught their reflections in the big mirror, then stared in shock.

Leah's face was blank and stiff, her golden eyes glittering with rage. "Let me *go,* you son of a bitch!"

she shouted. "You goddamn *bastard,* take your dirty hands off me! I hate you!"

Paul's face went white. His hands dropped slowly away from her body and he gazed in horror at the furious woman in the mirror, a woman that he remembered with such painful vividness.

But this time there was something different about her, something even more terrible than the Leah he remembered. Her face was suffused with rage, with a fury so potent that the small room seemed to rock and sway with the force of her anger. Paul felt a chill of fear when he stared at those glittering mirrored eyes and saw murder in their golden depths.

Finally, after a silence so profound that Leah's ragged breathing was clearly audible, he turned on his heel and strode from the room, gathering up his jacket and shoes as he left.

LEAH GAZED OVER THE DESK at Ken Holcross. Her hands were twisted tightly in her lap and her face was piteous with appeal.

"That happened on Wednesday evening, Leah?" the doctor asked gently. "Just last week?"

Leah nodded. "I don't know what came over me," she whispered. "When he grabbed me unexpectedly like that and wouldn't let me go, I just felt such a flood of...of rage. I couldn't control myself. I heard my own voice saying those words, screaming at him like that, and I couldn't believe my ears. It was so terrible," she concluded, brushing at the tears that trickled slowly down her cheeks.

"You say you felt a flood of rage, Leah. Were you aware of any other emotions?"

She looked at the doctor. "Other emotions?"

"Did you feel anything else besides anger? Distaste, maybe? Fear?"

Leah nodded slowly, thinking about the question. "Maybe fear," she said at last. "But that's ridiculous. Why should I be afraid of Paul? He's the kindest, gentlest, most considerate man...." Her eyes widened and she looked up sharply.

The doctor waited in calm silence, watching the play of thought and emotion on her expressive face.

"That's the answer, isn't it, Ken?" she asked finally. "When he grabbed me like that it reminded me of something from my past, didn't it? Some awful thing that I can't remember but still suffer from?"

"Yes, Leah," Dr. Holcross said quietly. "I believe it probably did."

"Do you know what it is?"

The doctor nodded with a cautious expression. "I think I do."

Leah leaned forward urgently. "What is it, Ken? What happened to me? Why won't you *tell* me?"

"Because I think you need to remember these things on your own. This particular experience is one of those you've only recalled under hypnosis, Leah. You didn't have any conscious memory of it even prior to your amnesia."

Leah was silent a moment, gazing at the doctor with an intent look. "Ken, I've been reading a book about hypnosis," she said abruptly.

"I see. And what have you learned?"

"When I'm hypnotized and I recall something, it's possible for you to make me retain it afterward, right? If you tell me to remember it with my conscious mind, then I will?"

The doctor tensed a little and nodded reluctantly. "That's usually the case, yes."

"Then why can't you do that for me? Why don't you take me back to these things that are bothering me so much, all the parts of my life I still can't remember, and just tell me to remember them? Then I could at least know what I'm dealing with."

Ken Holcross gazed for a long, thoughtful moment at the woman's passionate face and her unhappy eyes.

"I've never considered that a wise course of action in your case, Leah. I want you to integrate these hurtful memories into your life at your own pace, by your own will. You have a very strong will, but your emotional circuits could become dangerously overloaded if you're forced to remember too much before you're ready. In fact, your amnesia is proof of that."

"But what makes you think I'll ever remember these things on my own?"

"Your memories are returning in a very orderly fashion. You know they are, Leah. Your childhood recall is almost complete now."

"I know, but if these other things are memories that I never had consciously, even before the accident, why would they come back now?"

"Because," the doctor said with a gentle smile, "you don't just have a strong will anymore. You're a stronger person altogether now, Leah. You've had a marvelous holiday from trauma and the constant effort of repressing painful memories, and you've been allowed to experience love and emotional warmth unlike anything you've ever known. As a result, I think your mind will eventually be ready to receive and deal with the other painful memories."

"But maybe by then..." Leah began. Her face crumpled and she looked quickly down at her hands.

"What, Leah? What are you afraid of?"

"Maybe it'll be too late," she said in a low voice. "Maybe Paul will hate me by then, just the way he did before. I think he...he does already."

"He doesn't hate you, Leah. He was understandably troubled by a brief flash of regressive behavior, but I'm sure he's well aware of all the progress you've made."

"He's hardly talked to me since," Leah said, her voice barely above a whisper. "And when he does he's just polite, not warm and teasing like he used to be. And he spent..." Again her voice broke and it was a moment before she could compose herself. "He spent the whole weekend up at his cabin just like he always did when...when I was different. I'm sure he plans to do it again this weekend."

There was a brief silence, so tense and profound that both doctor and patient could hear the big wall clock ticking.

"What do you want me to do, Leah?" the doctor asked finally.

Leah looked up at him, her eyes blazing with purpose. "I want you to hypnotize me," she said. "I want you to bring out all those memories and tell me to remember them when I wake up. I want to know who I am and what made me like this."

Ken Holcross nodded reluctantly. "If I do that," he said finally, "I'll want to do it under controlled circumstances. I'll want to monitor your reactions very carefully, Leah. Maybe I'll even admit you to the hospital for a few days."

"I don't care. Whatever you have to do. I just can't live like this, Ken."

The doctor consulted his appointment book. "This weekend's the end of June," he said finally. "I always take my wife off to Banff for a romantic weekend on our anniversary—" he gave a small smile "—so that's out.... How about next Tuesday, a week from today?"

"All right," Leah said, swallowing hard and looking very pale all at once.

The doctor glanced at her sharply. "Leah? Are you not feeling well?"

She straightened in the chair and tried to smile. "I'm fine. I just feel . . . a little sick sometimes. Probably because I've been so upset."

Ken looked at her more intently, a suspicion beginning to dawn in his mind. "Leah," he said, trying to keep his voice casual, "have you been taking all your medications?"

Leah nodded, looking away from him and biting her lip. "Doris told me which ones to take," she said evasively, "but sometimes I get confused, and sometimes I don't remember...."

She glanced up at the doctor with a pleading look. He met her eyes silently.

"Up until now I've just felt so good," she murmured. "I didn't feel like I needed any pills, Ken."

The doctor summoned a reassuring smile, trying not to show his concern. If his suspicions were correct, then Leah Temple was about to face another huge complication in her life, one that she certainly wasn't prepared to deal with at the moment.

But next week when she was admitted to hospital would be soon enough to conduct the necessary tests

and decide on a course of action. In the meantime all
he could do was send the troubled woman home with
whatever small comfort he was able to offer.

And, Ken Holcross thought wearily, he could only
watch while she and her husband struggled to build a
relationship in the midst of fear and mistrust, of
darkness, sorrow and a fog of lost and disordered
memories.

LEAH WALKED SLOWLY along the narrow, leafy path
beside the creek, deep in her troubled thoughts. The
fresh air seemed to settle her stomach a bit, and she
wasn't bothered as much by the mysterious nausea
that still seemed to come and go randomly throughout the day. But she was so preoccupied with her unhappiness that she couldn't take much pleasure in the
beauty of the warm June afternoon.

Red-winged blackbirds trilled from their nests in the
tall rushes at the water's edge, and cedar waxwings
whistled softly in the poplar trees along the path.
Leaves rustled all around Leah's head, shifting and
moving in the mild prairie breeze against a sky so blue
that it dazzled her eyes. She heard a soft crashing in
the underbrush and looked up to see a white-tailed
deer bounding off toward the fields beyond the
wooded area, followed by two spotted fawns who
sprang behind their mother on long slender legs.

Long after the doe had vanished from sight Leah
stood with a wistful smile, watching the place where
the mother and her little twins had disappeared.

How wonderful, she thought sadly, *to be a bird or
a deer, with your babies safe beside you and nothing
in all the world to worry about except keeping warm
and finding enough food to eat.*

But even the birds and animals had problems, Leah reminded herself. They had to worry about men with guns, about traps and barbed-wire fences and polluted food supplies.

Still, animals didn't anguish over lost memories and murky hidden events in the past that still had the mysterious power to ruin lives....

Leah turned off the path and slid down the grassy bank to a big flat rock at the water's edge. She climbed onto the rough, sun-warmed surface and sat hugging her legs, resting her chin on her knees as she gazed at the rippling sunlit water with a brooding expression.

This was Saturday afternoon, a time that she and Paul had grown accustomed to spending together. Often they'd drive to the city on Saturday afternoon for a happy day of shopping and eating out, visiting the art gallery or the museum, going to one of the parks. Sometimes on warm days like this they'd choose instead to invade Heinz's well-stocked kitchen and pack themselves a picnic, then head out into the countryside to enjoy themselves.

Leah choked back a brief sob as she remembered those lazy afternoons. She saw herself lying on a blanket and reading while Paul ranged contentedly around in the woods with his camera, or the two of them cuddling and making love in some leafy, hidden place with the prairie sky arching silently overhead, and only the birds and animals for witnesses.

Those had been such blissfully happy times, but they were gone now as completely as if they'd never happened. Paul was all alone at his cabin, just as he had been the previous weekend, and Leah knew that she wouldn't be welcome if she joined him there.

Strangely, the rift had widened steadily, even though
Paul's outward manner toward his wife hadn't dras-
tically changed. He was still polite and considerate,
still expressed an interest in her day and conversed
easily with her when they ate their meals together. But
part of him was gone, and Leah knew that it wouldn't
be coming back.

Paul simply didn't trust her anymore. He believed
that the recovery of her memory was going to make
her cold and hateful again, and he wasn't prepared to
risk his emotions a second time.

Leah could hardly blame him. She shuddered as she
recalled the sound of her own voice screaming at him,
remembered the ugly face in the mirror that wasn't
hers at all but the white, twisted face of a stranger.

Leah had been stunned by the intensity of her anger when Paul had held her in that iron grip and refused to let her go. She'd lashed out with such
viciousness because she'd been almost suffocated by
terror and panic and a deep instinctive loathing that
had sickened her with its intensity.

If those feelings had always been part of her, it was
no wonder that she'd developed into such a bitter,
hard-edged woman. Leah shook her head blindly,
thinking about her miserable childhood memories,
wondering what had happened to that lonely, frightened child in her later years to make her so angry.

Me, she corrected herself automatically, breaking
off the head of a bulrush nearby and rubbing the vel-
vety brown surface absently in her hands. *Whatever it
was, it happened to me.*

But she still couldn't remember anything beyond the
fear and loneliness of her early years. Her childhood
had been empty and loveless, but Leah knew instinc-

tively that that state had no connection with the hideous flood of rage she experienced. If she could understand the source of the anger, maybe she could explain it to Paul and draw him near to her again.

The only way to repair things between them was to prove that his fears were unfounded. If she could recover her memory entirely, fill in all those sinister clouded areas where there was only darkness, then they might have a chance. Leah loved her husband and desperately wanted to be a good wife and make him happy. She simply couldn't imagine any of those feelings being altered by the return of adolescent memories, no matter how traumatic.

She stared across the water, her face pale with resolve as she thought about the week ahead and Dr. Holcross's promise that he would finally help her recover the hidden areas of her life.

But what were those memories going to be like? What terrible things had happened to her all those years ago? Again Leah shuddered when she thought of Paul's hands seizing and holding her and the choking mist of horror and disgust that had flooded her mind at that moment.

"Oh, Paul," she moaned aloud, tossing the bulrush aside and covering her face with her hands. "Paul, I'm so sorry, darling. I love you so much. I love you...."

Slowly she dropped her hands and frowned into the brown, shimmering water, struggling to capture the memories that crept to the edge of her mind. They hovered around her in the still air, so tantalizingly near that she could almost reach out and grasp them.

When she thought of Paul's hands and her own feelings of terror and panic, she could almost...

Again Paul's image drifted into her mind. She saw him laughing in the sunlight, tall and strong and golden, so handsome that her heart ached. And somewhere nearby was a dark, ominous cloud, some kind of threat to Paul's safety. She saw a confused, dreamlike scene in a dirty room, a ring glinting emerald in the harsh light, a man's gray stubbled face grinning at her....

The mental images faded slowly. Leah pressed her hands to her head, trying to hold the memories inside, but the sense of nearness was gone again. All she felt was a rising nausea and a kind of sick foreboding. She had the feeling that something terrible was going to happen very soon, and unless she could recover her memory she was powerless to stop it.

But her mind was gray and blank, mocking all her straining efforts to recall any personal event more recent than a lonely eleventh birthday in some long-ago foster home.

Leah crawled off the rock, her face bleak and sad, and climbed back up the creek bank to the path, turning to begin the long walk home. Far off through the trees she saw a flash of gold in the sunlight and recognized it as Bonnie's hair.

The girl must be walking down to pick up the newspapers. Leah considered calling out and running across the field to join her, but decided against it. The sun was dropping toward twilight and there was still a chance, even though it was remote, that Paul might come down from his cabin and want to join her for dinner. She should wash her hair and pick out something nice to wear....

Leah quickened her steps and decided to take a shortcut through the heavy wooded area behind their property, a path that she seldom traveled but still knew well enough to find her way along in the slanting afternoon light.

BONNIE TUCKED THE ROLLED newspapers under her arm and started up the road toward the farm, singing as she walked. She was flooded with well-being, wrapped like a princess in a rich, golden cloak of happiness.

The final frustrating plateau had apparently dissolved, because at last night's weigh-in she'd dropped almost four pounds. Bonnie's total weight loss now stood at thirty-one pounds, and she felt absolutely wonderful.

Soon she'd be able to stop dieting and implement her carefully planned maintenance program, eating a little more fruit and vegetables, increasing her daily intake of bread by a couple of slices and learning how much she could eat without starting to gain. It was going to be so much fun.

Bonnie raised her head and laughed aloud, running her hands over her flat stomach and down the wonderful slender line of her hips and thighs. For the first time in ages she wore a skimpy T-shirt and ragged denim cutoffs, and she had slim, tanned legs like the other girls at school. She felt like a prisoner released into the sunlight, or a butterfly that had just escaped from a bulky cocoon.

And she was getting so pretty. Bonnie knew how attractive she looked now that her cheeks weren't so fat. Her eyes looked bigger and her facial features were more defined. She even seemed taller, partly because she'd grown a bit while she was dieting, but mostly because she held herself proudly erect now instead of hunched over in an attempt to conceal her body. She moved quickly and easily, as light and graceful as a bird.

And her new attractiveness wasn't just something that she was aware of herself. Other people noticed it as well, especially the kids at school. The girls treated her with a new kind of cautious respect, and the boys looked at her with warm, speculative interest. It was almost scary, this unaccustomed sense of power that she felt. But it was also delicious.

Bonnie smiled dreamily, thinking about the new clothes her mother had spoken of last week. It had been the first time Anna had ventured a comment on her daughter's new figure.

"Looks like that baby fat is just melting away all of a sudden, Bonnie, isn't it?" Anna had said awkwardly. "I always thought it would, once you got to be a teenager and started getting taller."

Bonnie nodded, recognizing that her mother was still reluctant to make any direct reference to Bonnie's diet for fear of spoiling things. "I've lost quite a bit, Mom. I feel really good."

"Well, your clothes are just hanging on you," Anna said with gruff affection. "They look terrible. You need some new things."

"Mom..."

"Dad and I talked about it," Anna went on, her weathered cheeks pink with emotion. "He sold a few of his calves last week, and Paul's giving him a share of the money from the alfalfa bales, so I guess we can spare enough for a new wardrobe for our pretty girl." This time Anna couldn't keep the pride out of her voice. "Maybe we'll buy a few things when school's out, and then get a whole new wardrobe for next fall. What do you think, honey?''

Bonnie smiled again, thinking about the new wardrobe. When the time came she planned to ask her mother if she and Leah could go shopping together for clothes. Bonnie loved her mother dearly, but she knew that Anna would pick out shiny leather shoes with buckles, and dresses with tie belts and ruffled lace collars....

Bonnie grimaced, then turned as she heard a vehicle stopping beside her. Jody Muller leaned out the window of his battered old truck.

"Hi, doll," he said with a grin. "Where ya goin'?"

"I'm going home, Jody," Bonnie said calmly. "Just like always."

Jody shifted into gear and let his truck creep along beside Bonnie as she walked. He glanced quickly up the road and drummed his fingers on the wheel, then looked back at Bonnie. "Real nice day," he ventured. "Sure warm, isn't it?"

Bonnie realized with amazement that her presence actually made Jody nervous. She marveled at this complete reversal of the grim days just a few months ago, when she was the one who trembled in fear of what he might say. A heady wave of power surged through her, making her feel reckless and excited.

"What are you doing over the summer, Jody?" she asked, tossing her head and smiling at him the way she'd seen the popular girls behave when conversing with boys. "Getting a job?"

"I sure hope so," he said earnestly. "I asked Tom down at the service station if he needed a hand for the summer, and he said they were— Hey," Jody interrupted himself, trying to sound casual, "why stand there talking in the dirt? Hop in, okay? I'll give you a ride home."

Bonnie smiled again, tickled by the note of pleading in his voice. Jody Muller sounded almost *shy,* she thought in wonder. And all because he was talking to her, Bonnie McBride, and she was slim and pretty.

"I don't think so, Jody," she said primly. "It's just a little ways. I can walk."

"We could go the long way round," the boy said with heavy significance, eyeing her warmly in her brief shorts and T-shirt. "Then we'd have the chance to talk a bit, eh?"

Bonnie hesitated, feeling a little nervous now that the game was turning serious. For one thing, she didn't find Jody nearly as attractive as she once had. There was another boy she liked a lot better, Bryce Stebbings, who was on the football team and who'd made a point just last week of asking her how she'd done on her math exam. Bryce wasn't wild like Jody. He was quiet and nice, and even the teachers liked him.

Still, Jody had that exciting, restless look about him. And he sounded so pleading. He really was dying to give Bonnie a ride. She held this boy's emotions in her hands, and her sense of her own authority was unexpected and intoxicating.

"Well...maybe just for a little while," Bonnie said, smiling privately at the way his eyes lighted. "But I have to be home in half an hour," she warned as she moved around to the passenger side. "I have to water the chicks and do a whole bunch of chores."

"Sure thing," Jody said, leaning out with studied nonchalance to flip the door open, then winking at her as she settled onto the shabby vinyl seat.

Bonnie smiled back shyly, almost overwhelmed by the experience of riding alone with a boy. She turned to gaze out the window at the landscape flashing by as Jody drove rapidly along the prairie roads. The wind whipped at her hair through the open windows and she had a blurred impression of speed and dusty power and the male smell of warm skin and musky cologne.

"Jody," she said suddenly, "where are we going?"

The road was growing narrow and dark as the truck bumped along into an avenue of trees. Leaves rustled overhead and closed around them, shrouding them in dappled green stillness.

"We're not goin' anywhere. We're there," Jody said, switching off the ignition and extending his tanned arm along the seat, turning to grin at her.

Bonnie smiled back nervously, her heart racing. He seemed so close now that there was nobody else around, nothing in all the world but this dusty truck cab, the enclosing greenery and the muscular tanned boy next to her.

He leaned over to lift a strand of her golden hair with his finger and let it fall, watching her face closely. "Real pretty," he murmured. "You're sure pretty, you know that, kid? Just a real little doll."

His hand crept briefly onto her shoulder, then dropped to her bare tanned knee and edged upward.

All the breathless excitement of the adventure was gone now. Bonnie felt nothing but fear and revulsion. He was so close to her, so hot and sweaty, and his body gave off a rank smell of excitement that terrified her.

"Jody," she whispered, grasping his hand and trying to hold it away from her. "Jody, I have to get home. I promised my mom that I'd—"

"Your mom can wait," Jody whispered back hoarsely, pressing himself against her, swarming all over her with his lips and hands.

Bonnie felt herself invaded, felt his hands moving over her body, tearing at her clothes and touching her in places that nobody should ever touch. And he was so strong. She couldn't stop him, couldn't even struggle, because he had her pinned against the door of the truck.

She jerked her head away from his lips and screamed, a long helpless cry of terror that ebbed away into stillness on the warm summer air.

"Go ahead and holler," Jody said, laughing softly in her ear. "Nobody can hear you up here, doll. Just go on and yell all you like. It makes me more excited."

Bonnie screamed again and then began to cry, her scalding, helpless tears flowing down her hot cheeks as he continued his brutal invasion of her body.

CHAPTER TWELVE

LEAH HEARD THE BURST of sound dying away on the warm summer air. She paused abruptly, frowning in concentration. It sounded like a cry of terror, like that of some small animal in pain. Leah shivered, picturing a rabbit caught in a snare or one of those dainty little fawns trapped and thrashing helplessly under cruel barbed wire.

As she hesitated on the path, the muffled sound came again, making the hair rise on the back of her neck. Whatever living thing uttered those anguished cries, it was somewhere nearby, deep in the wooded thicket to her right.

"Stay on the path," Paul's voice warned sternly in the back of her mind. "Don't ever go into the woods by yourself, Leah. There're all kinds of dangers in there. Stinging nettles, snakes, lynx and cougars, even the occasional black bear wandering down from the mountains...."

His voice trailed off into memory. Leah took a deep breath and gazed with increasing apprehension at the dark undergrowth.

Maybe she'd just been imagining it. Maybe there was nothing in there at all.

Just then the sound came again, a high, keening scream of terror and pain, throbbing gradually into silence while the insects hummed and the leaves rustled overhead.

Leah turned and plunged into the brush, sweating and panting as she struggled through dense, gnarled branches that tore at her face and clothes and clutched at her legs. She was chilled with fear and her stomach began to churn uneasily as she pushed her way deep into the woods.

I'll get lost, she thought in panic. *God, what am I doing? I don't even know where I am....*

But the sound kept drawing her on. It was closer now but not nearly as loud, a sobbing, desperate whimper that stabbed at her heart.

Leah quickened her steps, fighting down the rising dread and nausea. Mercifully she stumbled at last through the dense growth and onto a rutted trail that curved into the trees in the direction of the sound. Almost light-headed with relief at the sudden ease of movement, Leah ran up the trail. She rounded a leafy bend and then stood still in horror, both hands covering her mouth as she stared.

An old truck stood in the clearing, partially turned so that Leah could see clearly through the open doors. There was a boy in the cab, a muscular adolescent in a black T-shirt, his weak, handsome face darkly suffused with passion. He was laughing, straddling a girl who fought and screamed on the seat beneath his body, her bright hair spilling down in a cascade of gold.

The girl was Bonnie.

Leah stood as if rooted to the spot, unseen by either of the young people locked in that grim struggle.

Dark thoughts and memories flooded her mind, rising in a black tide that roared in her ears and blinded her. She wanted to sink to the ground and curl herself up to ward off the searing pain of her memories, just wrap her body into a hard little ball that nobody could ever touch again, not as long as she lived. But there wasn't time to think of herself. Bonnie wasn't a dark, confusing memory from some distant past. She was a real flesh-and-blood person, a girl that Leah loved, and she was in terrible danger.

Leah drew a deep, shuddering breath, forcing herself to control her emotions and assess the situation. The boy lifted his head at that moment, still unaware of Leah's presence, and laughed aloud.

"Quit fighting, doll," he said thickly, addressing the girl who sobbed and struggled in his arms. "You're gonna like it. You'll just love it. See, I'm real good. Just ask anybody who's—"

But Jody said no more about his sexual prowess because he was suddenly incapable of speech. Something had grasped him cruelly by the hair and was hauling him out of the truck, screaming abuse at him, beating and flailing at his body.

Jody yelled in pain and surprise, then trembled with shock as he saw the demon that held him in its grasp. It was some fearful woman-monster from hell, a creature with a twisted white face and blazing eyes who continued to pour such fury and outrage onto him that he was struck dumb with terror.

The woman pulled his protesting young body out onto the ground, still clutching handfuls of his hair, and began to kick at his legs and ribs as the boy tried frantically to roll away and protect himself.

"Bastard!" the woman screamed. "You filthy *animal!* I'm going to kill you! Killing's too good for you, you dirty monster!"

Jody knelt by the truck, covering his face with his hands and hugging his elbows close to his body in a vain attempt to protect himself from the kicks and blows that the woman rained on him.

He had no doubt whatsoever that she meant what she said. Jody recognized her by now as Leah Temple, the rich guy's wife, a woman renowned for her bad temper and lack of control. And Leah Temple had completely lost it. She intended to kill Jody Muller with her bare hands, and it was increasingly clear that nothing was going to stop her.

His attacker paused for breath and Jody took a wild spring toward his truck, not even noticing that Bonnie McBride had crawled out and now sat rocking and sobbing on the ground nearby, her clothes crumpled and disarranged beneath her.

He leaped into the driver's seat, closed and locked the door and turned the key in the ignition, grinding the gears as he shifted and turned, praying that the old truck wouldn't stall on him. The passenger door slammed shut as Jody careered in a circle and went screeching out of the clearing and down the trail. He leaned forward desperately and clutched the wheel, his whole body still sweating and trembling with shock.

LEAH STOOD, HER HAIR in wild disorder and her face flushed, panting and gasping for breath as she watched the battered old vehicle disappear among the trees. Gradually the dark, murderous cloud began to lift and she came back to herself, remembered who she was and what had happened.

Her head was brimming with thoughts and memories, random impressions that swirled and pressed at her with powerful insistence, but she couldn't stop to think about them now.

Later, she promised herself. Later, when she was all alone, she'd try to understand what had just happened, and to sort out the flood of disjointed images that crowded her mind.

She hurried over and knelt by Bonnie, gathering the girl's trembling body into her arms, rocking her and crooning to her tenderly as Bonnie sobbed against her breast.

"Leah, he was... He tried to..." Bonnie choked and began to cry again.

"Its all right, baby. It's all right now, dear. It's fine. Nothing's going to hurt you. He's gone now. He's gone now."

Leah went on and on, murmuring soft words of comfort as she stroked the girl's tangled hair and patted her back and shoulders.

Bonnie's sobs grew quieter and she began trying to make faltering little adjustments to her clothes, kneeling to pull her shorts back up around her waist and refasten the zipper, then tugging at her torn shirt.

Leah handed the girl a couple of tissues from her pocket and watched as Bonnie mopped her tears, wiped her nose and struggled to compose herself. "What if... what if he comes back?" Bonnie whispered, gazing at Leah with terrified blue eyes.

Leah shook her head. "I don't think he'll be coming back," she said calmly, remembering the boy's look of ashen terror as he flung himself into the truck and turned to gaze wildly out the window.

"I thought..." Bonnie began in a choked voice, "Leah, I really thought..."

"What, Bonnie? What did you think?"

"I thought you were going to kill him," Bonnie said in a muffled voice, burying her face in her hands again.

"I was," Leah said in that same expressionless tone. "If he hadn't got away, and if I'd had a weapon in my hands, I would have killed him."

"Oh, Leah, it was so awful, what he did to me," Bonnie whispered, starting to cry again. "I was just so scared.... I was so scared...."

"I know you were, baby," Leah murmured. "I know how you felt."

She realized with a shock of recognition that she wasn't just saying those words. She really *did* know how Bonnie felt. She'd known for years, but hadn't remembered until now.

"Why was he like that?" Bonnie whimpered through her tears. "He acted like he hated me and wanted to hurt me. I never did a single thing to him, Leah. Why was he like that?"

"Because he's a weak and self-centered person, dear," Leah said quietly. "He has certain urges because of the age he is and the way he feels, but he doesn't make any effort to control them as he should. It's nothing to do with you. This wasn't your fault. I don't want you ever to think you were to blame for what happened."

"But if you hadn't come along, he'd have... In just a few minutes he was going to—"

"I know what he was going to do," Leah said, her face remote and sad.

He did it to me, a voice within her was screaming in agony. *He did it to me over and over again, all those years ago, and there was nobody to help me. Nobody ever stopped him. And I kept thinking it must be my*

*fault, that I'd done something bad to make him be-
have like that, until I felt so soiled and full of guilt that
I hated myself and everybody else in the world....*

Bonnie gazed up at the other woman with a pleading look in her eyes.

"Are all boys like that?" she whispered. "Are they
all awful like that?"

Leah thought of Paul, of his gentleness and consid-
eration, his strength and tenderness and quiet self-
control.

"No, dear," she said, blinking back the warm tears
that burned in her eyes. "No, all boys aren't like that
at all. Most of them are sweet and nice. Unfortunately, it's up to us girls to be able to tell the difference, and you have to be really careful."

Bonnie nodded and got slowly to her feet, leaning
against her friend for support. "Do you...do you still
like me, Leah?" she asked with a piteous, childlike
expression.

This time Leah couldn't hold back the tears. "Oh,
Bonnie darling," she whispered, taking the child in her
arms again. "Of course I do. I love you. You're a
wonderful girl, and all of us love you. Your parents
and Allie and Paul and I...we all love you. We always will. What that boy did, sweetheart, it meant no
more than being attacked by a bad dog. It's not any
kind of moral judgment on you. It was just...an accident."

As she spoke the words, Leah realized with a sense
of wonder that they were absolutely true. She felt
strangely liberated, so light and free that she was almost frightened, as if the burden of her repressed
emotions which had rooted her in place for so long
had been suddenly lifted. She was beginning to rise

and soar like a balloon, to drift and fly off above the clouds and into the wide blue heavens....

"Please," Bonnie said urgently. "Please, Leah, don't tell my parents. I just couldn't *stand* it if they knew what happened."

"I won't say anything, but I think you should tell them just as soon as you feel able."

"Why?"

"Because it's important to talk about it. For one thing, we have to make sure that boy doesn't do the same thing to any other girls. And it's important to tell the people close to you and give them the chance to show you it doesn't matter a bit, that nothing's changed and they still love you just the same."

Bonnie thought this over and nodded. "Okay," she whispered at last. "I'll tell them, but not right away, okay? In a couple of weeks, maybe, when school's out and I won't have to see him again."

Leah nodded and smiled, patting the girl's flushed cheek. "Whenever you're comfortable with it. Now let's go home, shall we?"

Bonnie swallowed hard and nodded. "Okay," she murmured gratefully, slipping her hand into Leah's and letting her head rest on the taller woman's shoulder.

Leah put her arm around the girl, holding her close, and they began to walk slowly along the rutted trail in the direction of the farm.

TWILIGHT SHADOWS lengthened, and the brilliant sunset colors faded to smudges of misty gray along the mountains. Leah huddled on the window seat in her room, gazing outside in brooding silence.

Sometime during the evening Heinz came to the door to ask if she wanted her dinner. He had been accompanied by Allie, who asked her if she wanted to visit the kittens. Leah was hardly aware of their presence. She couldn't recall what she said to them or the answers they gave, and she didn't even notice when they closed the door softly and went away.

Her mind was too crowded with memories and images, with recollections so brilliantly clear and sharp-edged that it hurt her to look at them. They'd begun swarming into her mind the moment she saw the dark-haired boy attacking Bonnie, as if that single picture was somehow the key to the locked room that contained her past.

Leah's whole life appeared before her, unrolling slowly in her mind like a technicolor film. She could see the succession of foster homes, the disappointment and cruelty and neglect, the boy who'd abused her so brutally when she was even younger than Bonnie.... Leah moaned softly and dropped her head onto her knees, huddling and rocking on the padded bench. Pain flowed over her, crashing through her mind like waves of molten lava.

Still, she recognized this as a different kind of pain, searing and agonizing but with a cleansing flame, so that memories stabbed and burned and left healing in their wake. Over and over Leah moved through the years of her life, examining her past, laying it open to the clean fire of memory and letting the images burn and shrivel until her suffering drifted away into the misty twilight beyond the windows.

She saw Allan, the boy in the foster home, so young and powerful and full of careless cruelty. Hatred rose in her, churned and twisted in her stomach until she choked with nausea.

Gradually, though, the hatred began to waver and then turned to pity. Leah wondered what had finally happened to Allan, where he was now and how he managed to live his life with the knowledge of what he'd done. Had he gone on to hurt other girls the same way? And was life punishing him as cruelly for his actions as it had punished Leah all these years?

She found that she didn't care. The world would look after Allan and see that justice was done. Paul often said that everyone finally got what they deserved out of life, and he was probably right.

"Our only concern is with ourselves," he'd said. "Our job, Leah, is just to control and look after what we can manage, and that's our own lives." Leah nodded, her eyes closed, recognizing the profound truth of this statement. She didn't need to be concerned with justice or retribution or controlling the behavior of others. Her only job was to discipline her own mind, feel gratitude for this miracle of restored memory and then learn to handle that gift properly now that she'd received it.

She squared her shoulders and drew a deep breath, lifting her head to gaze blindly out the window again as she traveled forward through her life.

With a kind of wondering amazement Leah watched the girl that she'd been, a child existing in conditions of incredible squalor and danger. She tried to imagine Bonnie or Allie living in some of the places that she remembered from her adolescence, doing the things and consorting with the kind of people Leah had known.

Leah found that she was now able to group all the troubled memories in perfect chronological order, even to recognize which were new memories and which were things she'd been aware of before her accident. It was a strange feeling of power, having her entire life available to her like this. She could run through it from beginning to end if she liked, or choose any particular moment and focus on it with instant recall.

She saw herself drifting into her later teens, wisecracking and street-smart, with more knowledge and grim experience than most people would ever acquire in their lifetimes. Shuddering with misery, Leah relived a brutal attack that left her half dead in a seedy apartment after a failed drug deal. She saw herself lying there, a nineteen-year-old girl racked with pain, making an anguished resolution to change her life. That was when she left eastern Canada, traveled west to Calgary and tried to make a new life for herself. She took a bartending course, got a legitimate job as a waitress and tried so hard to work her way out of the dangerous underworld and into some kind of respectability.

And then one night at work, she'd met Paul Temple.

Leah's face softened as she remembered that meeting, the way Paul had looked when she'd encountered him in the busy downtown lounge.

She realized now that she'd loved him from the first moment she saw him, although she never would have admitted that fact, even to herself. In those days Leah had been so hard-edged and cautious, so protective of herself and her emotions, love wasn't a feeling that she wanted anything to do with.

She'd only allowed herself to be attracted to Paul Temple because of his obvious wealth and assurance, and the knowledge that he could be her ticket to a better life. When it became clear that his interest in her was more than a passing thing, Leah had played her trump card, tantalizing him sexually and then holding him deliberately at bay until he was almost wild with desire for her, crazy to possess her.

But after they were married, Leah found that she just couldn't cope with the reality of life with a man. The repressed experiences of her childhood had been too devastating for her to overcome, and her fear and disgust over their sexual relationship had become a terrible destructive force.

Looking back with this new diamond-bright clarity, Leah could see exactly what their marriage had been like. She watched herself and Paul struggling to chart some kind of course through life while those childhood memories lay just below the surface of her mind, as dangerous as a shoal of submerged rocks grinding into the hull of a ship.

Still, there were times in their marriage when Leah had honestly tried to be a good wife. She could remember feeling guilty and frightened, usually when she'd been caught in some blatant bit of wrongdoing, and anxiously resolving to be a better person. But soon the familiar pain would rise up and engulf her once more with tides of bitterness and resentment that she could neither understand nor control.

And always there had been her anger, with its blinding, suffocating force that she turned on her husband whenever the feelings grew too powerful for Leah to suppress. She understood it better now, that depth of rage and loathing that had always been so impossible for her to manage.

But poor Paul.... How could he possibly have understood?

Leah shivered and covered her face with her hands, thinking about Paul's patience and kindness through those miserable years, his lonely despair, the times when he actually shed tears of bewilderment and anguish over her behavior.

"Paul," she whispered. "Oh, Paul, I'm so sorry, darling. I didn't know...I didn't know what I was doing...."

And then in the later years, Leah watched her anger and hostility slowly turning to hatred. She realized, looking back over her stormy marriage, that she'd only begun to despise her husband in earnest after he had turned away from her sexually and begun to talk about the possibility of divorce.

Her face was bleak with sorrow as she pondered the mysteries of the human personality.

I did everything I could to make him despise and reject me, she thought in wonder. *Then, when he reacted the way any normal man would, I hated him for it.* Suddenly the memories quickened, grew dark and murky and turbulent once more. Leah shivered with alarm and forced herself to be calm, to trace the progression of her life all the way to its recent past.

She saw herself developing an obsessive loathing of her husband, beginning to tell herself all the time that she wanted him dead and gone so he couldn't hurt her anymore. The idea of Paul's death had begun to consume her, as if by destroying that quiet accusing presence she could somehow manage to slay all her demons and find peace at last.

Leah began to shiver uncontrollably, knowing what was coming, dreading to examine the next part of her life.

But she knew, for Paul's sake, that she had to go on with this.

Moaning aloud in anguish, still trembling with revulsion, Leah saw herself making furtive inquiries, checking amongst her disreputable friends, arranging contacts. Finally she watched in wide-eyed horror as a distant, cold-faced Leah entered a restaurant with an emerald ring in her handbag, and sat down next to a big man with a vicious smile and gray, stubbled jaw.

"The carpet-cleaning man," Leah whispered aloud. "Oh, my God..."

She drew her breath in sharply and buried her face on her knees again, recognizing how her subconscious mind had strained to warn her, trying so many times to haul this dangerous, buried image to the surface before it was too late.

Leah gazed at the scene in the restaurant like a person watching some monstrous filmstrip, looking on in horror as she made final arrangements with the man, coolly gave him instructions and discussed methods of payment.

Finally she saw herself taking the emerald ring from her bag and dropping it into the man's grimy palm as if it burned her fingers.

The ring had been the cause of the attack out in the alley, Leah realized. She'd taken it to a couple of pawnshops earlier in the day to assess its street value, and a pair of thugs at the back of one of the stores must have seen the emerald and followed her, waiting for a chance to jump her. She remembered their faces clearly, and their anger when she had told them she didn't have the ring any longer. They'd started beating her, swearing furiously and kicking at her.

All Leah remembered after that was a flurry of pain and confusion, the sounds of shouting and running feet and the distant wail of police sirens. The next moment she was waking up in the hospital and looking at her hand, trying to recall the names of simple objects.

That had marked the beginning of the sweetest part of her life. But she couldn't allow herself to think about that now. She had to keep concentrating on what happened just before.

Grimly she forced her mind back to the meeting in the restaurant.

Leah Temple had actually hired a man to kill her husband. She'd given him her emerald engagement ring as partial payment of the contract, and even agreed to play her part by making her husband available to the assassin's bullet.

Leah's eyes widened in shock as she recalled the later visit from the carpet-cleaning man, his cautious inquiry about the "job" and her assurance that she still wanted the work done and fully intended to pay him as agreed.

"Oh, *no,*" Leah whispered aloud. "He must have thought... He still thinks I want him to kill Paul!"

"You just get him up there to that cabin," the man had instructed when they had met in the restaurant, "and I'll do the rest. I want it set for the last weekend in June because I'm leaving for Mexico early in July. Make it a Saturday night when you can be sure he'll be up there. I'll do the job first thing Sunday morning and they won't be likely to find his body until next day at the earliest. By that time I'll be long gone...."

The man's harsh voice faded. Leah shifted on the bench, groping through her memories, struggling to align them with her present reality.

The last weekend in June, she thought. *Saturday night...*

She got up quickly, crossed the room to her desk and switched on the reading lamp. It cast a warm pool of light into the dusky stillness as she studied her little gold-cased desk calendar. Suddenly she swayed on her feet and blood drummed in her ears, making her feel faint and queasy.

Today was Saturday, and it was the last weekend in June.

Her eyes closed and she crumpled to the floor.

LEAH HAD NO IDEA how long she'd lain unconscious on the carpeted floor of her room. When she opened her eyes and tried to sit up, the world was dark beyond the windows, her body was stiff and aching and her head throbbed where she'd struck it on the leg of the desk. But her mind was clear, all her memories still orderly and accessible.

She leaned against the desk, rubbing at her back and grimacing, trying to think.

Saturday night.

The plan was for the assassin to creep up the trail under cover of darkness in the hours just before dawn, position himself in the woods with a good view of the cabin's single door, and shoot his quarry when Paul stepped outside in the morning.

Then he'd make his getaway in a truck that a companion would have waiting below on the trail, and contact Leah within a few days to give her instructions on where and how to transfer the final payment.

Leah's mind moved sluggishly, frozen in panic. She clutched and pounded at her head, knowing that she had to think clearly, that Paul's very life depended on her ability to stay calm and reason her way through this nightmare.

But all she could think of was her husband's golden hair and shining hazel eyes, his broad shoulders and easy laughter, his intelligence and tenderness and the shy, sweet boyishness that he sometimes showed her when they were alone.

And all the times during their marriage when she'd hurt and disappointed him, shamed him and betrayed his trust . . .

Leah shook her head and bit her lips until they throbbed sharply with pain.

There was no time for that kind of indulgence. She couldn't afford to spend time thinking what a monster she was to have done such a thing or trying to analyze what had driven her to it. All those things could come later. Right now she could only think of the present danger and what she had to do.

Taking a few deep breaths, Leah got to her feet and moved stiffly over to gaze out the darkened window in the direction of Paul's cabin.

If she never did another thing as long she lived, Leah thought with grim resolve, she had to do this successfully. She had to find a way to save Paul's life because she was the one who had endangered it.

Briefly she considered going up into the woods, trying to find the hired assassin and let him know she'd changed her mind. Then she remembered his harsh voice in her ear as he leaned close to her in the restaurant.

"Make sure there's nobody else wandering around up there after dark, cupcake. When I'm ready to do the job I'll be so goddamn trigger-happy, I'll blow away anybody that comes within a half mile of me and ask questions later. And after it's done, I'll be out of there in a flash. I won't be hanging around for any chats."

No, trying to seek him out for a little business discussion was hardly a viable option. She had to think of some other way to thwart this dreadful plan.

But how? If she slipped up through the woods to warn Paul or called the police and sent rescue teams swarming through the hills, Joe might be scared off but he would certainly come back and try again as soon as he had a chance. He wanted the money she'd promised him.

Besides, Leah thought, staring into the darkness with a white face and dark, haunted eyes, warning Paul or calling the police would be the end for both of them no matter what happened. Paul would know what she'd done, and how could either of them live with that knowledge?

I'd rather be dead, she told herself simply, *than go on living and have Paul know what I did. I'd honestly rather be dead.*

As soon as the thought formed in her mind, Leah knew what she had to do. The plan was so simple and perfect that it seemed almost preordained.

She switched the lights on and dressed rapidly in jeans, a plaid hunting jacket and the sturdy hiking boots Paul had bought for her. Then she darkened her room again, took a flashlight from the hall closet and slipped out into the warm summer night, heading for the path behind the creek.

CHAPTER THIRTEEN

PAUL CLOSED HIS BOOK and leaned back in his chair, watching with quiet, brooding eyes as a moth circled and fluttered in the warm pool of light around the coal-oil lamp.

Finally he got to his feet, wandered across to the little enameled sink and washed his hands and face, then stepped out onto the veranda to gaze up at the sky. The night was black and still, dusted with stars so brilliant that he felt he could almost reach up and touch them with his fingers. Loneliness flooded through him, and an intense melancholy that was almost overwhelming.

Paul wanted his wife. He hungered for her company, for all the tenderness and happy laughter and warm sweetness that they'd shared during the past months.

But that interlude was all just an illusion. The happy, childlike woman who'd lived so briefly in his house and had twined herself firmly around his heart was not the woman he'd dreamed she might be. Those weeks of sweetness and trust were just a phase, a temporary aberration in the life of a cold and selfish person.

Paul shivered, still gazing at the starry blackness, remembering the spiteful face and bitter golden eyes of that stranger in the mirror, the woman who had shouted and cursed at him.

How could any man risk his deepest emotions with a woman like that? She was not only erratic but dangerous, Paul thought with another chill of fear, remembering the terrible look in her eyes.

In a less dramatic way, this pattern had repeated itself so many times before in their marriage. All through the years they'd experienced brief spells when Leah would make an effort to be nice, and he'd be tantalized and drawn to her in spite of himself. Then something would set her off and she'd be reduced to a screaming, vindictive monster all over again, just as she had the evening of the dinner party.

Paul leaned against the veranda railing and stared blindly into the darkness of the woods. Pale moonlight washed over his tall body and strong, tanned face as he pondered the mystery of his wife's behavior.

Ken Holcross had warned him about this. The doctor had even tried with uncharacteristic bluntness to let Paul know that his wife's condition was seriously unstable and that her new gentleness wasn't likely to survive the recovery of her memories.

But Paul hadn't wanted to listen and believe, because it was so hard to give up the wondrous sweet love that had filled his life and warmed his heart for these brief months.

Paul's shoulders slumped and he turned around to trudge back into the cabin. He picked up the lamp and carried it carefully up the rough steps to the sleeping loft, setting it down on a small wooden end table while he stripped off his clothes and climbed hastily under the chilly blankets.

The bed was handmade, a wooden frame strung tightly with hemp and padded with fresh pine boughs, then covered with a hard mattress of cotton ticking. The boughs rustled and creaked under the mattress, giving off a tangy, aromatic scent that Paul loved. He lifted himself on one elbow and blew out the lamp, then settled back on the mattress with his hands folded behind his head, gazing at the square of nighttime sky beyond the small window above.

Along with the loneliness, he had to fight against a desolate sense of entrapment and bitterness, and a deep resentment of his wife for placing him in this position. Back in April, just before Leah's accident, Paul had at last begun to feel in control of his life and his fate. He'd been to his lawyer, served Leah with divorce papers, started the cumbersome process of disentangling their business affairs and getting his life back into his own hands.

What could he do now?

Leah was getting better, but she was still far from healed. She wasn't capable of functioning in the world on her own, and he certainly wasn't brutal enough to force her out of the house in that condition. But the longer she stayed the more Paul suffered from the cruel mockery of fate, and the constant reminder of what his life could have been if only Leah had been a different person.

Physically she was everything he'd ever yearned for in a wife. No other woman would ever arouse him in the same way, carry him to such momentous heights of passion and then give him such sweet release. Leah was unique, and so utterly desirable that his body trembled with longing whenever he thought of her.

And Paul was intelligent enough to recognize that this appeal of hers wasn't all physical. He knew that there were other women even more beautiful and desirable than Leah. Still, they lacked the mysterious essence of her, whatever it was that drew him in such a basic and powerful way.

But her lovely body and her enchanting, childlike spirit were only part of a badly damaged personality. Mingled together, they created a woman who was infinitely alluring, yet so twisted and bitter that she wasn't capable of sustaining real intimacy with any man.

Paul shifted restlessly in the bed, wondering for the thousandth time just how far his responsibilities as a husband really extended. Because he'd married her, was he obligated to sacrifice the rest of his life in a hopeless attempt to help her find peace and fulfillment, to heal herself from childhood trauma and learn to be a warm and trusting person? And how much was he required to suffer in that attempt?

Paul was perceptive enough to suspect that his wife had begun to hate him before the accident. In those final months Leah often hadn't been able to conceal the bitter contempt in her eyes and voice, the hot flare of anger and loathing that she struggled to suppress whenever she looked at him.

It wasn't easy, Paul reflected with a small, bitter smile, trying to live with a woman who hated you. The constant tension in their relationship had made him feel uneasy and degraded, sometimes even eroded his confidence in his business dealings.

"Oh, God," he muttered wearily, pounding his fist against the mattress. "I want it all to be over. Why can't it just be *over,* dammit!"

Something caught his attention and he sat upright in the darkness, frowning. He tensed and strained, listening for the sound. After a moment it came again, a cautious rustle down on the veranda.

Paul shrugged and settled back against the pillows, trying to relax.

It was probably just a squirrel or a raccoon, he thought, trying to get at the trash bag strung between the cabin and the trees. Maybe the intruder was a wandering black bear, but that was no concern to Paul, either. The big door was stoutly barred, and he'd never had any trouble with bears here at the cabin. He respected their territory and kept his living areas scrupulously clean, so the bears never bothered him.

The sound came again, a muffled thumping and rustling noise, even more definite this time.

Paul slipped from the bed, pulled his jeans on and climbed down the ladder. He padded quickly across the lower room to peer through the window, then gasped in shock and sudden fear.

The moon was gone and the world was dark and still, so heavily shrouded in blackness that it was difficult to perceive objects. But Paul could make out the form of a shadowy human figure on the veranda looking at the door with concentrated attention, holding some kind of object concealed under one arm.

Paul reached for the rifle hanging near the door, checked the magazine and unfastened the safety catch. Then he unlocked the door soundlessly, eased it toward him on well-oiled hinges and leaned into the narrow opening.

"Who's there?" he demanded harshly. "Who are you, and what the hell do you want?"

"Paul?" a soft desperate voice said in the darkness. "Paul, it's me. It's Leah. Please let me in."

Paul hesitated for an instant, realizing with horror that he was actually afraid of his wife. Here in the darkness, miles from any other person, he was reluctant to let her into the cabin unless he knew what she held concealed in the crook of her arm. . . .

"Leah?" he said, stalling for time. "What do you want? Why are you here?"

She moved forward, dropping her hands so Paul could see the flashlight she held. He sagged with relief, and then felt another searing wave of misery. What a travesty of a marriage, when a man actually feared his wife! But he'd seen a murderous look in her eyes more than once, had caught the reflection of deeply banked fires that made him shiver. . . .

He stepped back abruptly and held the door open for her, watching in silence as she stumbled into the darkened interior of the cabin.

Paul latched the door and made his way across the room by instinct, searching for matches in their little nook above the sink. He lit the other kerosene lamp, then blew the match out and turned to look at his wife.

She stood white-faced and silent in the middle of the room, trembling with cold and shock.

"I was so scared," she whispered in response to his questioning look. "All the way up here I kept hearing things growling and moving around in the brush, and twigs snapping on the path behind me. Paul, it was awful. I was just terrified."

Paul found himself battling the old familiar urge to take her into his arms and wrap her in warmth and safety. Instead he forced himself to stand back and look at her unhappy face with cool detachment. He still felt wary and suspicious, troubled by her unexpected arrival in this remote place.

"Why did you come here, Leah?" he asked, more calmly than he felt. "What possessed you to climb all the way up here in the middle of the night?"

She hesitated, staring up at him, her eyes enormous in her pale face. "I was...I was so lonely," she whispered. "And I wanted to tell you something. I just wanted... Oh, Paul," she whispered, her voice breaking. "I was so scared...."

This time his need to hold her was more than he could bear. Paul moved forward and gathered her into his arms, embracing her tenderly, rubbing his hands over her trembling back and stroking her hair as she burrowed against him.

"It's all right, Leah," he murmured. "It's all right. You're here now, and the door's locked and barred. We're safe in here. Nothing can hurt us. Now," he said, leaning back to look down at her, "what was it you wanted to tell me? What's the matter, Leah?"

She hesitated, her face crumpling again when she tried to meet his eyes. "I'm so cold," she whispered, shivering. "Paul, I'm just so cold."

Paul gazed down at her, his face grim and taut as he battled with himself.

"Come on, Leah, " he murmured finally, giving in to all the clamorous urges of his body. "Come to bed with me. I'll hold you and make you warm."

LEAH MOVED AND STIRRED in Paul's arms, her whole body heavy and languorous with fulfillment.

I'm so glad, she thought with a brief, fierce surge of elation that was darkly tinged with sorrow. *I'm so glad I came here and we made love one last time.*

She moved her head on the pillow to gaze at his profile. He was so close to her that she could see the line of his nose and cheek even in the darkness, see the warm dense fan of his eyelashes and the little creases that rayed out from the corners of his eyes.

"I love you, Paul," she whispered, her voice breaking with sadness. "I love you so much. I hope...I hope you never forget how much I love you, no matter what happens."

His eyes opened and he looked at her in surprise. "What do you mean, Leah, 'no matter what happens'? Is something going to happen?"

Leah's mouth trembled and cold fingers of dread crept along her spine. But she forced herself to shake her head and smile, to nestle close beside him and run her fingers over his lips.

"Nothing's going to happen," she whispered. "Except," she added, leaning up to kiss his ear, "maybe we'll make love again before the night's over."

Paul chuckled and caressed the curve of her hip and thigh with long, gentle strokes. "Not a chance," he murmured. "Your poor husband's all worn out. Completely drained. Go to sleep, woman."

Leah cuddled against his long, warm body, so deep in love that she could hardly remember why she was here, and what was going to happen before the morning sun rose over the trees.

"Leah?" Paul murmured sleepily.

"Mmm?"

"You said before that you wanted to tell me something. What was it?"

Leah hesitated, wondering what to say. Suddenly, with numbing shock, she realized that this was the last conversation she and Paul would ever have. There were so many things she wanted him to know, and she'd never have another opportunity to tell him.

"Leah?"

"I just..." Leah's mind raced. "Something happened today that upset me quite a lot. I wanted to tell you about it, Paul."

His arm tightened around her. "What happened? What upset you?"

Leah told him about her walk, about hearing Bonnie's scream, running wildly through the woods and coming onto that shocking scene in the clearing.

"God," Paul muttered when she finished. Leah could sense the rigid tension of his jaw, feel the hard muscles bulging in his arms. "Lucky it was you and not me, sweetheart. I'd probably have killed the little son of a bitch."

Leah gave a shaky laugh. "I almost killed him myself, Paul. I really gave it a good effort, anyhow. If he hadn't managed to get away while I was trying to catch my breath, I'd probably be in jail by now."

Paul drew her close and rubbed his cheek against her hair, kissing her tenderly. "That's pretty hard to picture, Leah."

"Not if you understand everything that happened."

"What else happened?" he asked in the darkness. "What do you mean?"

Haltingly, her voice trailing off to a whisper at times, Leah told her husband about the stunning revelation of that moment, and the flood of memory that crashed into her mind when she saw Jody Muller attacking Bonnie.

Paul was silent for so long that she couldn't bear the tension. "Paul?" she murmured anxiously. "Are you all right?"

"Oh, Leah," he whispered, his voice husky. "Leah, darling...that's the memory that's been haunting you all these years? That boy, what he did to you.... That was the reason you were always so full of anger? And suspicious of me, and fearful of...of being with me?"

"I'm sure it was," Leah murmured. "I think that's what Ken was trying to tell me all the time, that I needed to recover that particular memory and learn to deal with it."

"Oh, Leah," Paul groaned, gathering her close to him and rocking her in his arms. "Sweetheart, I'm just so sorry."

"You're sorry?" Leah asked, bewildered. "Why, Paul?"

"For doubting you. For being so angry and impatient with you."

"Oh, Paul," she said, lost in sorrow. "It's not you who should apologize. I hurt you so much, over and over again."

"Darling, don't—"

"And," Leah interrupted him, taking a deep breath and forcing her voice to remain calm and steady, "I want you to know how truly sorry I am, Paul. I want you always to remember that I loved you, and that I was sorry for everything that happened between us."

"Leah, don't scare me like that! Why are you talking in the past tense? You're not going anywhere and neither am I. Not after we've made it this far."

"No," Leah whispered, burying her face in the warm curve of his neck and trying desperately not to cry. "We're not going anywhere, Paul."

"Leah," he went on, cuddling sleepily against her, his voice suddenly boyish and hopeful, "it's going to be different now, isn't it? Now that you've remembered all this we can talk to Ken about it and get some help for you, then go ahead and put it completely behind us. Life's going to be different now."

Leah sensed his new mood of optimism and her heart ached.

No, Paul, she told him silently, holding him in her arms and kissing his face tenderly as he drifted off to sleep. *It's not going to be different. There's no hope for us, Paul, because it's just far too late. Maybe if this had happened years ago, before it all went so terribly wrong . . .*

But there was no point in following that line of thinking, because it could lead only to misery and despair.

Leah lay awake in the darkness listening to Paul's quiet, even breathing. She stared up at the ceiling and waited for the first dim glow of dawn to wash over the rough logs.

There was no choice now. She had chosen her course of action months ago when she had set a sequence of events in motion. And now they had to be carried to their logical conclusion.

It made no difference that Paul was full of optimism right now, happy and hopeful about this new breakthrough. Leah knew how deeply ingrained his caution was, and how quickly new suspicions would arise if he sensed any change in her behavior.

She shivered, remembering the look on his face when he'd stared out at her as she waited by the door of the cabin.

He was looking at the flashlight, Leah thought in sudden understanding. He thought it was a weapon of some kind. Paul remembered the way she'd behaved the other night, and he was afraid she might have come up here to attack him.

And he was right, of course. Paul Temple's wife had planned to kill him in cold blood, and somewhere in the depths of his soul he'd understood and recognized that danger.

Once that monstrous fact was actually confirmed, once he realized and understood with his conscious mind that she had methodically planned and purchased his execution, how could they ever be expected to have a relationship again? What man could possibly live with that kind of knowledge?

Leah shook her head wearily and edged closer to Paul's long, still body, careful not to wake him. More than anything in the world she cherished these last few hours with him, the wondrous sweetness of their lovemaking and the feeling of warmth and safety as she nestled beside him.

This was the only thing that really mattered in life, Leah realized. All the things that people fought for and struggled so fiercely to obtain, like money and power and status... none of them meant anything at all. In the final analysis, all that mattered was love.

Love washed away pain, cleansed hurtful memories, healed and strengthened and restored. Love endured forever, long after all other human passions were spent.

Gradually the hours crept by and the velvet blackness beyond the window lightened and thinned, fading to a dull charcoal glow, then to a wash of silver.

Leah stared at the window, feeling a painful, gripping tension, a cold reluctance and dread. She sat erect, moving with infinite care to keep from disturbing Paul, and gazed down with brooding love and sorrow at his sleeping face.

He looked young and vulnerable in the silvery light of dawn, so gentle and handsome that her heart ached and tears gathered in her eyes, slipping unheeded down her cheeks. She leaned over softly and kissed the pillow close to his cheek.

"Goodbye, Paul," she whispered under her breath. "I love you so much, my darling." Then, still moving with that same silent caution, she gathered her clothes and slipped down the ladder into the chilly room below.

Leah dressed carefully and slowly, pausing every few minutes to listen and make sure there was no sound or movement from upstairs. She crossed the room and took Paul's bright red plaid jacket from its hanger, pulling it on over her sweater and zipping it to her chin.

Then from a hook above the jacket, she took down his distinctive orange hunter's cap and tucked her hair up out of sight beneath it, pulling the visor down low over her eyes. Finally she carried his tall hiking boots over to the door, stepped into them and laced them up as tightly as she could.

She stood for a moment longer, gazing around her at the silent gray room, the tables and chairs that Paul had carved with his own hands, the neat rows of books and supplies. Leah paused with her hand on the door latch, breathing in the rich scent of woodsmoke and kerosene, of pine and cedar and early-morning freshness.

Then she lifted the latch, eased the door quietly open and stepped outside.

She walked deliberately to the front of the veranda, trying to hold herself as tall as possible, though she knew that her body was still nothing more than a dim blur of color in the pale misty light of dawn. At the edge of the step she paused and looked full into the woods.

Come on, she urged silently. *Here I am, don't make me wait. Come on and do it....*

As the thought formed in her mind Leah heard a sound, not like a shot at all, but a muffled kind of burst that exploded softly in the air around her.

He must be using a silencer, she thought with mild curiosity, then recoiled in shock as the sound came bursting again and something slammed into her upper body with incredible force, spun her around and sent her plunging headlong down the steps to sprawl on the soft, matted pine needles.

Strangely enough, there was no pain at all, just a numbness that was followed by a warm, spreading sense of peace. Leah welcomed the dark tide that rolled over her. She gave herself up to it gratefully and moved toward the void with calm happiness, carrying Paul's image in her mind as she drifted away.

CHAPTER FOURTEEN

TIM CONNOR WAS HUDDLED in his lookout position, staring moodily down at the cabin, when he heard the door open and close softly and the muffled clatter of booted feet crossing the porch.

He drew his breath in sharply, wondering if Joe had seen their quarry emerging onto the porch. Tim was actually quite a lot closer to the cabin than Joe, even though Joe was the one with the gun. Tim sat about fifteen feet up in the branches of a spreading pine tree behind the little building; that vantage point gave him a partial view over the roof onto the lower steps and the front yard, although he couldn't see the door or the covered veranda.

Joe had chosen this spot for the lookout because Tim was able to watch the road below where the truck was parked, the path leading up from the farm and the surrounding clearing. The younger man was in an ideal position to sound a warning if necessary.

Joe had concealed himself about a hundred yards away on a small rocky knoll in the grove of trees directly in front of the cabin. From there he could see the door and fire a clear shot, even from such a considerable distance, what with the powerful telescopic sight fitted onto his rifle.

Tim had been in the tree for almost two hours and was growing steadily more cramped and uncomfortable. His mind, too, was beginning to play tricks on him, haunting him with doubts and fears that became more pressing as the sky lightened in the east.

He'd found himself wondering about Leah Temple and her husband, how happy they looked together and how gentle and sweet the woman seemed whenever she spoke to Tim. Was she really just faking it like Joe said or was the whole thing some kind of horrible misunderstanding?

And could he and Joe actually hope to get away with this? Could they kill a man like Paul Temple in open daylight and escape without punishment?

Tim shivered, thinking about Paul's broad shoulders and calm, steady gaze, the controlled power in his voice and person.

Oh, God, I want it to be over, Tim thought, listening tensely to those halting footsteps. *I don't want to do this. I wish I was a million miles away from here....*

For a brief, crazy moment he considered climbing down from the tree, telling Joe to shove the whole idea and shouting a warning to the man on the cabin porch. But as soon as he formed the thought Tim licked his lips nervously and glanced off into the distant grove of trees where Joe was crouching with his gun.

Tim knew that if he tried to back out now, Joe would kill him without a second's hesitation. He'd be just as dead as Paul Temple. And besides, there was all that money and the hope for a better life, far away from all this misery....

Tim groaned under his breath and shifted in the branches.

Suddenly he heard the first puff of noise and straightened, staring wildly down at the cabin and the edge of the step that was visible from his perch. Another muffled shot exploded softly in the early morning air and a bright figure tumbled into view, ending up full length on the ground while an orange cap rolled into the dust nearby. Tim shuddered and fought down a rising swell of nausea. With shaking hands he wrestled Joe's heavy binoculars from their case and trained them on the figure below.

"Make damn sure he's dead," Joe had warned him. "I can't tell from where I'm at. And don't start yelling, neither. If he needs another shot you wave this red flag at me. If he looks good and dead, wave the yellow flag and I'll meet you down at the truck."

"How will I... how will I know if he's dead?" Tim had asked his partner anxiously.

"Kid," Joe said with heavy irony, "you just look at him, okay? If he ain't moving, he's likely dead. Now, is that too tough for you?"

Tim shivered again. His hands shook so badly that he had to prop the binoculars against one of the pine branches near his face before he could manage to see anything.

He squinted down at the crumpled figure in front of the cabin, then gaped in stupefaction and slowly growing horror. The person on the ground was dressed in Paul Temple's clothes, in the same jacket and cap and boots that they'd seen on an earlier reconnaissance trip. But it wasn't Paul Temple who lay there on the path in a spreading pool of bright red blood.

It was his wife.

Tim's mind moved sluggishly as he gaped at the boyish light-brown hair, the slender body and delicate pale skin.

What in hell... Frantically he tried to think what to do. If he waved the red flag, Joe would fire another round of shots into her helpless body. If he showed the yellow signal, Joe would leave his post and hurry through the woods to meet him on the road down by the truck.

But we need to help her, Tim thought desperately. *We need to get her to the hospital or something. Maybe she isn't dead yet.*

Suddenly it was of vital importance to Tim, the question of whether or not Leah Temple was dead. He couldn't stand it if she was dead. He thought of her shy smile, her beautiful golden-brown eyes and the glow on her face when she cuddled the fat kittens in the barn. Fury rose and burned within him, hatred of Joe with his coarse smile and his ruthless animal cunning.

Without thinking further about what he was doing or what might happen, Tim flung himself out of the tree and pounded around the edge of the cabin to kneel by Leah's still body, touching her with shaking hands.

He heard a muffled curse from the grove of trees and saw Joe come running across the clearing, cradling the rifle in his arms.

"Goddammit, kid," he hissed furiously, "what the hell do you think you're doing? Is he dead or what? Get outta my way so I can..."

Tim looked up at the other man, his hands covered with blood, tears streaming down his cheeks.

"You bastard!" he moaned in agony. "You idiot! It's *her,* Joe. Can't you see that it's *her?* You killed her, Joe."

The big man looked coldly at the woman on the ground, then at his young partner. His face took on a wary, intent look and he swung rapidly into position, kneeling with his gun pointed at the cabin door.

Tim stared at the big man blankly through his tears. "Joe, what are you doing? We gotta get her to the hospital or something, don't we? Maybe they can help her. Maybe there's still time to—"

"Shut up, you fool," Joe hissed between gritted teeth. "Just shut up. Get away from her, you're blocking my shot."

Tim gaped at the big man in confusion.

"You *fool,*" Joe repeated furiously. "She didn't come up here all alone. If she's here, then Temple's here, too, and he'll be coming out in a minute to see what's going on."

And then Joe would shoot him as well, Tim realized, and make his getaway in the waiting truck. He'd leave both bodies lying quiet and still here under the morning sun, Leah Temple and her husband.

Everything had gone wrong, so horribly wrong. . . .

Paul appeared in the doorway at that moment, wearing nothing but a pair of blue jeans, his bare chest glistening in the morning light. Joe tensed and squinted into the sights of the rifle.

Tim suddenly couldn't stand it anymore. He couldn't bear the thought of any more pain, more blood and horror. He leaped forward with a scream of outrage and threw himself on Joe, driving him to the ground and clutching at the gun.

Joe grunted in surprise and then began to struggle violently, kicking and swearing as he fought with the younger man. Tim grasped the rifle barrel and wrenched it away, sweating and panting. With a wiry strength fueled by desperation he raised the rifle butt high over his head and brought it crashing down onto Joe's head and shoulders.

The big man's face stiffened in a look of comical surprise and he clutched at his chest with both hands. His eyes went round, then dropped shut as he sank to his knees and slowly unfolded to lie full length on the matted grass beside the step.

Paul stood on the veranda, looking down in confusion at the body of the man lying on the ground, then at Tim who stood facing him, the gun dangling broken and useless in his hands.

Tim moved slowly aside, and Paul saw his wife's slim, crumpled form, the bright hair against the grass and the spreading pool of blood.

Paul uttered a strangled cry and ran down the steps. He dropped to his knees beside Leah, lifting her lifeless form with gentle hands and turning her over to expose the bullet hole in the bright plaid front of the jacket.

Tim shuddered at the look of pain on the man's face, the deep anguish in his eyes.

"There's a... We got a truck parked down on the road just below, Mr. Temple," Tim said awkwardly. "If we could carry her down there, you and me, we could maybe take her in to the hospital...."

Paul needed no further prompting. "Take the door off its hinges," he said sharply, folding Leah's shirt front back to examine her blood-smeared chest, frowning as he tried to feel for a pulse. "Carry it down here right away, and then get me those old hiking boots from the porch."

Tim rushed to obey, humbly grateful for something to do, for the welcome feeling that everything was now in the hands of a stronger, better person and Tim didn't have to think anymore.

"What about him?" he asked fearfully, motioning toward Joe's prone, twisted body as he carried the heavy door down the steps and hurried back to the porch to get Paul's other boots.

Joe's head was bleeding freely from a deep gash in his scalp, and a mass of angry bruises already showed on his stubbled cheek and jaw.

"He won't get far on foot even if he regains consciousness," Paul said briefly, taking the wooden slab from the younger man and positioning it on the ground next to Leah's body, then jamming his bare feet into the boots. "Was he the one who did the shooting?"

Tim nodded and licked his lips. "Yeah. See," he began in agony, "we were..."

"Forget it," Paul said, lifting Leah's body onto the wooden door and stroking her hair with a gentle hand. "Let's just get my wife to the hospital, and after that you can tell me what happened. Take the front end, would you, Tim? You're the one who knows where the truck is parked."

Tim nodded humbly and hurried around to lift the other end of the makeshift stretcher, glancing with anguish at Leah's still, pale face. He paused for a moment to steady the slab of wood in his hands, then plunged off into the woods in the direction of the waiting vehicle.

THE SUMMER SKY was shell-pink and endless. It had a warm, pearly radiance that made Leah smile with sleepy pleasure. The warmth came from masses of drifting clouds that wrapped all around her and sheltered her body from pain and danger.

She wasn't completely safe from pain, she reminded herself. There was an intense fireball of heat in her chest, with sparks and sharp flares of agony radiating from it like the shining spokes of a wheel.

But that's just because I'm dead, Leah thought tranquilly. *A bullet went right though my heart and now I'm dead.*

She had a moment of sleepy surprise and pleasure at the thought of being dead, and paused to wonder what came next. What wondrous sights awaited her when she finally opened her eyes and the mists of pink cleared away?

Leah sighed and shook her head carefully on the soft clouds beneath her head.

It didn't matter what came next. All that mattered was that everything had finally ended. The horrible day had come and gone and Paul was safe.

Paul still existed in the world, still walked down the country lane by his house with that lithe, powerful stride and still lifted his golden head to the sunshine with the little squint of his hazel eyes that she loved so much. Paul was all right.

Leah sighed in contentment, then tensed.

Was Paul really all right?

She frowned, trying to remember the confusing sequence of events outside the cabin. She remembered the muffled first shot, and then the second that exploded inside her breast. Then there were grasping hands, running feet and anxious faces, but not Paul. She recalled shouts and fighting, though, and Paul was in that memory somewhere....

Oh God, Leah thought frantically, *what if they hurt Paul, too? Paul, where are you? I can't leave without knowing that you're all right. I love you, Paul. I love you so much. Where are you... ?*

"Now, just quit all that whimpering," a warm voice said nearby. "Stop it this minute, Leah. You're just fine, got nothing in the whole world to fret about. You just come back to us and start looking perky again. Your blood pressure's down in your socks, girl! You hear me? You wake up!"

The voice was so startling, cutting through the pearly rainbow mist with such harsh clarity, that it made Leah jump a little, then wince with pain.

What blood pressure?

Leah tried to imagine her blood pressure being down in her socks, tried to form a mental image of it. The problem was so bewildering that she opened her eyes, blinking away the pink mists to see a big, beaming, dark sun that warmed the whole sky.

The sun had eyes and lips and a jolly white smile, and was surrounded by curly black rays of light. It leaned closer and kissed her forehead. Leah gasped, afraid that the touch of the sun might burn or blind her, but it didn't. It just felt warm and sweet, and so did the gentle, enclosing arms and the soothing words that were whispered in her ears.

"Doris?" she muttered in disbelief, struggling to understand. "Doris? Are you here, too? How did you get here?"

"I drove here in the world's oldest living Volvo, sweetie, just like I do every morning. And what did I find when I came on shift? My own little Leah, back in all kinds of trouble again. I declare, child, you'll just be the death of me yet. You truly will."

This cheerful monologue was delivered in a firm tone amid a flurry of activity while Doris bustled around checking dressings, reading thermometers, taking blood pressure and jotting notations on charts, all the time pausing to make mysterious little adjustments that set Leah's body in a more comfortable position and eased the pain in her chest.

Leah gazed up at the big dark woman, struggling to understand. "I'm not dead?" she said finally.

Doris chuckled. "You damn well better not be. If you were dead, Leah Temple, we'd all just be *so* mad at you. You'd be real sorry, let me tell you."

"But I was... He shot me, didn't he? I felt the bullet...."

"Oh, he shot you all right, cupcake. That ol' bullet went right in here—" Doris poked a gentle brown finger at the massive bandage on Leah's chest "—shattered part of your collarbone and lodged against the scapula. That's your shoulder blade, back here, see?"

Leah's mind moved slowly, trying to absorb all this. "It didn't go though my heart? I felt like my heart exploded."

"I wouldn't doubt it, sweetie," Doris said, her face gentle and tender for a moment. "I wouldn't doubt it

for a minute. It must have hurt like hell. Actually,"
she added in a brisker tone, "just your collarbone sort
of exploded—that's the clavicle up here—and the
doctors did some pretty fancy work yesterday to patch
it all back together, let me tell you. And they had to
dig that ol' bullet out of your shoulder blade, too.
You'll have some big-time aches and pains for a while,
kid."

Leah nodded slowly, trying to absorb all this.

"Lucky you weren't six or seven inches taller,"
Doris went on casually, "or that bullet *would've* gone
straight through your heart."

Paul is six or seven inches taller, Leah thought in
agony. Oh, God, Paul... She gazed into the other
woman's face. "Is Paul all right, Doris?"

"He sure is. He's just fine."

Leah sagged with relief and turned away, suddenly
afraid to ask any more questions.

"It's Monday morning, about seven o'clock.
Breakfast time," Doris went on heartily. "Are you still
too sore to eat, sweetie? Need a little help?"

Leah shook her head. "I feel sick to my stomach. I
don't think I can eat."

"Well now," Doris said mysteriously, "that's another thing."

Something in the woman's tone caught Leah's attention. She glanced up sharply. "What, Doris?
What's another thing?"

Doris looked awkward for a moment. "I mean, that
you feel sick. See, I guess they had to...to use a lot of
local anesthetics during your surgery. They didn't
want to use a general, you see, and some of those

heavy local ones can make you a little queasy, sweetheart. You just relax.''

Doris's evasive look and tone increased Leah's
feeling of panic. ''Why didn't they use a general anesthetic? What's going on, Doris? Am I really all
right? Is Paul all right? There's something you aren't
telling me,'' she said with growing anxiety, heaving
herself up on the pillows and gasping as her wounded
shoulder exploded in anguish.

Doris eased the slender woman back down into her
nest of pillows and then glanced up with obvious relief as Ken Holcross came quietly into the room,
wearing his white lab coat, carrying his clipboard and
his tiny silver flashlight.

''Hello, ladies,'' he said mildly, smiling at the big
nurse and her troubled patient. ''What's up?''

Doris frowned helplessly at the psychologist. ''She's
just being a real bad girl, Dr. Holcross. She keeps
asking these questions like why we used a local instead of a general, and she's insisting on getting up to
check on things, and she tells me she's not going to eat
her breakfast.''

''Oh, I think she's going to eat her breakfast,'' Ken
Holcross said with a cheerful smile. ''Just give us a
few minutes, would you, Doris? I'll deal with our reluctant patient here.''

Doris sighed, then patted Leah's cheek as she passed
to show that she was just teasing. Leah and Ken Holcross watched as Doris crossed the room with a light,
graceful tread despite her bulk, and closed the door
gently behind her. Silence fell, warm and golden in the
early morning sunlight that flooded the room. The

doctor seated himself comfortably next to Leah's bed and waited, gazing down at his clipboard.

At last Leah turned to him, her face bleak. "A few weeks ago Paul explained to me the meaning of déjà vu," she said. "I certainly feel it strongly this morning, Ken. This has all happened before, hasn't it?"

"Well, you've obviously retained memory of the fugue period if you recall something Paul told you only a month ago."

"Oh, I remember everything," Leah said with touch of bitterness in her voice. "Every single, squalid, awful thing in my life from the age of four until yesterday morning on the porch of Paul's cabin."

Ken leaned forward with intense interest, flipping to a fresh page on his clipboard and snapping the point on his pen. "Everything, Leah? No gaps or cloudy areas?"

"None. I remember my whole life with extreme vividness. It's awful, Ken. When it all started coming back I could hardly stand the memories."

The doctor nodded at her in quiet sympathy, then turned back to his notes. "Was there a triggering factor, Leah? Something that brought back all the blocked memories?"

Leah told him about finding Bonnie and Jody together in the clearing, and the flood of murderous rage that had filled her mind at that moment.

"I really think I would have killed him, Ken," she told the doctor simply. "With my bare hands, if I could have."

Ken nodded thoughtfully. "Fifteen or twenty years of suppressed rage is certainly a force to be reckoned with, Leah. How do you feel about this boy now?"

"Which one? Allan, or the boy who hurt Bonnie?"

"Is there any difference?" the doctor asked gently.

Leah nodded. "I see your point." She was silent a moment, thinking. "I guess," she said finally, "that it doesn't feel like rage anymore. I think that's a feeling you can only have briefly and then it burns out. If I feel anything now, it's probably more like...disgust. Maybe even pity."

The doctor nodded approval. "That's very good, Leah. Very good. Now," he went on calmly, "we can move ahead through the years. You've fully recovered all your adolescent memories?"

Leah nodded wearily against the pillows. "I think I have. Ken...?" she asked with sudden curiosity.

"Yes?"

"Did you know all this stuff already? Did you know about how I lived and survived, the things I did when I was a kid and the people I hung out with?"

"Most of it," the doctor said. "After a period of initial resistance you began to respond quite freely under hypnosis."

"But you never instructed me to recall any of that stuff. I hardly had any memory of my life up to the time I married Paul. My life before coming out West and starting to be a waitress...it was all pretty much a blur to me."

The doctor nodded gravely. "It was my impression that those blunted memories were serving to hide something dreadfully traumatic in your earlier childhood. I hoped eventually to have it drawn out naturally, not through hypnotic suggestion. And I believe that's finally happened."

Leah drew a deep breath and gripped the edge of the sheet, staring up at the doctor's round, mild face.

"Ken..."

"Yes, my dear?"

"We can't keep putting it off any longer, can we? We have to talk about what happened."

"What happened, Leah?"

"You know. What I did, and why, and how Paul almost..."

Leah saw the doctor's troubled look and caught her breath sharply. "Is Paul...is he really all right? Tell me, Ken. *Tell* me!"

"Paul's just fine. He's outside pacing the visitor's lounge, demanding to be allowed to see you."

Leah turned pale in alarm. "How much does he know, Ken? Does he know about the...about that man? Does he know what I did?"

"None of us knows much as yet, Leah. Just a confused story from young Tim, who shut up as soon as he realized he might be compromising himself by talking. It appears that he feels responsible in some way for your injury, but we haven't established his involvement with the gunman, if any, or whether you were shot deliberately. It's all just a jumble of confusing stories and speculation."

Leah turned away from the doctor to gaze out the window at the square of summer sky. At last she took a long breath and began to talk, telling Ken Holcross how she'd felt her hatred for Paul growing with every criticism and rejection, how it had become a force so powerful that she could no longer deal with her emotions rationally and she'd finally begun to make inquiries about people who killed for money.

Ken leaned back in the chair, his face carefully impassive, making notes as he listened.

"So what do you think of me now?" Leah asked in a low, bitter voice.

"What do you mean, Leah?"

"Just what I said. What's your opinion of a woman who'd want to have her husband killed? Especially when he's a man who never did anything deliberately cruel or unfair in his whole life. What kind of woman would do a thing like that?"

The doctor was silent, gazing steadily into her anguished eyes.

"Tell me!" Leah urged. "Tell me what you think of me, Ken."

"You haven't finished the story, Leah," the doctor told her gently. "You haven't told me what happened after you started making these inquiries."

Leah sighed and settled back against the pillows, her body aching and burning with pain. "I heard about this man called Joe," she said wearily, her voice hardly above a whisper. "I made arrangements to meet him at a restaurant and took him my emerald ring as a down payment. We planned the whole thing that night, but when I left I was attacked by two men who'd seen the ring earlier in the day at a pawnshop. When I told them it was gone they started beating me. Next thing I knew I woke up here in the hospital and my memory was completely gone. End of story."

"I'm afraid not, Leah."

Leah gave him a quick, questioning glance.

"That doesn't explain what happened yesterday," Ken told her quietly. "How did you come to be at the cabin yesterday morning, Leah? Why were you wearing Paul's clothes?''

"I remembered,'' she whispered in agony, her eyes distant and full of pain. "After I saw Bonnie with that boy, I remembered everything. I knew what I'd done and that it was going to happen right away. It was too late to do anything. I couldn't phone you for help because you were away. And I couldn't warn anybody, not even Paul, because then he'd know what I'd done and he'd hate me so much. I didn't want to go on living if Paul hated me. I went up there,'' she recited in a toneless voice, "and spent the night with him to…to say goodbye, you know?''

She rolled her head on the pillow and looked at the doctor, who nodded calmly, motioning for her to continue.

"Then in the morning when it was still half dark I got up and put his clothes on and went outside on the veranda, knowing that they'd mistake me for Paul.''

"You wanted to die, Leah?''

She frowned, considering. "I knew somebody had to die because it was too late to stop them. And I didn't want it to be Paul.''

"You really love him that much, Leah?''

"I love him more than anything in the whole world,'' Leah said simply.

Ken Holcross passed a hand suddenly across his eyes and looked down at his clipboard.

"Ken?'' Leah said anxiously.

"Leah, do you want to talk to Paul now?''

Her eyes widened in terror. "No!'' she whispered violently. "Please, Ken, don't make me talk to him. I don't want to see him, ever again.''

"But you just said—"

"You're sure Paul doesn't have any idea what I did?"

Ken Holcross shook his head. "Tim is talking to the police right now, and I imagine he'll tell them the whole story. I take it he was involved?"

"I don't know. That man...Joe..." She paused, shuddering with distaste. "He told me he'd have a helper with him, and I suppose it could have been Tim. I guess Tim arrived at the farm right after we made the arrangements, didn't he? But you said—"

"He helped Paul save your life," Ken said. "Even if he was the accomplice, you probably would have died if he'd decided to run away and save himself."

"I hope they're not too hard on him," Leah said. "He's just a boy, Ken."

"Probably they won't be hard on him, considering his subsequent behavior and the fact that there's nobody to testify against him."

"What about the other man? What about Joe?"

"He's dead, Leah," the doctor told her gently. "Apparently they had a scuffle after you were shot, and Tim hit Joe with the gun to keep him from shooting Paul. He died of a heart attack during the struggle."

"Otherwise he would have shot Paul, anyway?"

Ken Holcross nodded.

"Oh, God," Leah moaned, covering her face with her hands.

The doctor sat and watched her quietly, waiting.

"And Paul doesn't know any of this yet?"

Ken shook his head. "He thinks the man was a poacher, out hunting illegally in the woods, and that

Tim was either helping him or else stumbled onto him and tried to stop him. He thinks you were shot by accident and Tim was preventing the other man from trying to cover up his crime.''

Leah's eyes flickered as she took this in. She gazed up at the ceiling, thinking hard, her lovely face drawn and taut with emotion.

At last she turned and looked directly at the man beside her. "I want you to tell Paul," she said. "I want you to go out there now and tell him the whole thing."

"Leah, there's no need to—"

"Yes!" she said, speaking so forcefully that the pain stabbed and flowed in her chest, spreading like a bright river all down the length of her body. "He has to know, Ken. We've had enough lies and evasions and terrible things going on just below the surface. From now on I'm never going to lie to anybody if I can help it. And if Paul hates me, that's the price I'll have to pay. I just can't be a coward any longer, or I'll be hurting him even more. I want you to tell him."

"Leah . . ." Doctor Holcross paused, his mild face troubled and uncertain.

Leah gazed up at him, still fierce with emotion, though a great, heavy wave of sadness and loss was beginning to wash over her.

Paul, she thought, knowing that she'd never be close to him again, never touch him or kiss him or gaze into his eyes. *Oh, Paul . . .*

"Before you make that decision, Leah," the doctor was saying, "there's something else you should know."

"Yes? What's that?"

"Leah . . . You're pregnant."

"What?"

"You're pregnant, my dear. I suspected it at your last visit and warned the hospital to test for it as soon as Paul contacted me about your accident. That's why they had to be so careful with the anesthetic during your surgery. You're probably about six weeks pregnant according to the gynecologist's estimate."

Leah's mind moved sluggishly. "That's why... the sickness..."

"Yes. You didn't have any mysterious illness at all. You just had morning sickness," Ken said, trying to smile.

Leah gazed at him, struggling to grasp what he was saying.

"The baby..." she began haltingly. "Has any of this... Did it hurt the baby?"

"Apparently not. They were very careful with medications during the surgery, and they've done several tests and an ultrasound since then. Everything's just fine, Leah."

She was silent again, her mind struggling to absorb this miracle.

"So," Ken Holcross began, "considering how Paul's going to feel when we tell him, don't you think it would be..."

"Paul doesn't know about the baby, either?"

"Not yet. The doctors left it up to me how to deal with informing you and your husband. I felt it would be wisest to tell you first."

"Don't tell him," Leah said abruptly, her mind beginning to work again. "Ken, I don't want you to tell him."

Her face was so grim and full of resolve that the doctor gazed at her in surprise.

"Leah..." he began.

"Don't tell him," she repeated firmly. "Paul's such a responsible man that if he knew about this he'd probably stay with me no matter what he thought of me, and that's the last thing I want. Ken, *don't tell him about the baby.*"

Baby, Leah thought in wonder, hearing her own words echoing in her mind. *I'm having a baby.*

She shook her head, remembering how carefully she'd always avoided pregnancy throughout her marriage, how many times she'd lied to Paul about contraception.

Paul wanted a baby so much....

"Just tell him about the gunman," Leah went on in a cold, strained voice. "Tell him I actually hired somebody to kill him, Ken. Tell him I'm so terribly ashamed and sorry and I'd give anything to relive that part of my life, but I can't change anything now. It happened and we have to face it."

"Leah, you don't have to do this."

"Yes, I'm afraid I do. Tell him, Ken," Leah repeated. "Tell him the whole story, and if he still wants to talk to me, tell him to come and see me. If he doesn't want to have anything to do with me, you can tell him I'm perfectly all right now, fully recovered and in control of all my faculties, and willing to give him a divorce on any terms whatever. He never has to see me again."

"Leah..." the doctor repeated helplessly.

Leah looked up and saw the misery on his face.

"A good therapist never shows emotion, Ken," she said gently, trying to smile. "Please, just go and talk to Paul. Tell him what kind of woman his wife is, and let him make his own decision."

CHAPTER FIFTEEN

LEAH LAY FOR A LONG TIME gazing quietly out the window at the summer morning. An orderly ducked through the door carrying a breakfast tray, but she shook her head and waved him away. Later she heard sounds and muffled conversations in the hallway, the trundling of carts and the busy clatter of cleaning equipment. Still nobody disturbed the silence of her room.

She watched opal-tinted clouds drifting across a pure sapphire sky, feeling strangely light and disconnected.

It's because I've lost everything, Leah told herself calmly. *I have nothing left to worry about, and that's why I feel so peaceful.*

She thought about Paul, tried to picture his reaction when Ken told him the whole story. If he couldn't bear to look at her after she'd shouted at him the night of the dinner party, how would he feel about such a gruesome disclosure as this?

Leah frowned briefly, then dismissed the thought.

Paul was gone.

He knew the truth by now, and he despised her. Leah knew that she deserved his contempt. She'd married him under false pretenses, deliberately seeking the luxury and security that he could provide her with, with no thought for what she could give in return.

She'd cheated Paul, had rewarded his kindness and all his efforts at patience and understanding with coldness and cruelty and deception. Only now when it was too late did Leah fully understand how much she loved him, how deep and strong and sweet the feelings were.

She sighed and gazed out the window again.

Lawn sprinklers on the hospital grounds below lifted slow, drifting sprays of water that arched into the sunlight, then dropped to the grass in gentle cascades of rainbows. The scent of damp flowers and freshly mown grass drifted in through open windows, and birds sang in the park across the street. Leah's throat ached at the beauty of the June morning.

Tentatively, holding her breath, she placed a wondering hand on her stomach.

A baby.

Leah trembled, trying to grasp the fact that a tiny new life was sheltered within her, a part of herself and Paul that existed in the world, growing safely and snugly inside her body through all this turmoil.

"I love you," she whispered to her baby. "I love you, do you know that? I'm not sure how we're going to manage, but I'll try to look after you and make it so you're never lonely or scared...."

Tears gathered in her eyes and slipped down her cheeks as she thought about her own childhood, and how desperately she wanted to give her baby a happier life.

"I hope someday you'll have a chance to know your father," she went on, aching with sadness, still murmuring to the small life within her. "He's the most wonderful man in the world. Oh, God, I hope you'll be able to forgive me for..."

Paul Temple stepped into the room and let the door close behind him as he stood looking at his wife. Leah tensed and stared back at him, wide-eyed and still, almost overcome by the sight of his big, golden presence, his beautiful jeweled eyes and strong, tanned face.

"Hello, Leah," he said quietly.

She tried to speak but the words caught in her throat. She could only gaze at him, drowning in love and sorrow.

Paul reached into the pocket of his leather jacket and took out a small plastic vial, holding it out where she could see it.

Leah bent forward, wincing at the sudden flare of pain that stabbed her chest. She frowned in surprise as she looked at the blue capsules.

"Sleeping pills," Paul told her briefly. "Bonnie gave them to me yesterday while you were having your surgery."

Leah looked up at him, still bewildered, watching as he opened the lid of the vial and tipped the pills into the sink in the corner, washing them carefully down the drain.

"Bonnie stole them from your medicine cabinet earlier in the spring. She told me she was planning to overdose on them and kill herself."

Leah drew her breath in sharply, gazing at her husband in shock and horror.

Paul tossed the empty vial into the wastebasket, crossed the room and seated himself by Leah's bed, taking her hand gently.

"Bonnie told me that you saved her life. You made her feel good about herself and gave her the incentive to get her life back under control. She's convinced she really would have died without you."

"Paul...I don't know what to say. I didn't know..."

"You've done so much for all of us, Leah, just by being yourself and loving us."

Leah continued to stare at him, confused by his words and manner, trying to find something to say.

She shivered, remembering the look of cold hatred in his eyes just a few months ago when she woke to see him standing by her bed for the first time. But there was no hatred in Paul's eyes now. They glowed warmly with love and tenderness, and a deep, settled peace that she'd never seen before.

"Paul..." Leah whispered, clearing her throat awkwardly, "Paul, didn't Ken tell you about..."

"Yes," Paul said gently. "He told me, sweetheart. And now we won't talk about it unless you want to. It's over, and I love you. I love you more than I can ever tell you, though I certainly intend to spend the rest of my life trying."

"But I...I hired that man to..."

"Leah," he said, his voice husky with emotion, "you were willing to die for me. You don't know how I felt when Ken told me that. The amount of love and courage it took to do what you did..."

She looked up in amazement at the tears glistening on his cheeks.

"Oh, Paul," she whispered.

"You remembered everything, all those painful memories," Paul went on, gazing down at her, his face taut with feeling. "You got your whole life back, and it didn't change you at all. You only wanted to protect me. I feel so ashamed, Leah."

"*You?*" she whispered. "Paul, why would you feel ashamed?"

"Because I didn't help you. I was so worried about myself and my own pain, and when things got a little rough I turned away from you. I'll never do that again, Leah. We're going to see things through together from now on. We're going to talk about everything you remember until all your pain is gone and there's nothing left that can hurt us."

Leah stared up at him, breathless and full of wonder. A small flame of happiness grew and trembled within her, soaring in her mind until she felt a real danger of rising in this new warmth and drifting back into the soft, rose-tinted clouds, losing contact with the world completely.

"Oh, Paul," she whispered, reaching out with trembling fingers to stroke his chest, his damp cheeks, his lips and eyelids.

Suddenly she remembered and smiled.

"But there's something we have to talk about right now, dear," she murmured.

Paul took her hand and held it to his lips, smiling down at her tenderly. "Not now. Just keep telling me you love me. That's all you need to say."

She shook her head. "Paul...oh, Paul, I don't know how to tell you this."

His face turned pale and he looked at her in quick concern. "What, Leah? What is it?"

Leah smiled mistily, so full of happiness now that she could hardly speak. "Paul, I'm going to...I'm pregnant, darling. We're going to have a baby."

Leah laughed aloud at the rapid play of emotions on his face. He registered delight, shock, concern, happiness, fear, all within a few seconds.

"Leah! Are you sure?"

"Ken told me this morning. He says I'm about six weeks pregnant, so it must have happened that very first night."

"And everything's all right? None of this has caused any damage?"

"Not a bit. Apparently Ken was smarter than any of us. He began to suspect a few weeks ago that I might be pregnant, and warned them right away to be careful with the anesthetic."

"Oh, my darling," he whispered in awe. "Leah, I just love you so much."

Leah wanted to answer, wanted to tell him how she adored him, but she was getting so sleepy. And there would be time later to tell him all those things.

All the time in the world, Leah thought in drowsy contentment, letting herself drift back into the warm pink mists of happiness as her husband leaned close and buried his golden head against her, just above their child's tiny beating heart.

She had a mystical sense of time and eternity, of destiny rolling full circle and finding a balance. Optimism surged within her, a feeling that the future was wonderful and goodness would triumph in the end. Violence and cruelty would ultimately be overcome by strong, caring men like this man in her arms. And the child in her womb would live its life surrounded by love and tenderness that would wipe away all the suffering Leah had ever known.

Someday, Leah thought drowsily, stroking her husband's hair with quiet, dreamy hands, life would be different for everyone. The world would be a wondrous place where men and women treated one another with gentleness and compassion, and the innocent were truly cherished.

And then, forever, to the ends of the earth, the children would be safe.

HARLEQUIN SUPERROMANCE®

THE MONTH OF LIVING DANGEROUSLY

LIVE ON THE EDGE WITH SUPERROMANCE AS OUR HEROINES BATTLE THE ELEMENTS AND THE ENEMY

Windstorm by Connie Bennett pits woman against nature as Teddi O'Brian sets her sights on a tornado chaser.

In Sara Orwig's *The Mad, the Bad & the Dangerous,* Jennifer Ruark outruns a flood in the San Saba Valley.

Wildfire by Lynn Erickson is a real trial by fire as Piper Hillyard learns to tell the good guys from the bad.

In Marisa Carroll's *Hawk's Lair,* Sara Riley tracks subterranean treasure—and a pirate—in the Costa Rican rain forest.

Learn why Superromance heroines are more than just the women next door, and join us for some adventurous reading this September!

HSMLD

Take 4 bestselling love stories FREE

Plus get a FREE surprise gift!

Special Limited-time Offer

Mail to Harlequin Reader Service®

3010 Walden Avenue
P.O. Box 1867
Buffalo, N.Y. 14269-1867

YES! Please send me 4 free Harlequin Superromance® novels and my free surprise gift. Then send me 4 brand-new novels every month, which I will receive before they appear in bookstores. Bill me at the low price of $2.71 each plus 25¢ delivery and applicable sales tax, if any.* That's the complete price and—compared to the cover prices of $3.50 each—quite a bargain! I understand that accepting the books and gift places me under no obligation ever to buy any books. I can always return a shipment and cancel at any time. Even if I never buy another book from Harlequin, the 4 free books and the surprise gift are mine to keep forever.

134 BPA AJJC

Name	(PLEASE PRINT)
Address	Apt. No.
City	State	Zip

This offer is limited to one order per household and not valid to present Harlequin Superromance® subscribers. *Terms and prices are subject to change without notice. Sales tax applicable in N.Y.

USUP-93R

©1990 Harlequin Enterprises Limited

**Relive the romance...
Harlequin and Silhouette
are proud to present**

by Request™

A program of collections of three complete novels by the most
requested authors with the most requested themes. Be sure to
look for one volume each month with three complete novels by
top name authors.

In June: **NINE MONTHS** Penny Jordan
                          Stella Cameron
                          Janice Kaiser

**Three women pregnant and alone. But a lot can
happen in nine months!**

In July: **DADDY'S
          HOME**   Kristin James
                   Naomi Horton
                   Mary Lynn Baxter

**Daddy's Home... and his presence is long
overdue!**

In August: **FORGOTTEN
           PAST**   Barbara Kaye
                    Pamela Browning
                    Nancy Martin

**Do you dare to create a future if you've forgotten
the past?**

Available at your favorite retail outlet.

Calloway Corners

In September, Harlequin is proud to bring readers four
involving, romantic stories about the Calloway sisters,
set in Calloway Corners, Louisiana. Written by four of
Harlequin's most popular and award-winning authors,
you'll be enchanted by these sisters and the men
they love!

MARIAH by Sandra Canfield
JO by Tracy Hughes
TESS by Katherine Burton
EDEN by Penny Richards

As an added bonus, you can enter a sweepstakes contest
to win a trip to Calloway Corners, and meet all four
authors. Watch for details in all Calloway Corners books
in September.

CAL93

Harlequin is proud to present our
best authors and their best books.
Always the best for your
reading pleasure!

Throughout 1993, Harlequin will bring you
exciting books by some of the top names in
contemporary romance!

In August,
look for
Heat Wave by

A heat wave hangs over the city....

Caroline Cooper is hot. And after dealing with crises all
day, she is frustrated. But throwing open her windows to
catch the night breeze does little to solve her problems.
Directly across the courtyard she catches sight of a man
who inspires steamy and unsettling thoughts....

Driven onto his fire
escape by the sweltering heat, lawyer Brendan Carr
is weaving fantasies, too—around gorgeous Caroline.
Fantasies that build as the days and nights go by.

Will Caroline and Brendan dare cross the dangerous
line between fantasy and reality?

Find out in HEAT WAVE by Barbara Delinsky...
wherever Harlequin books are sold.